Cowboy Shooting

On the Road

Richard M Beloin MD

authorHOUSE®

AuthorHouse™
1663 Liberty Drive
Bloomington, IN 47403
www.authorhouse.com
Phone: 1 (800) 839-8640

Published by AuthorHouse 02/21/2018

ISBN: 978-1-5462-2914-8 (sc)
ISBN: 978-1-5462-2913-1 (e)

Library of Congress Control Number: 2018901983

Print information available on the last page.

Contents

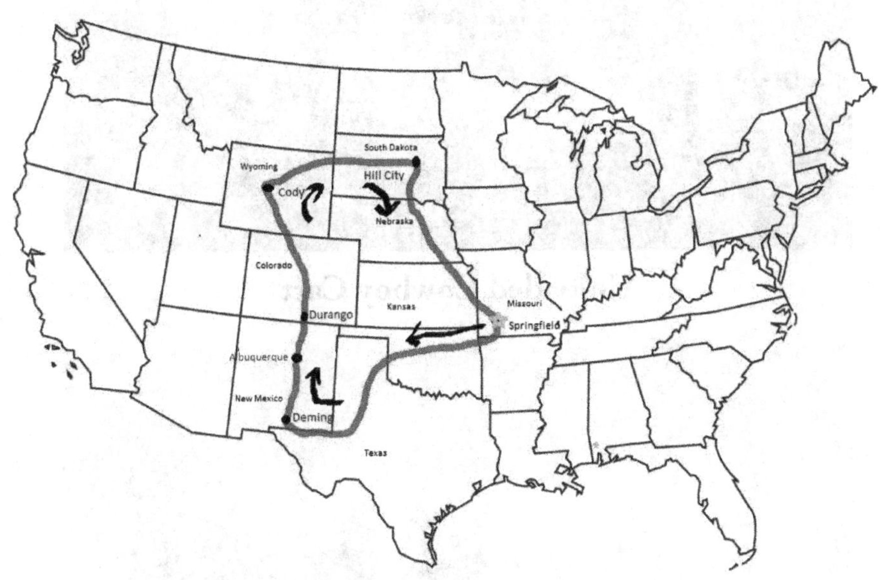

Circuitous Tourist Route

Unloaded Cowboy Cart

Loaded Cowboy Cart

Dedication

This book is dedicated to Curt and Sandy, who started the Sugarhouse Dancers, and were our companions and guides throughout our Western vacations.

Preface

This is a work of fiction with some true to life venues. The characters and shooting locations are fictional, and a figment of my imagination.

There are six bases that were used, over a week's time, to visit real local attractions. All these sites were visited by the author and his wife, while vacationing over several years.

Although the shooting events and locations were fictional, the safety rules, scoring methods and shooting classes were all real and part of the SASS Handbook. The Cowboy alias names are all fictional.

Special extensive reference to the Bar W Ranch is also a fictional location with fictional characters. The choice of the name, Bar W Ranch, does not depict or refer to the many registered Bar W Ranch's registered throughout the Western states, including Texas.

The Sugarhouse instructors are the only nonfictional characters. The partner dances, two-step, and waltz moves they taught are also real. All dances performed by the leading man and woman are real. Except for the Wild Horse Saloon, the dancing locations are all fictional.

The romance and interactions, of the leading characters, provide a comical and realistic relief throughout the book.

—Enjoy the shooting, romance and traveling over the American West—

Preface

CHAPTER 1

Changing Times

My life, as a practicing medical physician, changed drastically ten years ago. At age 51, I became a widower. My wife of 28 years passed away after a long chronic illness. With all three kids out of college, married and well settled, I found myself alone in a four bedroom two story house. I sold the family home and moved into a ground floor single story condo with a two car garage. The second garage was hopefully planned to be a workshop or a hobby room in retirement years.

My only hobby at the time was shooting an auto pistol at the local indoor range. This maintained my comfort zone with a handgun and was part of justifying a concealed weapon permit. With no other interests, I delved into my internal medicine practice.

During the next ten years several changes occurred in the practice of medicine. These changes were drastic and it changed my life long style of dealing and communicating with my patients.

The first was the evolution of a modern and complicated billing system. Whether you dealt with Medicaid, Medicare or a private insurance, the coding of services for payment became a nightmare. A simple office call was tied to sub coding with an illness that dictated the payment schedule. We now had at least 5 different office calls with a separate payment schedule and each had sub codes. The basic yearly physical exam was now tied to multiple sub codes. The simple coding system was now replaced by an intricate maze of possibilities. The worse of it all was that denials were very routine, which required the staff to call the insurance companies and find out how to code the service properly. Many times a second denial occurred despite all attempts to code properly. Frustration levels were high among the coding staff since our coders had to relearn the system they had trained for. This mess with coding promoted the next change.

The second was the new wave in "practice ownership". Local hospitals saw the frustration levels of their practicing physicians. The local hospitals had billing staff well experience in new coding methods since these code changes first appeared in hospitalized patients. Hospitals started purchasing medical practices and went into the business of outpatient medical care. The internal medicine group I belonged to decided to go this route and sold out to the local hospital. Suddenly, I became a salaried hospital employee after being in private practice nearly 25 years.

The third change, to kill private practice, was the idea that a physician could prosper as a salaried employee. It became impossible to find recruits as replacements in your group. The doctors coming out of training were looking for a salaried position and shied away from private practice–single and group practices. They wanted and found the security and benefits of a large employer and the local hospital fit that bill.

The fourth change was the new approach of night call and hospital care. The new crop of MD's were trained in one of two disciplines. One group was trained in outpatient primary care, while the other group was trained as physicians caring for the hospitalized patients. This last group has become known as the "hospitalists."

The third and fourth changes fueled the growing trend that a salaried physician either did office type medicine or hospital based medicine. This lead the office physician to abandon night and weekend call as well as transferring their patients to the hospitalists for inpatient care. Physicians started signing contracts for 32 hours per week of office work with benefits–that is four 8 hour days. I signed a contract for 5 days per week for a total of 40 hours per week. I needed all 5 days each week to care for the large practice I had developed.

The fifth and final change was the development of the digital medical record. On top of all the adjustments I had already made, I had to brush up on my 40 year old typing skills. For weeks I practiced at home until I could type 50 words per minute by using standard technique–not hen pecking. The real dilemma was how to add a laptop in the examining room without insulting the patient. Fortunately the hospital special administrative section gave us great proven methods. After several weeks, I learned how to properly exchange the hand written record for the digital system–and not interfere with my patient communication skills.

So this old dog had to learn new tricks. I incorporated all these changes and my days were busy, but my nights and weekends were long and empty, without night and weekend call. I found myself maintaining my practice but experiencing less personal satisfaction. It was clear that I was of the old school and had modernized into the new school. This is probably why I did not find the satisfaction that the younger physicians experienced. The new docs liked a guaranteed salary and fixed work hours without the hassle of billing, business expenses, night/weekend call, employees and the fluctuating bottom dollar.

My practice flourished over the years despite all these changes. Things were actually going smoothly until that fateful day when I experienced a personal medical catastrophe.

The first four days at the office were uneventful, actually operations were smooth and patient care was productive. Fridays were always unpredictable and could be business as usual or could be a havoc in progress. It seems that the staff, including myself, was tired from the first four days of the week and or were looking forward to the weekend.

The day started promptly at 8 am with a new patient referred for a cardiac evaluation. The patient and his wife were full of questions that needed my immediate attention. Consequently, I was 20 minutes late to get to my second patient. For reasons not clear, several patients also needed more time with me and so by noon I was very late. The staff instigated a corrective measure and cancelled a long yearly Medicare exam. I also elected to put off many of the typed notes to a later time. The result was that I finished my office hours only a half hour late at 5:30 pm. The billing clerk had already left at 5 pm, but the receptionist and my nurse always stayed until the last patient left the office.

As the cleaning service arrived, I moved to my private office to finish all the typed notes that were incomplete. I admit that I felt fatigued but attributed it to the difficult day. While I was typing I experienced a transitory double vision which I dismissed when it quickly cleared. I finally finished my notes an hour later. As I was closing my laptop I heard a "pop" in my head that was accompanied with flashing blue stars. An explosive headache ensued and I screamed out in pain. As the cleaning lady came in my office to check on me, suddenly everything went black and then there was nothing.

The next thing I recall was being on an ambulance gurney being wheeled into the ambulance. The ride to the hospital was interrupted with periods in and out of consciousness. I finally woke up in a large and busy ER. The ER physician did a quick history and exam and astutely told me that he suspected an intracranial subarachnoid hemorrhage.

Fortunately the headache had lessened since receiving a mild analgesic and after stabilizing my vital signs that showed a fast heart rate and elevated blood pressure, I was transferred to the radiology department for an emergency head CT scan. In a short time the ER doc and radiologist came to inform me that the CT scan confirmed a mild to moderate hemorrhage and suggested that an enhanced CT scan be performed to locate the origin of the bleed–presumed from an aneurysm.

> *The enhanced CT is a form of angiogram produced by injecting a dye thru the IV line that lights up the arteries in the brain and can locate an arterial aneurysm.*

This enhanced scan did confirm the location of the aneurysm and the fact that it was presently not bleeding. By the time I got back to the ER, I noticed a slight weakness of one arm and leg and a mental dullness with lack of clarity. I was then admitted to the hospital for further management. It was the next day when I had a meeting with a neurosurgeon and an interventional neuroradiologist. The issue at hand required a decision whether to proceed with a surgical clipping of the aneurysm versus an endovascular coiling procedure.

I had been informed of this meeting ahead of time and took the opportunity to explain to my two sons and daughter what the two choices involved before meeting with the doctors.

> *The surgical clipping is an invasive open cranial procedure which involves applying a metal clip at the opening of the aneyrysm to close off the opening to blood flow. The endovascular coiling involves the insertion of a catheter in the femoral artery and directing a micro catheter via the aorta to the carotid arteries and then to the intracranial arteries. After locating the aneurysm under CT imaging, a coil is electrically released into the aneurysm. The coils are made of platinum, are the size of a human hair and have a spring/coiling memory.*

> *The coils are left in the aneurysm and induce clotting of the blood in the aneurysm. This clot prevents blood from entering the aneurysm. For years surgical clipping was the "gold standard". The endovascular coiling has been performed since the early 90's. Recent articles have been showing a likely long term benefit of this coiling technique over surgical clipping.*

I met with the surgeon and the neuroradiologist and they presented their own approach respectively. The risks of either method was well detailed as well as their potential complications. Both methods took into account that I had suffered some mild neurological deficiencies when the aneurysm ruptured. At the end of the discussion, I was comfortable with my decision–I chose the endovascular coiling method. My kids who were at the meeting were also comfortable with my decision.

Thanks to modern technology and an experienced neuroradiologist, the procedure went well without complication. The coils were instilled in the aneurysm and proof of the clotting was proven later by CT imaging. The remainder of my hospital stay was uneventful except for the physical therapy for my arm and leg weakness as well as a baseline evaluation of my impaired cognition. I was discharged from the hospital after a five day stay. The discharge planner scheduled me for outpatient physical therapy and for a follow up visit with the neuroradiologist with an enhanced CT scan.

The month of physical therapy was so beneficial that on my last visit with the therapist, I had no residual weakness. The impaired cognition did not change. Basically I was experiencing memory deficits that were not conducive to medical practice. One month later, my cognitive skills had not improved, and was told by my neurologist that such impairment may last many months or may be permanent.

I had now been on temporary disability for close to three months when the group chairman of my private practice invited me to a meeting of the group's senior physicians. The early discussion covered my present cognitive impairment and then the subject matter moved on to the potential for permanent disability. The discussants pointed out that this medical catastrophe occurred while on the job and that stress of the difficult last day had certainly contributed to the event. This approach meant that I would qualify for permanent disability under the group's plan. One physician pointed out that continued medical practice could lead to a re-bleed or worse. Another pointed out that working with impaired cognition was a high liability for me and my group–not mentioning that our malpractice insurance could refuse to insure me or that the new hospital employer could refuse to reinstate me.

And so the extended discussions continued along these lines. The chairman closed by recommending that I accept the group's long term disability benefit–not knowing that the insurance carrier had already approved my disability up to age 70. It was also pointed out that I would also be eligible for Social Security benefits at age 62 and would likely qualify for Social Security Disability benefits after being disabled for one year. These benefits along with my old Keogh, IRA and now current 401 plan would provide my financial security.

The decision was a difficult one. After practicing medicine for over 35 years, it was not easy to let go of a profession that had been so rewarding. When I reviewed the pros and cons on the matter, it always came down to the same conclusion. I could not risk the liability for myself and my group, but more significant, I could not risk the potential damage to my patients. It was also crucial that I not expose myself to the stresses of medical practice, that could be the cause of further neurological complications.

After a long week of personal soul searching, I informed our senior partner that I would retire. I was still reluctant but understood the reason for my decision. My reluctance was based on two issues. The first was walking away from the practice of medicine, but the real frightening thing was, "what am I going to do with my life?" I had no hobby and no major interest outside of medicine. I NEEDED A SECOND LIFE!

And so my story begins.

CHAPTER 2

A Second Life

A knock at the door and there was Jack, my next door neighbor. "Come in Jack, how about a morning cup of coffee?" "Yes, a coffee sounds great." "Well, what brings you here this fine Saturday morning?" "Thought I would check on what you are doing tomorrow." "Well Jack, I have nothing planned as usual. I am sure you are aware that I am having difficulty finding a hobby or a regular activity to fill my days. I have tried golfing, hiking, card playing, reading and even tried dating but nothing is going well and I am still trying new endeavors."

Jack looked at me and said, "I guess that is why I came to see you today. I have known you for 10 years since you moved next door. I was working at a cable TV company and you were busy with your practice, and so we never got together much except for our visits to the indoor range for pistol shooting. I retired one year ago and immediately got involved with a shooting sport that I had eyed for a long time."

"They are having a shoot tomorrow at the local club and I hope I can convince you to join me as your guide." I thought about what he said and for no reason I gladly said I would be happy to join him on this tour.

Jack replied, "That is wonderful, now this sport is called Cowboy Action Shooting, but I do not want you to Google it. I want you completely ignorant of the sport so I can present it to you the same way it was presented to me". *What I did not realize at the time was that Jack was planning some "Shock and OMG" as well as some personal introductions, and had already acquired two books on the subject!*

I almost cheated and nearly opened Google to look up the sport on Cowboy Shooting. Fortunately I resisted and Sunday AM arrived. Jack picked me up and we headed to a local shooting range within 10 miles of home.

Sunday day 1. We arrived early at the club and only the organizers were present at the clubhouse. Jack explained that I was a tenderfoot–meaning that I was a newcomer and knew nothing of the sport. He actually refined his statement by saying to the man that I was being introduced to Cowboy Action Shooting(CAS) in hopes that I would join the sport. The organizer came up to me and said "welcome to the Desperados, my name is Ranger Rooster, I am president of this club and range master for the shoots." *I just realized that members of CAS use alias names.* He further added, "you are lucky to be guided by P–Shooter, and I am certain that under his guidance, we'll see you again."

Jack, or I should say P–Shooter, showed me around the clubhouse. There was a registration counter, a display table where members place their wares for sale, and many round tables for lunch and meetings. The clubhouse also functions as a dance hall when the club hires a country band, and removes some round tables to create a dance floor. I also saw an elevated bench/bar that opens during dances to provide liquid refreshments.

On our way back to the parking lot where participants were arriving, I asked Jack, "why did you take the name of P–Shooter as your alias?" His answer, "the first time I came to a shoot, one of the local cowboy shooters told everyone that I was a well known auto pistol shooter in the competition world. At registration, since I had not taken an alias, someone yelled out P–Shooter and it has been my alias ever since."

P–Shooter explained how alias names were chosen. "It was often based on a profession, location, work ethics, habits, physical appearance, past criminal record and on and on. For example a name like Diamond Bandit would likely be a local jeweler, Iron Man would be a welder, Otto-Driva would be a German race car driver, and Ditch-Witch would be a lady excavator operator and so on. Now you can imagine the origin of alias names like Booger Joe, Big Dufus, Scruffy, and Sassy Dame."

Arriving at the parking lot, I noticed that several participants had arrived. Jack pointed out, "note that there are cowboys and cowgirls. The shooters are unloading their cowboy carts which is a two wheel L shaped wagon like an old plow. There is a top box for ammo, a rack for long guns, a bottom box for accessories that also serves as a seat and two holsters attached to the upright handles for pistols." *I was looking at these cowboy carts and noticed that some were commercial products but most were made by the shooters themselves. These had a personal flare that seemed to match the dress and decor of either a cowboy or cowgirl.*

The next thing Jack pointed out was the dress code. "Look at the men's costumes. Yes, they are costumes of the 1800's and so they are period correct clothing between 1800–1900. The man's pants are either canvas or a tweed with buttons for suspenders, without belt loops, and buttons instead of zippers. The shirts are full, partial buttoned fronts or shielded "bib" fronts. They have long sleeves and banded collars. Mandatory accessories include the cowboy hat and cowboy boots. Many cowboys wear vests for insulation or for show."

Jack then described the ladies costumes, "they have the option of wearing the same costume as men but often substitute the banded collar shirt for a long sleeve blouse. However, many wear a gingham type dress of the pioneer days or a flashy costume of the era..... etc etc. Some wear riding pants as a costume approaching the late 1800's. Other optional accessories include bonnet, apron, chemise under the dress, ankle length skirts and vests. There is more individuality with women costumes which adds to the flare, beauty and fantasy of the sport."

I watched the men load their cowboy wagons. Something caught my eye–a cowboy was working hard to pump air in his wagon tire. That is when Jack jumped in and said, "today most cowboys use hard rubber tires instead of pneumatic tires. There are too many thorns, sharp plant products and cutting rocks that cause flats with pneumatic tires, whereas the hard rubber type is the standard west of the Mississippi."

The wagon loading process was a universal system from one wagon to another. Jack volunteered the sequence of events. "They start with the long guns to be placed in their racks. The rifle's lever is left open and the double barrel shotgun in open. Some shooters use a period pump shotgun and the slide on those is open. The revolvers are placed in the wagon holsters or in the bottom box. Ammo goes in the top box and any other accessories go in the bottom box. Used ammo bags are attached to the wagon and the last item secured to the wagon is a large beach umbrella–for sun or rain protection. The cowboy then puts on his boots and hat, secures his belt and holsters, and can use an extra belt for his shotgun and pistol/rifle ammo slides."

While watching several shooters getting ready, Jack and I heard a loud "@#$%^&**(% I forgot my *******ammo". Jack added, "par for the course, at least he didn't forget his holsters like he did last month. Guess you can understand why his alias is Alz Homer!" *This made me think that were I to entertain this sport, a check off list would be in the cards for me, especially since I still have memory deficits from my aneurysm rupture.*

Jack continued, "after the wagon loading is done, the shooters head for the clubhouse to register and get their coffee and donuts. They then circulate, socialize with other club members, look for visiting shooters and new shooters to welcome them to their club. Everyone then waits for the 9 AM Shooter's Meeting."

Suddenly an SUV pulls in and parks right next to us. *Jack turned toward the vehicle but not before I saw a smile on his face. WOW, I could not believe my eyes, but it was real. I saw a tall and slim woman with a friendly face, a natural smile, well endowed, skinny legs and beautiful short blond hair in a "Princess Diane" style. I thought, great genetic inheritance. I knew that my jaw had dropped open and would be tongue tied if forced to speak. I came out of my reverie and heard Jack say.* "Doc Derby, I would like to introduce you to Lady Slipper. This cowgirl is a well known shooter in this club and other surrounding clubs. Doc Derby is my neighbor and today I am introducing him to our sport."

Lady Slipper stepped up to shake my hand and welcomed me to today's shoot. I finally got a few words out, and I did notice that she in turn was giving me a full going over, as I had done. She then proceeded to load her gear and get ready. We were able to carry a conversation as she multi tasked her prep work and her responses. After she was ready, we escorted her to the club house where the next step shortly followed, the Shooter's Meeting.

The Shooter's Meeting was a mandatory attendance for all shooters. It started with the Pledge Allegiance to the Flag. The Range Master who wrote the stages ran the meeting. Posse's were assigned. He announced that this shoot would be following SASS rules, went over convention rules such as only lead bullets allowed etc etc, and pointed out that this club requires that the loading and unloading tables be manned at all times. He reminded all shooters that everyone was a safety officer and any questionable activity should be brought to the range officer's attention. After some shooters asked questions or made announcements, the meeting was terminated and the shooters headed to their posse's starting stage.

As Jack and I were considered spectators, we stayed this side of the split rail fence. Jack then proceeded to describe the full sequence of events. "The range officer gathers the posse and reads the scenario. He describes the sequence of each firearm. For example: you shoot the 5 pistol targets from left to right on the first pistol and right to left on the second pistol. The rifle 5 targets are shot by double tapping targets 1,5,2,4,3 in that sequence, the three shotgun targets are shot four times in the sequence 1,2,2,3. Targets 1 and 3 are knockdowns and must go down or are a miss. So the sequence is pistols, rifle and shotgun is last."

Jack continued, "a shooter's name is called to the loading table. He loads his rifle with ten rounds and loads each pistol with 5 rounds(allowing the hammer to fall on an empty chamber). The loading officer confirms that this was done properly. The shooter is then called to the shooting line. At the buzzer, he shoots his stage and then takes his long guns to the unloading table. All guns are then brought to the wagon and the shooter is done this stage. The range officer reports to the scorekeeper this shooter's shooting time for all four guns and adds 5 seconds for every miss and 10 seconds(procedural) if a target was shot out of sequence. He will repeat this sequence at the next stage but with a different scenario and shooting sequence. The next stage starts after all posse members have finished with their first stage." I then said, "OK, here we go, the first shooter is now moving to the firing line."

The range officer(RO) says, "is the shooter ready(shooter says yes) and the RO says, stand by, and the buzzer goes off." BANG The shooter lets go his first round and blasts thru the stage with incredible speed, and WOW-OMG my world changed forever.

I was shocked and could not believe my ears and eyes. For the second time today my jaw dropped and it took some time to regain a degree of reality. I turned my head and looked at Jack. He softly said with a million dollar smile, "YEP, I thought that would do it, guess you are hooked, heh!" I then looked at the posse and saw Lady Slippper looking at both of us with a very approving smile and a thumbs up sign.

Jack then analyzed what this last shooter did. "His name is Papa-Grand(he owns the local hotel–The Grand). He shot 4 guns for a total of 24 rounds. He drew both pistols from holsters, reholstered, transferred the left pistol to the right hand and back, ran 8 feet to the table holding the rifle and 6 more feet to the table holding the shotgun–all in 33 seconds. After one year of shooting this sport and many practices, my best time for this stage is 44 seconds." I was impressed with Papa Grand and P–Shooter.

I then watched several contestants step up and shoot the stage.

Lady Slipper was next to shoot. She shot with a great "stage presence." She had a stable shooting stance, superb accuracy, moved quickly and efficiently between staged firearm, and just simply appeared very sure of herself. Her shooting time was 45 seconds for this 24 round stage.

I watched the next two stages without explanations from Jack. I was taking mental notes of things to clarify with Jack but because I had so many questions, I started writing them down on a note pad. When we got to stage 4, the RO announced that this was the last stage before lunch. He then pointed to a large wheel and said, "yes, this is the new Texas Star. For everyone, let me explain. There are 5 plates attached to the wheel–2,4,6,8 and 10 o'clock. The idea is to shoot the 10 o'clock plate first. This leaves the right side of the wheel to be overweight and so the wheel will turn counter clockwise to the right. Now if you quickly shoot the 2 o'clock plate then the counter clockwise rotation will stop. If you miss this 2 o'clock plate, get ready for a spinning wheel. Your choice then is to chase this plate or wait till the wheel stabilize. Then restart with the 8 o'clock plate and repeat the process. You start with pistols, then rifle and finally shotgun. Once the five plates are down, you shoot the leftover rounds on that green dumping target."

The first shooter was the RO who expertly demonstrated this shooting method. It looked easy! Then the next shooter missed the second plate at 2 o'clock and all hell broke loose. It was a nightmare for the shooter and he ended up shooting all his 24 rounds at a madly spinning Texas Star. That included all his four shotgun rounds. I was impressed that the Texas Star was likely an anathema to many shooters. I then looked at Jack and found him with a smile from ear to ear.

Lunch time at the clubhouse. The menu was classic for a period correct trail meal which included: homemade baked beans sweetened with molasses, crispy salt pork and biscuits. Desert was canned peaches.

Lady Slipper joined us for lunch. That is when I said, "it is now clear to me that this tour was well planned, so it is time for you to give it up," Jack looked at Lady Slipper who nodded yes, and she started to say, "our club is experiencing a drop in membership and all club members were given a challenge to find some new shooters." Jack then added, "I decided to team up with Lady Slipper on a 50/50 basis. I would find a candidate, provide his first guided tour, spend a week with him to shop for firearms, clothing costume, reloading equipment and help him build a cowboy cart. I would then teach our shooter how to reload safely using a modern reloader. After my week, Lady Slipper would then take over and spend a week at the range with the shooter. She would guide him through the correct method of shooting this sport, from the loading to the unloading table, including the important firing line. Her goal was to certify that this new shooter was safe, well informed, had the proper technique and was ready for his first solo run at a real Cowboy Action Shooting event."

There was a long time spent without a single spoken word. I then said, "it's incredible that you would both be willing to invest a week of your time and expertise, to claim me as your student, and achieve your goal. I gladly accept your proposal and would be happy to become a Cowboy Shooter. This dedication to the sport is honorable and I hope two things will happen. The first is that I will become a respectable shooter, and the second is the hope that I would have the opportunity in the future to do the same as you are now doing–bringing a newbie into the sport. Thank you so much and I am looking forward to the next two weeks. I promise you both that I will give you 110 % of my effort and attention."

After lunch, we watched the last two stages of the day. That is when Jack said, "After lunch is when the fun starts. The post lunch contestants are logy, both physically and mentally, and you are going to see some bloopers." As predicted, the first shooter was called to the firing line and stepped forward with his pistols. The RO says, "this stage includes rifle and shotgun, don't you want to get your long guns?" So I understood what Jack meant. Through out the stage we saw several other bloopers. One contestant at the loading table was seen attempting to load the other contestant's rifle! A tall shooter on his way to the firing line forget to duck at the bank's door! A portly shooter's gun belt fell to the ground while shooting his rifle! These bloopers alerted me to some realistic events that can occur when you are not focused–coffee or a caffeinated drink at lunch might help.

At the end of the day with all firearms and gear reloaded into vehicles, all contestants gathered at the clubhouse for awards. First, second, and sometimes third place winners were handed awards for each shooting category. Jack pointed out that at age 61, I would be shooting in the Senior category. Jack then said, "look at the top shooters in this category. They will be the ones to try to beat some day."

On our way home, Jack explained that all the days of this coming week were planned in a purposeful sequence. He was very specific that he did not want me to go on line tonight and attempt to research this sport. He then handed me a book titled Cowboy Action Shooting by Richard M Beloin MD. He then said that my job for tonight was to read this book cover to cover. He even said that I should take notes since this book is clearly written with a lot of usable information.

I thanked Jack again and he stated that he would pick me up at 8 AM. We were heading 50 miles away to a unique cowboy gun shop for firearms, shooting accessories and accoutrements.

CHAPTER 3

Setting Up

Monday day 2. On the way to the gun shop, a few topics came up. "Well Jack, when you introduced me to Lady Slipper, you said my cowboy alias was Doc Derby. Where does that come from?" He answered, "Even if you are retired you will always be a doctor. Since you live on Derby Lane, I thought the name would fit you well. As a doctor, you can still dress in traditional 1800's period garb. You can also dress up with a fancy doctor costume of the 1800's. That upgrade costume would consist of a fine black striped tweed pant, silk white shirt with bow tie, a red fancy vest with a pocket watch on a gold chain looped in the vest button hole, black flat heel cowboy boots and a fancy black derby hat of the times." I countered, "I thought the derby hat had a hard felt, short rim and round crown! Isn't that a modern hat design?" He answered, "the derby hat was designed in 1849 and was a standard feature with city folks in the Old West. It is true that a dandy often wore a derby hat, but it was the usual wardrobe of doctors, lawyers, judges, undertakers and a slew of other business people." With that in mind, I recalled seeing a photo of Bat Masterson as a lawman wearing a derby hat. As we closed this subject, I was satisfied with my assigned name.

The second subject was about the book on Cowboy Action Shooting(CAS) that Jack gave me to read last night. "The book you handed me to read was a masterpiece. I read it slowly and did take notes. It was so well written and informative that I read it a second time into the late hours. By adding the contents of this book to my touring experience yesterday, I feel ready to embark in the process lying ahead."

As we were approaching the town where this gun shop was located, Jack explained, "this store is not just a gun shop. It is a mercantile that specializes in cowboy guns, accessories, accoutrements and anything a Cowboy Shooter can ever need or want. It serves at least a dozen cowboy shooting clubs within 150 miles and you will enjoy Ed and Eve."

As we entered the Cowboy Mercantile, I experienced instant retinal overload. Although the storefront was only +- 25 feet wide, the depth of the store was impressive. There was a center isle with displays on both sides of firearms, reloading equipment/components, leather products, a large garment section, cowboy carts and many other retail items.

We were greeted by both owners, Ed and Eve. Jack spoke up and said, "everything we discussed last week is a definite go." Ed answered, "well doc, why don't you step into the wardrobe section and Eve will help you with your selections. I will start collecting the items that Jack has already selected." Jack simply smiled.

I went through the garment choices. I selected four pairs of pants. A striped grey, striped blue, beige cotton for hot weather and a fine twill for my doctor costume. Picked up the shirts to match the traditional pants and a white shirt for the doctor costume. Selected two hats, one was a traditional cowboy hat in light grey, and of course a black derby. To finish the doctor costume, I added a charcoal frock coat. When it came to cowboy boots, Jack suggested a mid calf black square toe with a flat heel. "The high cowboy heel boot was to secure their foot in the stirrups. When you stand all day, flat heels are much more comfortable and an aggressive high traction sole is preferable for wet terrain."

After trying on for size, we carried these accoutrements to the cash register. Next to the cash register was a window display of handguns, and next to that was a long narrow work table loaded with stuff. That is when Ed spoke up and said, "all this stuff will round up everything you will need to participate in this sport." I had little notion as to what everything was for, fortunately Ed went on to describe each item: "this is a Marlin Cowboy rifle in 38 special. Jack will help you with an action job. Since I am a certified gunsmith, I repaired the dreaded "Marlin Jam". This is a Marlin production defect that will wear a lever part and cause a jam of the rifle." As Ed paused, I asked Jack what an action job was. He said, "polishing every moving part with 400 to 800 and finally 1200 grit sandpaper for metal. You will appreciate the smoothness of the lever action."

The next item was a double barrel 12 gauge shotgun by Stoeger. Ed added, "I have done no modifications on this shotgun since Jack will do them with you." Finally Ed gets to the pistols, "these two pistols are stainless and short barrel Ruger New Vaqueros in 38 special. Like the other firearms, action jobs and modifications are your responsibility. I may add that I have included all the modified springs and parts you will need to perform the desired changes for all four firearms."

Then Eve took over, "the remainder of the items chosen by Jack include the following: a black double holster/belt rig by Black Hills Leather to include a shotgun slide and spare 38 special slide, a brass vibratory tumbler with corn media and a Dillon Square Deal B reloader. This is the Dillon RF-100 primer loader which Jack will explain."

"In this section are reloading components to include, primers, powder, 4000 lead bullets, 38 sp. brass and all the components to load 12 gauge shotgun shells. This box has all miscellaneous items and tools for shooting or reloading, all the tools of the trade."

The last item was a classic cowboy cart. Ed explained, "this is the L-shape model with a top and bottom box, plow handles as the uprights and 16 inch hard rubber wheels. It has hooks for brass bags and an anchor for an umbrella. The plow handles are pre drilled, and I have added holsters on the uprights. These carts are built by a local retired carpenter. Jack did not include it on his list since this is a new item." I could see that Jack approved of the quality construction.

I stood there and was amazed at all the stuff I needed. I sarcastically but politely asked Ed if I was missing anything and to my dismay he said, "well yes, here are two hard gun cases. The large one is for the rifle and shotgun and the small one is for the two pistols." He then unceremoniously waved me to a chair and said that this was the only free item in the store. He then poured in each ear, a warm liquid mixture of silicone and hard foam, to form my personal ear protection. Jack had been rather quiet through out this shopping spree and finally chimed in, "I am glad I called ahead so you could get any item that had to be ordered, and especially glad you had time to collect or order the parts needed to perform action jobs and modifications. Guess it is time to pay up." While Ed was adding this up, Jack and I start loading everything in his truck. I was glad the truck had a hard bed cover over most of the goods, but clothing and guns went in the truck's back seat. Ed then gave me his bill and I pulled out my credit card and a check. Ed quickly said, "sitting on a large order for payment from the credit card is not the best for cash flow. If you are paying cash by check, I will give you a 6% discount." Well I answered, "here is a check for the full amount, I am certain you gave me a fair price and I appreciate the great service." I could see that Jack approved.

On our way home, I discussed the likelihood that it will take forever to learn the specifics of all this technology, especially the reloading science. Jack confidently answered, "nonsense, by the end of my week with you, you will master all this technology and will be ready for your training with Lady Slipper."

Upon arriving at home, we unloaded his truck of my possessions and proceeded next door to Jack's garage. We ordered a pizza for lunch and I took lunch time to make a mental picture of the garage layout. Like me, he had a two car garage for one vehicle–his truck. The second bay adjacent to his condo had been converted to a gun room and reloading center. I specifically noted that the reloading bench was the same as mine. He had a real gun safe for his firearms, plenty of free standing floor shelves and a few on the wall above his reloading bench.

After lunch, Jack said "this afternoon is dedicated to teaching you how to reload safely and properly. The first thing is to choose your powder. I use Clays but other powders are popular with Cowboy Shooters to include Titegroup, Red Dot and Trail Boss. The reloading manuals show a Clays charge of 2.5 grains(velocity 800fps) to 3.5 grains(velocity of 1000fps). I load 3.0 grains for pistol and 3.5 grains for rifle." He then showed me how to add primers to the magazine tubes of the reloader and add powder to the hopper.

He then started reloading and explaining every station of the reloader. "Station one is where you add a case. As you pull the cycling arm, the case is sized and the old primer is popped out. Station two adds a new primer and drops the powder in the case. Station three is where you add a bullet and cycling the arm seats the bullet in the case. Station four is where the case mouth is squeezed into the groove of the lead bullet–this last stage is called crimping. So every cycle, as you add a case in station 1 and a bullet in station 3, a new loaded round falls in the catch bin on pulling the cycling arm." He then went into great detail regarding this simple reloading procedure and an hour later I was ready to start reloading.

At first I was slow, cautious and under Jack's verbal assistance. I quickly picked up the pace and by the end of loading the first 100 rounds, I was reloading independently. In the next hour I loaded 100 rounds and was feeling comfortable with the process.

We then took a break and Jack showed me how to operate the Dillon RF-100. "This machine accepts 100 primers in a platform hopper and automatically adds all 100 primers into a tube to be transferred to the Square Deal B reloader." He showed me all the tricks to keep this machine running smooth without snags.

We then discussed several features of this reloader and some common snags that need readjustments. He then suggested that I go ahead and spend an hour reloading to see how many I could load in this time frame. Everything went smooth as this machine was a real marvel. Jack just watched and at the end of the hour I had reloaded almost 225 rounds. That is when Jack said, "you seem comfortable reloading and you have a nice cadence. I can see that you are well focused on the job. Eventually you will increase your speed and production. I can easily produce 400 rounds per hour on a regular basis. I have done 500/hour but it is not as pleasant as 400/hour."

The last thing we did was to review reloading for 12 gauge shotgun shells. Jack had a retired single stage MEC Sizemaster reloader that he donated to my cause. The steps were very similar except for three. The first was that I had to resize the cases so the brass bases were returned to their original shape. The second was that I had to manually move each shell through all the stages and then pull the cycling arm. The third was that I had to add a plastic wad between the powder and birdshot. That was the difference between a progressive reloader(Square Deal

B) and a single stage reloader(MEC Sizemaster). Jack pointed out that I don't need many shotgun shells and a single stage shotgun reloader is adequate. For example at a regular shoot you generally shoot 25 shotgun rounds, 100 pistol rounds and 100 rifle rounds. He also pointed out that when you go to the range to practice, you need pistol and rifle ammo–not shotgun ammo.

After my loading tutorial and a quick dinner, I went to my local Home Depot to finish my first days events. I picked up two 5 foot free standing heavy duty plastic shelves–36 inch wide. I also picked up a 27 inch high shop stool which would match my 36 inch high reloading bench. The big ticket item was a fireproof gun safe. The remainder of my order included several 10 inch wide pine boards, shelving hardware, two 3 foot LED shop lights, assorted hardware and a gallon of paint.

When I got home, I painted the reloading bench and the pine boards for shelving. The paint was a durable decking grade with primer. The late evening painting session meant that I could use the bench and build the shelves in the AM.

Tuesday day 3. This was my day to organize and build myself a gun room and reloading center. The unused second garage next to the condo entrance was slated for a major do over and designated use. First, I moved out all and anything that would not fit in my man cave. The first thing I did was to assemble the shop stool and the two free standing shelves. Despite "some assembly required", the shelves and stool were finished without too many expletives.

The next was the reloading bench, I was pleased that the bench was 16 feet long by 24 inch deep. It was sturdy and there was a bottom shelf 10 inches off the floor the width and length of the bench–another storage site. I secured the bench to the wall studs with 3 inch angle irons.

The reloading bench was finished by building four 6 foot long shelves over the bench.

Next was power source and lighting. The two shop lights were installed on the ceiling and the power cord plugged into the many electrical outlets. LED lights produce a silent white light. No more humming of old style shop lights. There were four outlets to cover the 16 foot bench which would serve the power demands.

After lunch it was time to fill up shelves with my supplies. The bench's left side was for the brass cleaning tumbler and the shotgun reloader. The bench's right side was for the RF-100 and the Dillon Square Deal B reloader. Bench shelves were loaded with corresponding accessories to match the bench reloaders. Heavy items such as lead bullets and birdshot went on the bench's lower shelf. The remainder of the "stuff" went on the free standing plastic shelves. After adding the firearm safe and the cowboy shooting cart, the garage space looked occupied.

The remainder of the afternoon was spent on installing the Square Deal B reloader. Opening the box and finding so many parts to assemble seemed overwhelming. The installation DVD was placed in my laptop and I followed each step meticulously. I paused the video till each step was correctly performed and then restarted the video for the next instructions. An hour later the press was up and running.

I stood back and viewed my work–I was pleased. I then called Jack and asked him to check things out. When he arrived, he looked at every nook and cranny. He stated, "very nice, very well organized and user friendly. The room shows pride in your work. Tomorrow is day four. In the AM, I would like you to reload pistol, rifle and shotgun rounds. Take your time and always maintain a good comfort level. If you hit a snag, I will be home so just call me. In the afternoon we are going to modify your firearms and perform action jobs!"

Wednesday day 4. By early AM I was at my reloading bench. I set the powder charge a 3.0 grains for pistol ammo. Loaded 100 Federal small pistol primers and opened a box of 125 grain lead bullets in 38 special. I then started to reload. Within two hours, I had loaded 500 rounds of great looking ammo that met all the specifications of the published data. To be on the safe side, I called Jack and asked him to come inspect my loads. After his careful examination, he said "by my measurements with a dial caliper, this is perfect ammo. I am taking some rounds and your two Ruger Vaquero pistols to the indoor range to do some testing, and will explain why I am doing this when I return."

While he was gone, I changed the powder charge to 3.5 grains and proceeded to reload 500 rifle rounds. I then cleaned the reloader and put away the reloading components. I specifically placed all my primers in freezer type zip lock bags. These bags seal the primers from humidity which could cause deterioration of the priming compound.

Shortly thereafter, Jack shows up with Italian subs for lunch. During lunch Jack explained what he had been up to. "I took your pistols and your loaded ammo and test fired both. As expected, both had a POI(point of impact) several inches below the POA(point of aim). This is a common finding with cowboy pistols. It is caused by Ruger barrel groove characteristics, short shooting distances and low powder charges. The last two are "par for the course" in cowboy action shooting. We will correct that today and match the POI to the POA."

We then started our home gun modifications and action jobs. The first thing Jack did was to open the armorer's tool kit that Ed had provided. He then said, "this kit includes all the tools you will ever need when working on your guns. It includes: specifically designed multi size tips for straight, phillips and allen screws. Other tools are: armorer's pliers, brass and plastic tip hammer, fine and medium India stone, brass and steel pin punches, micro file kit and protective rubber sleeves for vice work. We will use all these tools today."

The Stoeger double barrel shotgun was first. Jack took out Ed's box of spare parts, selected the Stoeger parts and said, "Unscrew the small factory sighting gold bead and replace it with this large gold bead from Slix-Beads. The original had a diameter of.12 inch and the replacement has a diameter of.22 inch. This large bead will make target acquisition much easier. The next thing is to replace the soft factory firing pins with hardened stainless steel. You use this special three pronged tool to remove the bushing that holds the firing pin and spring."

"Replace the factory firing pin and spring with the stainless steel one and use this extra power rebound spring. Place blue locktite on the bushing threads and tighten the bushing. The locktite prevents the bushing from backing out and locking the gun. Now do the same with the other pin."

Moving on, "the shotgun is new and does not break open easily. Using 400/800 grit sand paper, work the male and female ends of the hinge till it opens easily–but not so loose that the gun will close when placed in a gun rack. The next step is to polish the chambers. I brought my flex hone brush for 12 gauge. Place the brush on your drill and polish the chamber using this honing oil till the chambers shine like a mirror."

While I was honing the chambers, Jack explained, "a smooth and polished chamber allows the shooter to shuck out the spent shells. Shucking means to perform a quick jerky shotgun rearward/forward motion and the shells come flying out–saving time from removing each spent shell manually. This is feasible if you are using smooth shotgun shells with a brass base–not ribbed shells with steel bases."

The last shotgun modification was the safety. Jack explained, "it is not illegal in CAS to dismantle the safety. Since you are a beginner in this sport and have no experience with long guns, I strongly recommend that you leave the safety as is. The seconds saved in time is not worth the potential danger with a newbie. In time, you may choose to dismantle it."

"Your biggest time saver is the fact that Ed gave you a shotgun with a single trigger compared to the double trigger option. Now use these changes along with the light load I gave you–low charge, 1 oz. of 7.5 shot in a 2 3/4 inch shell and you are good to go. In case you wondered, these modifications on all four guns are all SASS legal."

The next firearm is the Marlin Cowboy rifle. Jack went into Ed's box and took out the appropriate parts. "You will hear from shooters how they had installed "short stroke kits" on their more expensive rifles. There is no such kit available for your rifle. However of all other similar rifles, this Cowboy model has the shortest lever action."

"The first modification is the sights. We are changing the front sight bead from.09 inch to a larger "Grabber" gold bead measuring.13inch. We then will replace the rear Buckhorn sight to a Marble sight, which is a flat top for easy target acquisition. Both these sights are appropriately matched and your POA will match your POI up to 50 yards with the powder charge of 3.5 grain previously mentioned."

The next step was the action job. Jack made me watch an internet video on dismantling this rifle. He then proceeded to dismantle it in a matter of minutes and moved to the actual action job. "We need to sand each part with the three grits–400,800 and 1200." With both of us working we were done in short order. We then exchanged the stock two piece firing pin for a one piece firing pin.

He added, "as we are reassembling the mechanism(as per video) we will be replacing some springs. The mainspring and lever plunger spring were exchanged for reduced power springs. The trigger safety spring was slightly bent to decrease its strength." He then finished the assembly.

I thought we were done but Jack said we had to cycle a round, with the safety on, to make sure the gun functioned properly. To my surprise there was a glitch as the round attempted to enter the chamber. Jack exclaimed, "as I expected." He then removed the lever slide that holds the extractor and said, "the tip of the extractor is too sharp and needs to be filed down." He used the micro file in the armorer's kit and minimally rounded the tip. He added, "this is a do and check process. File a bit and then reassemble the slide and retry to load a round." He did this filing three times and had it perfect. The round smoothly entered the chamber without hesitation.

He then added the two last parts. "We add a leather butt cover to prevent the stock from sliding off our shoulder. We also add a lever wrap to speed up the lever action." When I wondered why a lever wrap was of any use, he explained, "the lever hole that your non trigger fingers fit in is too large and as you work the lever there is too much play. With the lever wrap, your fingers are more secure and this leads to a more efficient and time saving action."

The pistols were next. Jack selected more parts from Ed's box but he left some parts in the box. Jack starts.

"The Ruger New Vaquero is a great pistol. It reminds me of an Everready battery–it shoots on and on and on without breakdowns. The first thing we will do is to correct the discrepancy in the POA/POI. The inches of discrepancy were exactly the same as I found in my own guns and the correction will be the same. The stock front sight is.30 inch high and we will file it down to.25 inch."

He took the hard rubber sleeves in the armorer's kit and placed them in the vise to protect the pistol. With the pistol secure, he filed and checked often with calipers. This was another do and check process since you cannot add metal if too much is removed. At the end, he filed a 45 degree angle at the top rear of the sight. This apparently has a high light reflection to help with a quick sight picture acquisition.

The next step was the action job. After watching the disassembly video, Jack proceeded quickly. I could not believe all the small parts that came out of this pistol. I asked him how on earth we were going to reassemble it. He answered with a smile, "not to worry, been there, done that." We buffed every part with the same three levels of paper grits and Jack added, "after watching the reassembly video, we will reassemble with different springs." The reassembly was slick and neat. We changed the hammer spring to a reduced power of 14 pounds and the trigger spring down to +- 2 pounds. We also changed the base pin spring to an extra power spring to keep the base pin in place. The second pistol was altered in the same manner.

Jack brought up the subject of short stroke kits for the Vaqueros. "There are presently two gunsmiths that I am aware of who provide these kits. One is based on tig welding/cutting and the other provides a drop in kit. This kit with a lowered hammer can shave off 15-20% time in one handed shooters like gunfighter and duelist categories. It is generally believed that it does not provide much benefit in the traditional two handed shooters like ourselves."

Jack announces, "tomorrow is Thursday day 5 and my last day for me. Lady Slipper is starting with your training on Friday. Let's meet at a local family restaurant at 9 AM for breakfast at these directions....... I have several subjects on my list that I had to cover with you. Since you purchased a cowboy cart instead of building one, we are an entire day ahead. After my closing remarks, I suggest that you do some shooting on your own before you take on Lady Slipper's tutorial and training. After your shooting exercise, do some extra reloading because you will spend a lot of ammo next week. Also tonight, go to this website and do a bulk order of bullets. Use this other website for powder and primers–time to order is before you run out. These two internet retailers will deliver your order within two business days."

Thursday day 5. On route to the restaurant, I spotted a sign that said "Dusty's Shooting Range" and made a mental note to ask Jack about it. The restaurant was really an old fashion diner and was moderately busy. Jack pointed out, "When this crowd leaves, the place will be empty till lunch. We will be able to stay in our booth and finish our talk." The waitress came and we ordered.

"You may have noticed Dusty's range a mile from here. This is where you will spend the next days with Lady Slipper. Dusty maintains six cowboy stages for practice seven days a week. He charges $10 for a three hour attendance and $20 dollar for all day. He repaints the targets and reorganizes them each evening. He is open from 9am to 5pm. He is usually at the range but if he is not present, you leave your money in the enclosed metal box and write your name on the envelope provided. This is a good man and he will get to know you–he likes to talk but he is not bothersome once you start shooting. SASS operational and safety rules apply."

The food arrived, was very good and plentiful. Jack then started, "You probably noticed that there were parts left over in Ed's box. These are spare parts for all four guns. It is impossible to maintain every part in these guns that a gunsmith would carry. I have chosen the problem ones you need at home for quick repairs. Any other part is ordered through Brownell or Numrich parts. For the Stoeger shotgun, you have a set of firing pin rebound springs, a mainspring, two hammer impeller springs and two top lever springs.

The Marlin rifle has an ejector/spring and an extractor/ spring. The Vaqueros have extra 14 pound hammer springs, a reduced power trigger spring, hammer plunger spring/pin, pawl plunger spring, gate detent spring and a transfer bar. Guess you are getting the idea that springs are important– they break or weaken and need replacement."

"The next item is your holsters. Two holsters, belt, slides for shotgun and 38special rounds is called a "Rig". You have a high end tooled black rig. Basically keep it clean. If your pistols are sticking in the holsters, place your pistol in the holsters and store them in the safe to stretch the leather. Spray silicone inside the holsters before a match and the guns will easily pull out. Other quality points include flared out tops, exposed trigger guard, angled away holsters, 2 in drop holsters below the belt and a comfort tapered belt. You have a shotgun slide that snaps over the belt buckle and a 38 ammo slide placed in front of your right holster.

"The remainder of my list includes quick tips and I will just quickly go over them.

- You have 14 pound hammer springs on your Vaqueros. That means you need a soft primer for ignition–stay with Federal primers since they are the softest. If none available use Winchesters.
- Make an order tonight at Dillons. You need a spare parts kit for your Square Deal B reloader and add this list of springs..............!

- With the same order, add a 7 hole cartridge gage from EGW. I test all my competition ammo for splits, high primers and other defects which can lock up a gun.
- Also with the same order, add a shooting timer. Lady Slipper will show you how to use it.
- Keep your loaded ammo in clear wide mouth plastic containers with a sealing twist cap.
- Load your pistols rounds with nickel plated case, use brass for rifle. This separates the different powder charges of 3.0 vs. 3.5 grains.
- Clean your guns regularly and spray the internal mechanism with cleaning spray powder blasts followed by light gun oil. A clean and well oiled firearm will give you better service.
- Polish your brass after each shooting event. Clean brass not only looks good but it sizes with less resistance in your reloader. It only takes one hour if you polish the brass in the tumbler after getting home. It takes longer if you wait for days."

"You have read the book on Cowboy Action Shooting and here is the latest book from the same author. It is called "Reloading–A Practical Hobby". You will learn so much more about reloading and I am sure you will find it full of usable information."

"This terminates my portion of your tutorial and I will check with you during Lady Slipper's training. You are well equipped with the tools of the trade. It has been a pleasure guiding you to this point and you made my job easy because of your dedication and focus to learn."

I answered with a sincere Thank You and shook his hand in gratitude.

I drove into Dusty's range and found three shooters going through the stages. Dusty was in the office/clubhouse. I introduced myself and Dusty pointed out that Jack had given him my life's history. We had a pleasant talk and then paid for three hours of range time. For an extra $6, he gave me a red spray can to paint my own targets.

Out comes all my gear and guns without the period clothing. Jack had suggested that I wear my cowboy boots and hat. It takes a while to get use to walking steadily and shooting a rifle without hat interference.

I headed out to Stage 1 and to the loading table with my four guns and ammo. Each pistol was loaded with 5 rounds with an empty chamber under the hammer. My reading explained why this was necessary. Some pistols do not use a transfer bar and the firing pin is attached to the hammer. With these guns, a dropped gun may discharge if there was a round under the hammer–not so if your gun has a transfer bar.

I then shot five quick pistol rounds at the freshly painted pistol targets and was shocked to see the results–I never hit a single steel plate. I shot again but this time I took slow and careful aim at each target. This time I had all hits near center. This meant two things. The first was that the front sight filing did assure that POA matched POI. The second was that operator error was the cause of the initial five misses. I had to slow down and aim. I was a newbie and had to act like one.

I stayed with the pistols for another hour and gained confidence as my speed and accuracy improved gradually. I then changed to the rifle. Loading the rifle simply involved adding ten rounds to the lower tubular magazine. I took several shots and was surprised to discover that you can miss a 16 inch target at 16 yards. The old adage, "a gun will not automatically seek the target for a hit–you need to place the sights on target."

I did the same with the rifle, shot it for an hour. I got to a point that I could rack the lever smoothly and keep my eyes on the targets. I also noticed how smooth the lever was cycling–the result of our action job. I again became comfortable with the rifle and was ready to try the shotgun.

Loading the shotgun required a special technique. You could not load a double barrel shotgun one shell at a time–it was too time consuming. The book on Cowboy Action Shooting clearly demonstrated the proper technique. Using the advantage of the shotgun slide which has slots that hold two shells, grab two shell with the left hand as the shotgun is held almost chest high. Then apply the shells simultaneously at 45 degrees on top of the chamber mouths. Then simply lower the shells and push them into the chambers. Once practiced, it can be a quick and smooth process. I used my iPhone and researched a video showing this technique. The expert made it look so simple. I figured it will take me a long time to get good at performing this maneuver.

I took two shots at shotgun knockdown targets and was surprised to have one still standing. This told me that a few pellets that is a hit on fixed targets will not work on knockdowns. You need to be on target. The last thing to practice was shucking the spent shells. I had polished the chambers using the flex hone brush/oil. The quick rearward and forward jerking motion sent the spent shell flying out of the chambers. I then spent a half hour practicing the shotgun.

For the last half hour of my shooting session, I shot all four guns in succession. Slow at first then as fast as I could without too many misses. I then headed home to place my order with the Dillon Blue Press. I then cleaned my guns and started reloading. I figured that I would need a lot of ammo for the next training days with Lady Slipper.

For personal reasons, I was really looking forward to my days with such a lovely woman!

CHAPTER 4

Lady Slipper

Friday day 6. I arrived at Dusty's range at 7:30 AM thinking I would be early and would have time to get my gear ready. As I pulled up to the office, there was Dusty and Lady Slipper with a coffee in their hands, a smile on their faces and basking in the morning sun. I stopped, joined the gathering, and Dusty offered me a cup of coffee. Small talk ensued and finally got to paying for range time. Lady Slipper suggested that I pay for two full days since other plans were in the works for Sunday. She did mention to Dusty that we would be back on Monday.

We then headed to our vehicles to unload my gear. While walking I noticed how Lady Slipper was dressed. Other than a cowboy hat and boots, she was wearing form-fitting jeans and a sleeveless blouse that highlighted her full bustline. *How does one keep a focused and professional demeanor?* With all my gear loaded she stated, "the goal of this training session is to show you how to shoot efficiently, safely and according to SASS rules. This will be accomplished within one to five days, or whatever you need. At the end of your training you will be ready to perform a "solo" run in a real cowboy shoot–and feel at ease during your performance."

"This morning, you are free to proceed on your own. I will be watching you and if I see a safety or SASS rule violation, I will yell STOP. This means you freeze on the spot, even if your gun's hammers are pulled back, YOU DO NOT FIRE. It is extremely important that you have a clear mind-set about this command. Any shooter who disregards this "stop order" and continues to fire will get a Match D/Q. I should add that all shooters on your posse are technically safety officers. This means that anyone who sees a safety violation can yell out STOP even if the RO did not see the actual violation."

The training session starts. I pick up the loading block of ammo, holster both pistols, pickup my rifle/shotgun and take two steps toward the loading table, STOP. "The long guns are carried pointing up at the sky, not at the ground." *Great way to begin the day especially when I knew that to start with!* I finally got to the loading table and loaded all my guns. STOP "You load the pistols and rifle but you do not load the shotgun until it is time to shoot the shotgun on the firing line." *That one I did not know.* So I then turned around to bring my loading block back to my cart and STOP. "If you wish to bring your loading block back to your cart, you must leave your pistols on the loading table. Most shooters find a way to attach it out of the way to the back of your gun belt. I have a lanyard on my loading block and I installed a hook on my gun belt to hold the block out of the way." *This was also new info and worth doing.*

I forgot to mention that before loading my guns, Lady Slipper had described the shooting scenario–a simple one. First pistol, shoot the pistol targets(1-5) left to right. Second pistol, shoot the pistol targets right to left(5-1). Rifle, shoot the same as the pistols. Left to right on first five shots and right to left on next five shots. Shotgun, shoot the three knockdown targets left to right. After shooting at all three targets, if any knockdown did not fall, all knockdowns are shot until they fall.

So I then proceeded to the firing line and Lady Slipper was the acting RO. This is when I heard the classic commands. "Does the shooter understand the course of fire?" I answered Yes. "Is the shooter ready?" I answered Yes. "Stand by!" Several seconds elapsed and then the BUZZER GOES OFF and my brain froze. I had no idea which gun to fire first or recalled anything of the shooting sequence. That is when Lady Slipper literally started laughing.

"OK, you just experienced your first 'fruit salad' syndrome. This can occur anytime in even the most experienced shooter. It means that the buzzer triggers a barrage of electrical impulses to your brain, and unless your are well focused on the shooting sequence, you will fail to engage the proper physical sequence. Later on I will give you some tips on how to avoid this dilemma. If you are ready, let's try again."

The shooting sequence went well and I did not hear that dreaded stop word. Lady Slipper said, "nice job, you hit every target in the proper sequence. A bit slow but at least you did not shoot me or yourself in the foot." That lighthearted comment just simply softened all the stop commands I had received. I then picked up my long guns and turned to go to the unloading table. STOP. "You turned toward me and you pointed the shotgun at my nose. Sweeping someone with an unloaded gun is a Stage D/Q. Always turn away from the RO."

I then proceeded to the unloading table and Lady Slipper acted as the unloading table officer. She made me show that the open shotgun was empty. I then racked the rifle's lever to show her that the rifle was empty and left the lever open. I then unloaded the pistols of all five spent shells. She then made me turn the cylinder a full turn to show her that the pistols were unloaded. So I finally survived my first shooting sequence with only four STOPS and one FRUIT SALAD. I then brought my guns to the cart, reloaded the loading block and replaced my spent shotgun shells.

"You are now free until the posse finishes this stage and moves on to the next stage. This is when you take a few minutes to read the next stage scenario." She then hands me a booklet of scenarios for the rest of the day.

Why did I even suspect she was not thinking ahead. I read the next scenario and put the booklet down.

Lady Slipper then asks? "So what do you do until the next stage? This is when you join the work crew. The least favorite job is picking up brass and shotgun shells. Take these tools and go to work" With a smile on her face she hands me the stage's routine 3 foot pickup tool with a rubber tip, and a wooden cane with a bucket bolted to the end of the cane. With this tool you pick up the spent shells without bending over–not good for some old backs. It is also some club rules that prevent pistols from falling out of holsters or sweeping shooters as one bends over. As a newbie, picking up brass will be appreciated by all. Later on we will discuss the other duties of posse members."

Moving on to the next stage, Lady Slipper reads the scenario and asks if there are any questions about the shooting sequence. She then informs me that she will act as the loading table officer and will clarify the standard loading techniques. "Your pistol is loaded as follows: Load one, skip one and then load four more. Close the loading gate and click the cylinder into the lock position. Verify that there is an empty chamber under the hammer. Then lift the gun up to my line of sight and show me that there is an unloaded chamber under the hammer. Repeat with the next pistol. The rifle is on the table with the action open. Close the lever and lower the hammer under control of your thumb. Never dry fire any gun anywhere because that will result in a Stage D/Q." I then loaded the rifle with 10 rounds and waited for the command "next shooter."

Somehow I shot this second stage with one pistol miss but no stop command. The next stage also went well until I put my rifle down on a vertical rest. I guess I put the rifle down too fast and it fell to the ground. Yet I did not hear the word stop. She explained later, "this event was classed as a 10 second penalty as long as the rifle was empty and did not break the 170 degree rule. If the fallen rifle had broken the 170 degree rule(explanation to follow), it would be a Stage D/Q. Also, many clubs now use tables as long gun rests instead of vertical rests–thereby avoiding this situation."

That was it for the morning session. We left all our gear in the office with Dusty and headed to the local diner for lunch.

The diner was nearly full so we knew we had a long wait for our food to arrive. That did not matter to Lady Slipper since she had many subjects to discuss. "Let's go over the unfinished topics left open this morning. First, what is probably a rare but serious situation that leads to a stop order–a squib load. Even with auto indexing progressive presses, anyone can load a bullet on a primer without adding powder. The primer will propel the bullet into the barrel where it will stop. If one fires another round, you can imagine that a gun can blow up and likely cause injuries. The shooter may not recognize the light explosion of a primer without powder–trust your RO, spotters or posse's STOP order."

"The next is how to prevent a fruit salad syndrome. As a newbie don't rush to be an early shooter. Stay back and pick up brass. Before all the shooters start shooting, run the sequence in your head again. Repetition is the best aid to focusing."

"Here are several that do not need long explanations. What is the significance of a Stage D/Q? Answer–if you are competing then the game is over. You then finish the day as a JFF(just for fun). Why pre check your match ammo in a cartridge gage? Answer–to pick out high primers and other defects that may lock up a gun. Why do clubs set up some of their own rules? Answer–because they may have had a bad experience in the past. My favorite one is to not rack a rifle lever until the rifle is lifted to eye level. To prevent a close accidental discharge which may cause a Stage or Match D/Q. Why do we use loading blocks? Answer–a loading block holds 10 rifle rounds and two 5 round holes for pistol. Prevents over loading a firearm."

"The next two require more explanations. The 170 degree rule states that any firearm muzzle has to stay within 170 degrees in all planes and down range. This includes left to right and ground to sky. If the muzzle is in this plane it will have its muzzle down range–away from other participants and spectators. Breaking the 170 rule is a Stage D/Q."

"Finally the last one covers other duties of posse members. The other jobs include: time/score keeper, loading table officer, unloading table officer and spotters. We have three spotters that watch each target for a hit or a miss. The use of three is to prevent a tie. If one spotter has to abstain because he was distracted, the other two make the call. If these two spotters cannot agree, then the benefit goes to the shooter with the least number of misses. Now add the RO and one brass picker and you have a minimum of 8 workers. That is why the ideal posse has 16 members–8 work while 8 shoot and the process then reverses. That way everyone works and the posse moves along smoothly."

Our order finally arrived and we had a quick lunch. Lady Slipper was eager to head back to the range. She gave me the agenda for the afternoon–tips and techniques on drawing and shooting pistols efficiently and accurately.

Lady Slipper put her holster rig on with unloaded pistols. She then said, "in slow motion I will describe and show how to draw and shoot the first round. First step, firmly place your right hand on the pistol grip and quickly snatch the pistol out of the holster, with your trigger finger out of the trigger guard. Step two, point the pistol down range and bring your left hand to support the pistol as the barrel points 45 degrees off the ground. Step three, lift the pistol up to the target and use your left thumb to cock the hammer. Step four, as you are very near the target, move your trigger finger into the trigger guard and fire as the sight picture places you on the target." She then loaded one pistol and demonstrated this fluid motion several times–each time faster than the last. Finally she said, "use the timer to start me, when I hear the buzzer I will draw and hit the target." On the buzzer, the pistol came flying out of the holster and in a flash she hit the steel target. "WHOA" is all that came out of my mouth. She then explained, "I have been practicing my draw for over a year and you don't have to be that fast. The point is that in competition there is no room for a languid draw. You have to be alert and quick to get the pistol safely on target." With an unloaded pistol I then practiced the draw repeatedly until Lady Slipper approved the speed and technique. I then drew and fired the pistol several times.

The next tip was how to efficiently cock the hammer without wasting time. The answer, "as soon as the first round is fired, move your left thumb to the hammer and as the pistol is moved to the next target, cock the hammer. When the pistol arrives on target, fire. This holds true whether the next target is adjacent such as target 1 and 2, or whether the next target is far such as 1 and 5. It is of note that a beginner should fire when the front sight is in the target center and with a momentary pause, whereas the experienced shooter will start squeezing the trigger as soon as the front sight passes the edge of the target, leading to a smooth continuous movement from one target to another–the pistol is always moving."

Lady Slipper demonstrated this technique in slow and fast motion. I then practiced this technique until I picked up the correct speed and rhythm. "The next tip is the safe gun transfer. Assuming you are right handed, after the first pistol has fired all five rounds, holster it. Make sure the pistol has entered the holster by snugging it tight in its place. Many a shooter has missed the holster and dropped a pistol to the ground, this is a Stage D/Q."

"The next step is to snatch the left pistol out by using your left hand. This is followed by transferring the left hand held pistol to the right hand while pointing the pistol downrange. The remainder of the sequence is then the same. The important point is to securely do a gun transfer without dropping a loaded gun, this would be a Match D/Q."

I then practiced this proper technique till I got it right. Most important, I could appreciate a firm gun transfer versus the flimsy loose method I had been performing. All that was needed was to increase my speed which would come with practice. Lady Slipper then added, "I am going to quickly mention some tips and then you can practice on your own."

1. "When you are ready to shoot as you are approaching the firing line, loosen your pistols in their holsters, even if you had sprayed them with silicone."
2. "Don't cock your hammer prematurely. I used the 45 degree rule where it is actually 5 feet. Cocking a hammer within 5 feet is a 10 second penalty."
3. "Keep in mind that an accidental discharge(AD) within 5 feet of the shooter is a Match D/Q. An AD between 5 and 10 feet is a Stage D/Q."
4. "If you need to move to a specific spot to shoot your pistols, do not draw on the move. Wait till you get to the designated location and face downrange. I have seen experienced shooters draw while moving and find themselves breaking the 170 degree rule–it is not worth it!"
5. "If your pistol breaks and you cannot finish the five rounds, follow the club rules on how to proceed. Two common choices are: Stop, claim a broken gun and hold the muzzle up for the RO to confiscate–a reshoot will follow. The other method is for you to put the pistol safely on the table pointing downrange and continue the firing sequence–every round left in the broken pistol will be a miss. The same rules hold for rifle and shotgun. This is one subject that is worth clarifying when shooting at a new club."

"Go ahead now and shoot your pistols as I watch." The first five strings of fire went well and I found that increasing my speed came naturally. Then it happened. I was cocking the hammer when my thumb slipped off the hammer and I heard a click instead of a bang. STOP. "Well I knew that this would happen as I saw you increase your speed. You were going too fast! As the hammer slipped before it got to full cock, the cylinder partially turned, but it was enough to pull the primer off the firing pin–resulting in a click. Now in this case, you slipped the hammer on the fourth round. This means that you have two unfired rounds left, that is round 4 and 5."

"Go ahead and resume fire." I fired the next round but the next one was a click. I know I looked dumbfounded but Lady Slipper quickly explained. "After that last click, the RO will loudly say–one more, go around. You have to cock the hammer and fire each cylinder till it goes bang. That could mean one or several dry fires till it goes bang. With each dry firing, you had better be on target or you will end up with a miss when it does go bang. A slipped hammer is a hard way to do this sport–it is better to slow down and avoid this irritating situation."

To train me on managing a slipped hammer, Lady Slipper had me intentionally slip the hammer and then cycle the cylinder till the bang arrived. It took a while to get use to this, but it was a good exercise.

Friday evening, end of day 6. "Tomorrow AM we will discuss the tips for shooting the rifle and shotgun." I then asked, "what is there for evening entertainment in town." She answered, "the local hangout is a place called the Country Roadhouse. Many of the cowboy shooters gather every Friday and Saturday night. It serves the usual burgers and sandwiches and these are the nights that they have a DJ. This is a dancing spot where we do line dancing, country two-step and country waltz." I added, "I know how to two-step and waltz. I was raised in Texas where dancing always included these dances. I two-stepped all through high school and college. It has been years since then but I suspect that I can likely jump in and follow my partner." Lady slipper quickly came back, "well in that case, I would love to introduce you to the festivities. Pick me up at 7 pm and I will call ahead and reserve a table for two." "Great, where do you live?" To my surprise she answered, "I live in the same condo complex as you do. You live at #24 Derby Lane and I am at #97 Derby Lane." "Wow, a small world! What is the dress code?" She said, "jeans, cowboy shirt, boots and hat."

When she answered the door, I immediately got an eye full. She had a welcoming smile and was wearing designer jeans, a western ladies blouse and an expensive cowboy hat. Even her cowboy boots were high end. An attractive woman dressed to a T–unbeatable. Off we went.

The Country Roadhouse was spacious and well decorated in a western decor. A large dance floor was surrounded by tables for two or four and the stage was already set up for the DJ. The host seated us and a waitress took our order–I had a draft beer and Sue had a white wine. I said, "On a social event, I feel I should call you Sue and hope you will call me Wil." "I agree."

Refreshments arrived and Sue took the opportunity to explain how the club was organized. "Tables are for couples–married or just dating. The single women sit at tables in groups and the men stand at or around the bar. At 9 PM the DJ starts the dancing. He usually starts with several line dances and the floor fills with 80–90% women. The men in attendance are historically two-steppers or waltz enthusiasts. Very few men do line dancing. People come here to dance!"

"When a two-step or waltz is announced, the single woman who wants a partner will stand up at their table. They are quickly partnered up by the single men. If a woman stays sitting, she will not be asked to dance. Those women who do not want to dance also take the time to visit the ladies room. Single men do not ask ladies to dance if they are with a date at a table. There are several slow dances, what is referred to as "belt buckle polishers" and these rules of etiquette still apply. Since there are usually two women to each man, all the single men get plenty of opportunity to dance. In short, all who come here want a good time. We don't have fights over hormonal drives."

My question was, "I am certain that some of these single men and women will return as paired-up dates. How do you keep and adequate supply of singles to maintain this social pattern." She countered, "not an issue, there are plenty of guests waiting to enter. The room occupancy is 200 persons. The bouncers will keep a head count and will close the doors at 200. Just look outside during intermissions and you will find a line of people waiting to enter. There are always people leaving early and the bouncers will replace the count accordingly. It seems that there is an early crowd that comes for dinner and dancing till 11 PM and a crowd that comes later till closing at 2 AM. In actuality, there are more singles after 11 PM."

We ordered dinner. I took a house Cowboy Burger with coleslaw and Sue took a large salad covered with chicken. During dinner, I jokingly said that since we were sitting at a table for two, that would appear to me that we were on a date. With a smile she said, "Yes it would appear so." As we finished dinner, the DJ was getting set up as it was approaching 9 PM. We both headed to the rest rooms before dancing started.

As I was busy at the urinal, a fellow appeared to my left and said, "well, aren't you the lucky one, partner? On a date with Sue Austin! How did you manage that? She has been dancing here for a year and has never come with a date. Many of us have tried to escort her but she has universally declined! This is a great gal so be kind!"

I gracefully thanked him for the information and filed it for future discussion.

The dancing started with line dances and the DJ announced three oldies to start the evening–watermelon crawl, boot scootin boogie, and tush-push. This filled the floor since everyone seemed to know these dances. Sue gracefully announced that she better do these dances because she does not know all the newer line dances. I watched and saw many beautiful women, but very few could hold a candle to Sue.

Sue had natural rhythm and clearly mastered the different moves with grace. Actually her body slithered like a seductive nymph. I knew I was staring at her but I could not keep my eyes off her! After the three dances she admitted that she just loved to dance.

The next dance was a nice two-step. I said, "guess it is time to do the quick-quick-slow-slow!" The song was Adilida by George Strait. The DJ started the song and then started the dancers by calling out "5-6-7-8". I started without stumbling and because the tune had such a good beat, I quickly loosened up. I could tell that Sue was right with my tempo. I didn't know who was leading but we were traveling at the same speed as the other dancers and I was the actual driver. That is when I got bold and went into reverse and Sue became the driver. After several basic steps I swung her back into reverse and resumed driving. I then directed her to perform a simple outside turn and then a simple inside turn. That is when Sue says, "Wow some old tricks never die." I then informed her that this was the limit of my memory bank and we continued traveling with the rest of the dancers to the end of the song.

That is when Sue gave me a huge hug and was smiling ear to ear. She finished by saying, "Will Summer, you never cease to amaze me. Who would have thought that you not only can shoot but you can dance–it's going to be a hell of an evening."

Ernie had been eyeing Sue and her date since they got here. He turned towards his buddy Stan and said, "Look at that, Sue shows up here with a date. That's the first for her. Isn't it a shame that it could not have been one of us dancers who have been trying to date her for a long time." Stan came back, "boy you are really steaming about this Ernie. It is what it is and best to leave it alone," "Well what has this dude got that we don't have? Guess we need to find out don't you think?" "This kind of thinking and behavior will get you in trouble–walk away and move on Ernie."

Ernie kept thinking, *I suppose she will start holding hands and even do a slow dance. In a whole year she has not danced a slow dance with any of us. I wonder if this dude can do a country waltz. I know I am upset, actually I am* ****** *off!*

After the two-step, the DJ announced three newer line dances. Sue said that she knew the first, Tennessee Waltz Surprise, and would dance it. She certainly knew the dance, it was fast but Sue had no trouble maneuvering the complicated steps. This dance certainly fit the category of exercise.

The next announced dance was a country waltz. I looked at Sue and said, "time to do the long-short-short." The song was, Someone must feel like a fool, by Kenny Rogers. The DJ started the song and then started the dancers by calling out "1-2-3". I almost froze, but Sue sensed my hesitation and gently pulled me into the "long, short, short". The song was a classic for a smooth and elegant waltz. It took a few basic cycles before I remembered to sway into a "skating" mode–veering right and left as if skating on ice. Sue recognized the skating and said, "YES". I knew that I should be reversing since no one can dance in reverse continuously without getting hip muscle fatigue. So I went for it and managed to accomplish the feat fairly well. I stayed in reverse until my legs were sore and then swung Sue back in reverse. The dance finished and to my surprise, people were clapping to express their pleasure with the DJ.

Ernie was watching intently and again said to Stan, "the way that fella did a waltz, he has danced before. He starts stiff-like but quickly gets in the groove. The way he is progressing, he is going to eventually show us off. We can't allow that! I am going to scout these two. Do you know where Sue lives?"

Stan was shocked. "You cannot do this. Scouting her is a good way to be charged with stalking! I am not telling you where Sue lives. If you continue with this obsession, you are heading for trouble, and I will have no part of this."

Ernie was thinking, *I am going to follow these two tonight and find out where they live. That way I can better plan my revenge.*

The dancing continued with several line dances that Sue ignored. I found it hard to carry a conversation when the music was so loud and you were not dancing. We found ourselves scooting closer and eventually we were almost in each other's lap. She did not seem to mind and I was a willing participant. Then they announced a slow dance which would be followed by an intermission. The song was, For The Good Times, by Ray Price.

I said to Sue, "is this when you go to the ladies room? She answered, "yes, only if you don't ask me to dance!" "Well, that's an invitation I cannot pass up." We started to slow dance formally as friends. The song inherently had sentimental and loving lyrics such that we started moving closer. My hand moved from her upper back to her lower back and she followed by raising her left arm upwards and her hand reached my neck. We danced in unison and glided effortlessly on the floor. When the dance finished we walked to our table and held hands. After sitting down, I attempted to let go of her hand, but she held on and we ended up holding hands like teenagers. The afterglow came to an end when the waitress showed up to take our second drink order.

The intermission started and I took the opportunity to bring up the subject I was informed while in the men's restroom. Sue listened carefully and did not look surprised. She said, "I was expecting this but not this soon in the evening. He was correct. I started dancing here one year ago when two of my girl friends insisted that I try it. I loved line dancing and continued coming with them on weekends. Eventually I learned to two-step and waltz, which required a male partner. I danced with all the single men–as dancing partners. I did not take any man home and I never dated them nor did I ever come as their platonic escort."

I thought this over and touched her hand and asked, "why are things apparently different tonight." She smiled and added, "The doctor who treated my post divorce depression told me several months ago that it was time to rejoin the human race. He told me that I had too many "what if's" in my life and was using these excuses to maintain my reclusive life. My doctor went as far as stating that it was time to allow a man in my life, it was time to let go of living alone and always being in control. He also reiterated that it was time to allow a male companion to share my world. That was four months ago and then you showed up. I will sound forward but I was immediately and unexplainably attracted to you."

I put my hands up and said, STOP. Sue suddenly broke out in spontaneous laughter–"guess I deserved that!" I looked at her and sincerely admitted, "I also cannot explain my feelings but I have felt this same attraction from the moment I saw you. I am sorry if I pushed you to this personal admission, but I will never do it again." We just looked in each other's eyes and held hands again. *I knew that something special had just happened and I hoped that it would continue and progress.*

I cannot believe it, Sue and the dude are doing a slow dance. She has never danced a slow dance with any of us. They started as friends but now they are cheek to cheek and their bodies are enveloped. Finally the dance is over–but now they are holding hands. That's enough. I will know where you all live by tonight!

The dancing resumed, the DJ announced a lively two-step to bring the crowd alive, Small Town Saturday Night by Hal Ketchum. We joined in and realized you had to move with the other dancers, We were traveling rather quickly around the perimeter of the dance floor. It felt like the running of the bulls–we had to avoid getting trampled. The one thing I noticed that the faster the two-step, the less turns and movements were observed. I did direct Sue into some turns and she was able to do them because of her physical prowess on the dance floor. I then recalled that the man directs but the woman performs. *I thought, I like it when the woman does all the work.*

The song came to an end but the DJ kept everyone on the floor. He announced a medium tempo two-step and he expected more turns, spins and complicated movements. The song was, Me and Bobby McGee by Roger Miller. The tempo was perfect for executing turns and multi-movement groups. I remembered how to bring my partner into sweetheart position and promenade around the floor. I then said to Sue, "what do I do now?" She asked if I knew how to do Around the World. I nodded with uncertainty, she said "follow me." Starting in sweetheart position she turned in front of me and headed to my left, then behind me and she moved to my right where she did a 360 degree turn back to sweetheart. All I could say is, "what happened." She laughed and said, "nothing new, the woman always does all the work!"

Sue then said, "since we are still in sweetheart position, let's do the pull-through." I said, "never heard of it." Before I knew it, she pulled in front of me and stood on my left, then slid behind me to get back on my right into sweetheart. She did all this without a single turn. *Guess that is why it is called a pull-through.* We then went back in standard position and finished the dance.

When we got back to our table, I commented that I needed some practice. We agreed that we would get together in my gun room and practice these movements that I either forgot or never learned. The next dances were line dances, but Sue never got up to dance. I think we were enjoying our company too much to separate.

During our break, I asked her, "where does your alias Lady Slipper come from?" She responded, "I was born and raised in Minnesota. The state flower is an orchid called Lady Slipper. It is a very slowly growing plant that can take years to bloom with a multi lobed orchid. It took me many years to come out of seclusion just like it takes many years to produce its first flower. I guess the similarities caught my eye." *I thought, the flower is beautiful like its namesake!*

The next dance was a waltz, Last Cheaters Waltz by Boz Scaggs. The dance floor was packed. It was clear that the two step and waltz were the main staple of this club. After all, everyone could dance from singles to couples. All the dancers were following floor etiquette by dancing on the perimeter in counter clockwise fashion. Some couples were doing "buckle polishing" in the center of the floor. The song was one of my all time favorites. I was so pleased to see that we performed this dance as well as anyone else.

The dancing continued. We talked, we laughed and just enjoyed the evening and our company. With every hour it got easier and more natural to maintain a conversation. The topics seemed to just pop up and hold our attention. We danced often, but sometimes several dances passed us by because we were so deeply involved in a mutual topic.

The DJ announced a slow dance to be followed by an intermission. The song was, I Overlooked an Orchid by Mickey Gilley. We looked at each other when he said the word Orchid–was it fate or divine? We started dancing to this lovely song and without hesitation came into each other's arms. Before I realized it, I had both my hands on her lower back and she had both hands around my neck. Somehow, it felt as if we had fused into one person. We wove back and forth and we were never aware of our steps. We were in our own world and the passion kept growing–then the song ended. We looked at each other and then it happened–we kissed. The kiss was real and sincere, yet impossible to describe. As we separated, Sue said, "oh my heavens", with a glow on her face.

The lights came on and the DJ made an announcement. "It is close to midnight and I know some of you will be leaving. Because of popular demand, for the next three Saturdays, we will be teaching you a weekly partner dance, like two step, a couple's dance. The three dances will be the Blue Rose, the El Paso and the Texas Waltz. Come early since the free teaching session will start at 8 PM sharp. To give you a preview, in the center of the dance floor are our instructors, Ben and Dixie. I will play the song Blue Rose by Pam Tillis and the instructors will present a short version of the dance. The music starts and Ben and Dixie started dancing, as if there was no one watching. Jaws were dropping and people were smiling. The music suddenly stops and the place exploded with applause and whistling. The DJ says, "looks like a winner, see you tomorrow night for our first lesson. Remember 8 PM sharp and you need a partner–this is not a line dance."

On our short drive home, Sue said, "tomorrow is a work day for us. I have a full agenda to cover. How about coming over at 7 AM and I will have breakfast ready. That will put us at the range by 9 AM." "I agreed and asked if we were going tomorrow night for dancing, dinner and our first partner dance lesson." She answered, "Yes, I would love to." We were home in 15 minutes. I walked Sue to her door and said, "this has been the most pleasant evening I have had in 10 years." Before I knew it, we were in each other's arms and kissed." She said, "it was also the best night of my recent life, goodnight."

As I left I noticed a black jeep Cherokee parked across the street. What I did not realize is that he followed us home.

Saturday day 7. I was up at 6 AM to get ready and load up all my gear and guns. I used my check list which had not yet failed me. I was at Sue's place on time. She greeted me with a smile and a warm hug. A full breakfast of scrambled eggs, home fries, toast and coffee was ready. We managed to eat and talk over an hour. We were on the road by 8 am. Dusty was already at work. I unloaded my gear and headed for the first stage of the day. Sue then took over.

"This AM we will concentrate on the rifle. Load your rifle and then place it on the right table, place the shotgun on the left table for this exercise." On the way with both long guns, I carefully placed the shotgun on the left table and then the rifle on the right table. STOP, "wow that is early in the morning for a stop order" Lady Slipper came over and said, "As you laid your rifle on the table, I noticed that you intentionally placed it so the entire lever is past the edge of the table. I know you did this so you can quickly access the gun and the lever. However the trigger must be left over the table and only the finger loops of the lever can hang over the table edge."

"All rifle scenarios this morning will be, shoot five left to right and repeat with the last five rounds." "At the buzzer I start shooting, after two shots" STOP. "You shot target 1 and then moved the rifle to target 2 and racked the lever. That is a waste of time. As you are moving from target 1 to target 2 is when you should be racking the lever. That way as you arrive on target 2, all you need to do is fire." I finished the cycle and she commented, "you nicely lifted the rifle to chest high before racking the lever for the first shot–that was great!"

"For the next exercise, I am going to load your rifle and will explain later." With the rifle properly staged, I commenced shooting on the buzzer. On the fifth shot all I heard was a click. STOP. "Now you know you have a live round in the chamber but it did not go off. Two things will cause this. Either you have a defective(or absent) primer or a high primer."

"Let's assume you have a high primer. Upon firing, the firing pin pushed the high primer deeper in the primer pocket. Now if you fire again, the shot will go bang. So just pull back the hammer and fire. BANG. Yes, I had slipped a round with a high primer. Now if you pull the hammer back and it still goes click, you have a bad or absent primer. Eject the round and continue firing. Once the rifle is empty, you can load another round from your slide."

"Well, that is an excellent teaching tool. Had you not planted the defective round, it could have taken months before I experience the actual high or defective primer–which would likely have occurred during a real match."

"For the next exercise, stage your rifle on the right table and the shotgun on the left table. After shooting the rifle, carry the rifle with the lever open to the shotgun table and then shoot the shotgun." At the buzzer, I empty the rifle, open the lever, point the rifle downrange and walk over to the shotgun table some 10 feet away. STOP. "I actually knew that I had done everything correctly. So what on earth is going on now?" Lady Slipper very softly asks, "are we going to mosey along to the shotgun or are we going to move it–pronto? Time is money in this game. You need to hustle as safely as you can and get to the next gun ASAP." *I have to remember, this is a fast sport. We not only try to shoot fast, but we also have to move with gusto–safely.*

"I want to add, if you are shooting your pistols first and have to hustle to the next table, make sure that your last pistol is holstered before even turning toward the next gun. Then hustle over. Your Black Hill holsters will hold the pistols from bouncing out if they were firmly inserted. Shooters with economical rigs have holsters that can loosely hold pistols. These shooters will hustle with both hands on their pistols."

"For the next exercise, load the rifle and then turn around for a few seconds." *Without hesitation I complied.*

I wonder what she is up to this time. On the buzzer, I shot at the first target and heard a CLICK?

Lady Slipper proudly steps to the firing line and says, "you know you have a live round in the chamber and you got a click. Proceed and do the maneuver I just taught you." So I pull back the hammer and get another click, I eject the round and bring another and fire. I get another click. I stop myself and say, "I give up, what did you do and what is going on?" Lady Slipper softly says, "look at the rifle next to the hammer. Is the red flag on the cross bolt safety showing. No. Well something or someone put the safety on since red means ready to fire."

Out of her pocket comes a small zip-lock bag with a small black donut–an O-RING. She explains, "this o-ring fits in the groove of the cross bolt safety and prevents the safety from going on–as it happens when you place the rifle on a table or accidentally place pressure on the receiver. With the o-ring in place, the safety is technically dismantled and the potential problem goes away. This is a legal modification."

"For the next exercise, I want you to shoot your rifle as fast as you can and I don't care if you miss, then put the rifle down on the table and run to the shotgun. Let us see what happens." I followed her direction and pushed myself and cycled the action as fast as possible and really did some speed shooting. "OK, the result is as follows: You had three misses, you threw down the rifle on the table and broke the 170 degree rule, the lever accidentally closed and you only fired 9 rounds(the tenth round is right there on the ground). So let's analyze each event."

"The misses were simply because you were going too fast for your current ability. Breaking the 170 rule is a no-no in this sport. Place the rifle down, don't throw it, and always take the time to place it pointing downrange. Remember that special attention to safety relaxes the RO when you come up to shoot. The shooter who throws his rifle down and does other aggressive moves, keeps the RO tense and there is no need for that. The lever that falls closed is no longer a safety or procedural violation under this new rule. At the end of the shooting string, the shooter picks up the rifle and shows the RO that the rifle is unloaded by racking the lever –before going to the unloading table."

"Now jacking out a live round as you just did is a common problem with all the fast shooters we have. The issue is how to manage it. First, if you or the RO or the spotters do not notice the jacked round, you end up taking a miss when the brass picker finds a live round on the ground. More than likely the RO will likely yell out– one more. In which case you take 5 seconds to load one round from your slide and hit the target. Now if you miss the target you have lost 10 seconds. Some shooters just ignore the jacked round and just take the 5 second miss.

This leaves a bad taste in people's mouths and labels you as a GAMER(more later at lunch). So the proper thing to do is to load one round and aim well. A hit means you have lost 5 seconds for reloading just like the gamer's 5 second miss, but with more respect!"

"For the next exercise, load your riflle and I am going to change the targets. At the buzzer, I started shooting and suddenly I could not see the third rifle target when my rifle was ready to fire. So I had to move several steps to the right and, STOP. "Yes, I intentionally moved some targets so you would have a blind spot. The rule is you cannot move both feet with a loaded and cocked gun. What you have to do in this case is to keep your left foot planted, stretch out your right leg to move your right foot and your body to the right, till the blind spot clears. This rule is also true with pistols and shotguns."

"The next is a quick statement on protocol. It is customary to limit the number of shooters at the loading table to two. This gives the loading officer the time to do his job and allows the correct elbow room for the two loading guns. It is also customary to allow one shooter at the unloading table. There is more checking to be done by the unloading officer, and more brass for the shooter to gather from the posse's brass picker. Many times the unloading officer will help bring brass or a long gun back to the shooter's cart."

"The final exercise of the morning is a mechanical rifle failure caused by the operator." With a loaded rifle, Lady

Slipper racks the lever and fires away–CLICK. "So what happened, well in this case it is not a high or bad primer. It is a case where I did not push the lever forward enough to bring up the next cartridge. The lifter was not engaged. Watch me move the lever and at the end watch the lifter engage and lift the round up with a metallic clang. The technical term for this is, the lever has to be racked to it's apogee to engage the cartridge lifter. Here, try it for yourself and watch the internal mechanism. You have to see it to believe and understand these details."

"The significance of this will be appreciated when you start developing speed without adequate focusing. I know it is corny but the firearm is a mechanical tool and you are the operator–the gun will not operate on its own."

"Let me add one tip before we head out for lunch. Shoot your own guns. You know what each firearm requires to properly function. The more you practice and shoot, the sooner your firearms will be an extension of your arms and hands. Shooting other people's guns is a novelty but it adds nothing to your hard earned dexterity."

The diner was a familiar and welcomed site. We were late for lunch because of the involved training session and a large breakfast to boot. We ordered, I had a hot chicken sandwich and Sue had a toasted western sandwich. As the coffee arrived, I asked if we were on business or social time? "We are on business time and the topic till our food arrives is The Psychology of Shooting–theory and practicality."

"First in theory. Why do cowboy shooters clearly exhibit the will to shoot fast and accurately? The answer is, that we shoot as well as we can because we love the sport and it becomes a matter of pride and honor. Some say we do this to win awards, or to look good in front of our friends. In reality, I feel good when I shoot well."

"For practical purposes, speed and accuracy separates the cowboy shooters into three groups, Traditional, JFF and the Gamers. There are sub groups which is a subject for another time. The traditional shooter is a two handed shooter who likes to compete against shooters in his category. In our case, you are 62 and I just turned 60, so we are in the senior category, but separated into mens and ladies groups. The problem being, the traditional group also has the Gamers in this group."

"The Gamers in my opinion are shooters that participate for the thrill of winning. They shoot and move fast with an aggressive intent to be better than anyone else. In their own way, they are not evil, and many believe that they help to promote the sport. Some of us try to emulate them. They often introduce new shooting techniques and accessories. Their performance can be dramatic and entice new shooters in the sport."

"The downside of being a Gamer is the fact that they need a reason or an excuse for their misses, procedurals and safety violations. Of course the RO or the spotters are always to blame! Over the years clubs have found a way to slow down Gamers. Some stages have small targets, targets farther than usual, moving targets or complicated scenarios that require memory and slowing down. We all get irritated with these target variations, especially so with Gamers."

"The Just for Fun class(JFF) attendance is getting very popular. Some say it is because of our aging members. Others attribute it to failing vision or health. Many just like the slower and more relaxed pace of this group without the Gamers. This group has many happy members who don't mind taking longer to shoot a stage. They enjoy the extra time to visit with their friends and posse members."

"In recent years, some clubs have experienced a process of natural selection controlled by the shooters at registration. Shooter are signing up with their friends and chosen members into one of these three groups. That way you, as a non gamer, do not have to watch a Gamer blow through a stage in 25 seconds. This can ruin anyone's psyche."

"For more on the practical side, how do you deal with misses, procedurals, and D/Q's?" A miss is a miss and nothing will change that. It is only a 5 second penalty and you need to get over it. If you don't, a miss will lead to more misses. A trick I used in the past was to ask someone how many I missed. Irrelevant of the count, it is still a small percentage of the 25 targets per stage."

"Procedurals are a 10 second penalty but you can only get one per stage. Once you know you made a procedural error, don't minimize it by shooting the remaining rounds on the easiest target. This kind of behavior is disrespectful and can lead to a Spirit of the Game penalty of 30 seconds(more later). Once you know you are getting a procedural, try to shoot the remainder of the stage the way it was intended."

"D/Q's are another matter. A Stage D/Q means you are out of the competition. Everyone will likely get one if you shoot long enough. It can happen to anyone. The only recommendation is to finish the day by shooting as well as you can. It is good to go home knowing that despite a bad day, you can go home with dignity."

"A match D/Q is the worst demoralizing event a cowboy shooter can experience. In a later discussion, I will review the events that lead to Stage and Match D/Q's. If you experience a Match D/Q, you are not allowed to continue shooting. You have to put your gear away. Then do the only honorable thing possible, return to your posse and take over a job and work to the end of the day."

"The other issue is letting other shooter's times and misses affect your own productivity. It does not matter that a shooter has now shot nine stages without a miss or procedurals. It also does not matter that the shooter ahead of you just shot a 29 second stage. If a shooter ahead of you gets a Stage D/Q, are you going to let this stir you up so badly that you shoot poorly or worse. Remember, check on your misses and your shooting time and that is it. Nothing else matters. How you did in relation to other shooters will be on the master score card available after a match. That review will be beneficial in the long run."

Lunch came and everything was delicious. After taking care of the bill, we headed back to the range–still in full business mode!

"This afternoon we are covering the shotgun and more exercises to cover all three guns. When shooting at a 9 yard fixed shotgun target, it is hard to miss. Very rarely, a clear miss several feet away from the target will be called a miss by the spotters. The problem with shotgun targets are knockdown targets. The rules of engagement for shotgun knockdowns are outlined by the RO for each stage and or match." "A common directive is: there are four shotgun targets. Shoot them left to right. Target 1 and 4 are knockdowns and target 2 and 3 are stationary. If a knockdown fails to fall, after the string of four targets has been engaged, you may then return to the standing knockdowns and shoot at them until they fall. In other words, eventually all knockdowns must go down."

"At other times the RO directs all shooters to keep shooting at a knockdown until it is down and before you proceed to the next target. There are even other methods of engagement, that is why you must understand the RO's direction before the shooting starts."

"I am aware that Jack gave you his light load 12 gauge recipe, I use the same recipe and it is quite user friendly with low recoil. This load will work on knockdowns, but you must take the time to put the bulk of the pellets on the target center. Some shooters shoot at the top of the target to take advantage of a better fulcrum point. The problem with high hits is that they can be too high with too few pellets–resulting in a failure to drop. I suggest that you aim at the center of the target for uniform results. This stage has 4 knockdowns, go ahead and shoot at them. Shoot some in the center, some low and some high. You will see what I mean"

I proceeded and shot at them, every time the four targets were down, Lady Slipper pulled on the cable and all four targets came up. After shooting some 25 rounds, it was clear that targets shot low did not go down. High hits had a 50% failure caused by a lack of pellets on the target. My dead center shots were all effective.

Lady Slipper added, "These light loads are easy on your shoulder. Compared to the economical field grade shells from box stores, our light loads do not bruise your shoulder like the field loads can."

"Most stages have 4 shotgun targets. Your slide holds 6 shells. Six rounds is enough when you have stationary targets. When you have knockdown targets, six rounds is not enough. Since I have an extra 4 loop slide, I am giving it to you. Place it behind your right holster. Get in the habit of replacing your used shotgun shells at the same time you reload your loading block for rifle and pistol ammo. You will occasionally forget to replace your used shotgun shells, that is when the spare 4 pack at your side will be greatly appreciated. Also, you will eventually fumble the double shell loading and a shell lands on the ground–where it is dead. Basically, you never have too many shotgun shells on your body."

"The recent changes in scenarios is the addition of Cowboy Clays and the Texas Star. The Texas star will be used with pistols, or rifle or shotgun. Using a shotgun on the Texas Star is a real pleasure. Not so easy with the rifle or pistol."

"Cowboy Clays are very popular, probably because our older population of shooters have all shot Trap. The clay launcher is usually operated by a club member that is a non shooter. This minimizes the chance of injuries when reloading the machine with clay birds. The scenarios include singles and doubles which is easily done with a double barrel shotgun like ours. Many clubs do not count a miss or count your time, whereas if you hit a clay pigeon, you deduct 5 seconds off your time for the remainder of the stage with pistols and rifle. In my opinion, Cowboy Clays breaks the monotony of standard stages."

"At a recent shoot, I saw something new, Cowboy Rabbits. A machine lying on the ground shoots a special hardened clay pigeon to roll, hop and scoot on the ground. The rabbit travels right to left at a fairly good clip. Shooters were laughing and obviously enjoyed the new event."

"That basically covers the shotgun. FYI there are two other types of shotguns used in CAS. A pump shotgun with an external hammer which dates to the 1800's. A recent addition is the lever action shotgun which also dates back to the 1800's. They also can load two shells like the double barrel but IMHO they do not provide an advantage over the double barrel shotgun–it is a matter of preference."

"Now let's get back to shooting all three guns. Load and shoot this next stage of 24 rounds repeatedly. I will watch and add tips when the occasion arises." On the first string, while shooting the pistols, I got a click. Lady Slipper jumped in and said, "I am glad this happened, so you likely have a bad primer–since you did not slip the hammer. I doubt you have a high primer like you can have with a rifle. A high primer in a pistol locks the pistol since the cylinder will not rotate. The RO will tell you to go around and fire six more time. If it does not go bang, place the pistol on the table, downrange, and proceed to the next gun–you will get a miss for the misfired round.

If it did go bang, I hope you were aiming and did not get a miss."

"This next stage has 10 long range pistol targets at 25 yards. It is not common to have this event, but knowing how to deal with it is important. First, you do not have to compensate your sight picture, the bullet will get there. The important technique is to loosely hold the pistol with your shooting hand and use other hand to hold the pistol up and cock the hammer. To prove my point, hold the pistol as if you are ready to shoot. Now squeeze the grip hard with your shooting hand. Do you see what happens? The barrel is shaking all over the place. Now loosen your shooting hand and let the left hand hold the gun up. The barrel and sights become stationary. Give it a try with both methods."

I shot all 10 rounds and experimented both ways. It was no surprise to find that Lady Slipper was right on–again!

The next stage had pistol and rifle knockdowns. Lady Slipper explained, "these knockdowns I am told are set to drop with a 125 grain bullet traveling at 700-750 fps–with a center hit. For an advantage, I load my pistols with the rifle ammo which has 0.5 grains more of powder–assuming your pistol ammo had 3.0 grains and the rifle ammo had 3.5 grains of powder. The pistol knockdowns are 16 inches wide and at 7 yards. The rifle targets at 16 yards are 10 plates on a rail. The first plate is large, the second is smaller and by the tenth plate it is the size of a coffee cup. This rail with falling plates is a riot. If you miss a plate, you have to shoot it till it falls since the next smaller plate is not yet accessible. Your misses are set by the number of plates still standing after 10 shots. Go ahead and try them out."

The pistol targets had to be shot center or high to fall. All low shots were a failure. There were 5 pistol knockdowns for 10 pistol shots. After all ten shots, the standing targets were misses. If you put down all the 5 knockdowns, with left over pistol rounds you then shoot at the large dumping target at the side, to empty any remaining pistol rounds.

The rifle targets were more of a challenge than I expected. You had to slow down and aim. The first time I had two plates standing. Eventually I got them all down. The last plate was more like a tea cup.

The next exercise was the flinch. I loaded my pistol with 5 rounds but instead of placing an empty chamber under the hammer, Lady Slipper had me spin the chamber. She added, "now you do not know when the hammer will fall on the empty chamber. Let's see what happens!"

I started shooting and on the 4th shot it went click. I did act surprised when I found the tip of the barrel point down almost 30 degrees. "What happens is that the shooter unconsciously applies a slight downward pressure in anticipating an upward muzzle jump of the barrel. We all look foolish when this happens–the flinch."

"Some of us start flinching while shooting our pistols. This is especially true if you shoot magnum loads at the range–yet it can happen even with light cowboy loads. The cure is retro training. This is done by loading 5 rounds and then spinning the cylinder. You have no idea when the hammer will go click. The idea is to try to prevent the downward dive when the gun does go click. This is an exercise you should do often–until the click no longer leads to a barrel dive."

"The last exercise involves sweeps. A sweep is a dictated firing sequence. The simplest example is to shoot your first pistol left to right and the second pistol right to left. There are too many sweeps to commit to memory, When the RO announces a sweep he will be very specific on how to perform it."

"The common sweeps are double tap, the Nevada sweep and the skip. The double tap is straight forward: with the pistol you place two shots on target 1 and 2 and one shot on 3. With the second pistol, you place one shot on target 3 and two shots on target 4 and 5. That way each target got a double tap. With the rifle, just place two shots on each target–5 targets equals 10 rounds in the magazine."

"The Nevada sweep is simply and continuous motion back and forth from one target to another. In the rifle targets are shot 1-2-3-4-5-4-3-2-1-2. Same for the two pistols. The skip requires some concentration and memory. The classic example is, hit targets 1-5-2-4-3. Gamers don't like this sweep because it forces them to slow down and aim!"

"So let me see you practice these sweeps with both the pistols and the rifle." I went ahead and started shooting, I quickly realized that you had to think of what you wanted to do, a few times I found myself reverting to the simple sweep. Like anything else, practice is the only solution. Best to make the mistakes now–I don't give myself procedural penalties!

Lady Slipper then puts her hands up and yells, STOP. With that smile and that look she says, "That does it with the two days of didactic training. I have covered everything on my list. Tomorrow we are heading out some 70 miles to a big yearly county shoot. Several local clubs get together and put on this event. You will learn many things. We will be spectators so we can dress casually–and bring a camera.

Monday we will begin a two day event of practice with my supervision. By Tuesday evening you will be on your own. You will have three days to prepare for your solo shoot at a real CAS event."

"During these last two days, I will cover at lunch the remaining three topics: the dedicated practice/muscle memory, the RO1 class, and review the penalties and D/Q's. Right now we have to get going. You have an appointment in one hour for an eye exam and choosing proper cowboy safety glasses."

I had learned not to question Lady Slipper's planned and organized schedule. "Well Lady Slipper, are we now still in business mode or are we transitioning to social mode?" Without hesitation, Sue walks up to me and plants the most amazing kiss on my lips then adds: "does that answer your question." Meanwhile my hat had gone flying to the ground and I heard clapping and whistling.......... Dusty and several shooters had been watching!

We got to the optometrist and I had my eye exam. The doc summarized my findings. "Your near vision is perfect which will allow you to see your sights clearly. Your distant vision can be improved. Look in the machine, this is your natural eyes and this is with glasses." I told the doc that I had no idea! He added, "you will see distant targets much better and give you quick target acquisitions."

"I recommend OSHA approved high impact polycarbonate clear lenses with side shields. For heavy sun I recommend magnetic clip-ons, lightly tinted in the color of your choice. Most cowboy shooters like the very light green tint because it does not require adjusting to the background and it does not distort the targets. The color yellow is popular with some shooters especially the ones that put these glasses on as they get to the range. Cowboy shooters use the tinted light green clip-ons as a last resort.

Also, do not get polarized or antiglare in your clip ons–they can hinder target visibility IMHO."

I left the optometrist with my detailed prescription and handed it to the attendant. She said, "looks like you are a cowboy shooter with this prescription." She helped with the frame selection and got it down to three choices. Sue put all three samples on my face and made the final choice with an approving smile–a lightweight titanium charcoal frame. The attendant then directed us to come back in one hour and the manufacturing plant in the office rear would have my glasses ready. I could not believe how technology had adapted to our fast world–or was it the other way around?

So we left and Sue made the following suggestion. "Lets get a quick burger and be back in one hour to get your glasses. Then you can drop me off at the house. We will have time to get ready and be at the club by 7 pm. I will make reservations for a table like last week.

Saturday night is dress up night. Wear your best western dress pants and shirt–and make the shirt a red one."

And so the next chapter of our lives was in the works!

CHAPTER 5

Home Invasion

Saturday evening day 7. I arrived to pick Sue up at 6:30 PM. As the door opened, I saw her wearing a gorgeous low cut one-piece red dress with cleavage, and a flared/pleated skirt–with an open slit on the side. She just looked hot and lovely. I commented, "with my red shirt we almost look like a matched couple." She countered, "and when we walk in the club holding hands, there should be no doubt!"

We arrived thinking we were early, but the place was already filling up. It appeared that people were looking forward to the free dance lesson. We did walk in holding hands, and heads did turn. Sue whispered, "I told you so." I tried to walk with a straight face and a non committal gait. Sue was swashing those hips and making her dress open at the slit with each step. How any woman could walk like that and maintain a neutral face was beyond me. Finally we got to our table and ordered our usual draft beer and white wine. I commented to Sue, "a cover charge of $5 barely pays for the DJ and certainly not for our instructors fees." She explained that, "The owners do very well with alcoholic sales that they can pay the balance not covered by the cover charge."

The DJ came to the microphone and called couples to come up. The single men quickly paired up with the single women. The DJ then noticed many women still standing, but there were no more men to partner with. He then says, "this is a partner dance, and you ladies can ask a lady to be your partner." A ruckus was the result, every single woman in the hall got up and paired with another lady. The floor was full with a single file of anticipating dancers.

Sue introduced the couple in front and behind us. In front, "This is Ernie Blackwell and Monica Greene. Ernie is a Cowboy Shooter by the name of Blackie. Behind us is Stan Winslow and Kelly Grimshaw. Stan is also a Cowboy Shooter by the name of Sloe Winn. Sue then introduced me as, "this is Wil Summer who lives in my condo complex. He is training and will soon solo his first Cowboy Shoot. His alias is Doc Derby." Stan quickly asked, "does that mean you are a real doctor or something similar?" I answered, "retired medical physician."

The DJ then introduced the instructors, Ben and Dixie. He started the song Blue Rose by Pam Tillis and B&D performed a longer version of the dance. The music stopped and Ben went over the steps. He covered the first

8 steps and made sure that everyone got them. Then he explained the next eight steps, and on, till the entire dance was taught, and everyone could do all the separate steps properly. He then started the music and people started to get in step. It did not take long for all to be actually dancing. I could not believe that I could do it as well.

I did notice that Ernie seemed a bit uncoordinated compared to Stan and also did not seem very interested in meeting me. I wondered, *is that secondary to natural clumsiness or is it secondary to alcohol or drugs? I made a mental note to keep watching this guy!*

The DJ mentioned, "I will play this song twice more this evening as part of the lesson. If the dance goes well the second time, I will speed up the third one a bit." And so the evening of dancing began. Sue got up to do a line dance and this fella, Ernie, was staring at Sue. I could see why, when she did a 180 or 360 turn, that dress slit kept opening up. When Sue joined me at our table, I saw that Ernie was still staring at us.

We got up to do a medium tempo two-step. At the end of the dance, Sue excused herself and headed to the powder room. I then spotted Ernie talking to Stan and then he headed for the exit. I followed him outside and hid behind a pillar. I then saw him enter a black jeep Cherokee and head out. *I thought, that is not good!*

On reentering the hall, I sneaked up to the bar next to Stan and made some small talk about Cowboy Shooting. I then asked him where his buddy, Ernie, was?

He answered, "he is just an acquaintance and he had to go back home to get his wallet." *Strange I thought, how did he pay for his cover charge and the several drinks he just had? Must be carrying a tab on credit! Really!*

Ernie was thinking as he drove his car to Derby Lane, *thanks to last night's scouting, I know where she lives. I will pick her front doorlock, go inside and unlock the window to her guest bedroom. This will give me a quiet access tonight to the back of her house.*

Fifteen minutes later Ernie came back in time to do the second dance to Blue Rose. People did very well and the next time the tempo would be picked up. We danced several two-steps, waltzes, and wonderful slow dances. It was such a pleasure to be her partner. Sue could almost dance independently which made things easy for me. Between dances we agreed that this week, we would spend some time practicing turns for these dances–my gun room was to become a dance floor!

During the next intermission, I pointed out to Sue that Ernie was staring at us. She came back, "A lot of people are checking us out." I didn't add the black jeep situation. She added, "Ernie is a strange guy. Once he starts drinking, he gets paranoid and possessive. I found that the only way to deal with him was to dance with him early in the evening, and later try to stay away by dancing with other guys."

At eleven o'clock, the DJ announced, "let's do the third Blue Rose before you are too drunk to remember the steps. This time we will do the dance to Toby Keith's, Who's Your Daddy."

The D/J was right on. It required moving along at a good clip. Yet the tempo was perfect for this dance. Everyone was pleased, the applause and smiles were enthusiastic. The D/J mentioned that the dance next week was the El Paso, to be taught by another couple in the same dance group–The Sugarhouse Dancers."

Since we had an early day tomorrow, we decided to head home. Neither of us noticed that a certain black jeep followed us. When we got to Sue's condo, Sue realized she did not have her house key, so she stepped down the entrance, lifted a brick and took a key. She unlocked the door, replaced the key and brick, and pulled me into her house and closed the door–no formality, "would you like to come in?"

"Would you like some decaf coffee and a pastry?" While preparing the coffee, I said to Sue, "I know Jack told you my long and short term history, but I know very little of your past." She kept working and said, "You are right, so here is a Cliff Note summary. I had a great marriage and life with my ex and we raised two great daughters over the past 30 years. One day out of the blue, he announced that he wanted a divorce and was leaving me to marry his secretary. I was so shocked that it took several months before I was able to seek the help of an attorney, to fight an attorney. Thanks to my daughters, they put me in contact with this lady lawyer who saved my life."

"It took 18 months to get the judge to sign the divorce agreement because of the haggling over my alimony. The result was a 50% division of assets, health insurance to age 65, a generous monthly alimony to age 65, and a one time payment to cover my mental anguish. The alimony would terminate prematurely if I remarried."

"The next 3 plus years was a sad time. I went into a profound depression. I had to quit work as a research technician, and my psychiatrist had a difficult time finding the right anti-depressant for me. Eventually the meds kicked in, and Jack got me started in CAS. The rest is history. I started shooting, dancing and I came out of my shell thanks to my doctor and Jack. Then I met you!"

I pondered on all this information and said, "life dealt you a bad hand. You were jilted and humiliated, it is no wonder you had a prolonged depression. Occasionally, time heals all but very slowly and with medications. You know Sue, I will always have good memories of my wife and medicine–just like you will have of your good years with your ex. Despite our past, we still have our children and we both still have a life to live." Sue smiled and shook her head in agreement.

As Sue was bringing the refreshments to the couch, I noticed that black jeep parked on the street. Sue nonchalantly went to the window and dropped the

Venetian blinds. Before she closed the slats, I saw the jeep's light come on and then the car took off.

Ernie had been waiting already 15 minutes when the blinds came down. *Well it don't look good for tonight. It looks like this dude could be spending the night. Whatever happens, I am not waiting another minute. It is still early in the evening to find a contact for the night. I will try again tomorrow night. Her day will come soon!*

We were sitting on the couch, side by side, but eventually turned and faced each other. Things quickly progressed from kissing to wandering hands–as I was working that slit in her dress. Suddenly, I said, STOP. We were both startled and then started laughing. Sue interjected, "I wish I had never used that darn word. One day we are going to hear that command at a shoot and we are going to start laughing when we realize we heard it tonight–knowing what we were up to!"

"Sue, the way things were going, we were heading for your bedroom. She paused and said, "that would not be so wrong, would it?" I came back and said, "actually that would be wonderful since I feel that is what we both want. So hear me out."

"Two weeks ago I was lost. Trying to find a hobby and redefine my life's direction. Without warning the light bulb went on. I was exposed to a potential hobby and I met a beautiful woman the same day.

It has been an eight day whirlwind–the happiest I have been in over ten years. Now that I found you, there is the good possibility that I found what I was unknowingly searching for–a companion. Someone that I can respect, trust, care for and possibly fall in love with. The bottom line, I do not want to live alone any more!"

"Lovely lady, you just make me feel alive. I want to be with you all the time. To think you could be my companion, I am not going to ruin that possibility with a quick roll in the sac. If we were to hook up, I am certain that this level of intimacy would be part of our lives."

A long silence followed. Sue wiped some tears and started, "oh Will, days ago I fell hard for you. Unexplainably, during our first training day, I did not know how to deal with my feelings. I had been away from the social graces for so long that I did not know what to do or how to act. I know I pushed myself on you, but I did not want to do anything that might ruin our chances at a relationship. I also do not wish to live alone anymore."

"Sue Austin, hear this. You do not have to do a thing. I am head over heels crazy about you and I am not going anywhere. Let us enjoy each other and develop a bond. Things will evolve naturally and I am sure we are on the right path." We passionately kissed goodnight, and I planned to pick her up at 5:45 AM with coffee and donuts.

Sunday day 8. We were on the highway by 6 am. We had a 70 mile trip and we wanted to be at the range early to visit the vendors before the shoot. By 7:30 am we were at the food vendor and Sue ordered coffee and two orders of Huevos Rancheros. I asked what that was, "fried eggs over fried corn tortillas, and topped with a tomato-chile sauce." Wow that was delicious.

We quickly went over to the vendors. I went to the components section. Sue showed them her SASS membership card and we were instantly approved as buying customers. Sue then went to the ladies garment section and I purchased 5000 bullets, 5000 primers, several cans of powder, and all the components to load 500 shotgun shells. I loaded everything in a wagon and brought these components to my SUV. When I returned to the vendors, I went to the SASS table and signed up for a membership. My card would come in the mail with an assigned number and my alias. They mentioned that my number would be next in a sequence of members–and would be in the 200 thousands.

Sue came back with several new outfits. Some for Cowboy Shooting and some for dancing. We then walked around to see the scenarios. This club has permanent facades on each stage. We saw their 10 stages to include: livery stable, jail, tonsorial shop, saloon, hotel lobby, gambling hall, bank, soiled dove house, gallows and a court-house. A lot of work went into their construction and the attention to detail of the 1800's was exquisite.

Each facade was connected to the next with a boardwalk. I took photos of all the stages and a panoramic shot of the entire array–and sent the photos to Ranger Rooster.

During the Shooters Meeting, I counted 100 plus shooters. We moved out of earshot and Sue said, "I brought you here so you can appreciate how an upscale SASS cowboy range functions. You will see many of the issues we discussed and plenty of bloopers." We then placed our eye and ear protection on and stood behind the spectator's fence.

The first shooter was the RO. He was a fine smooth shooter that hustled between guns and shot the stage clean in 35 seconds–no misses or penalties. I commented to Sue, "if the other shooters perform like this one, there won't be much to learn." She just smiled and I knew that was not to be the case.

Sue pointed out, "look at the next shooter up on deck. He is busy talking to the shooter loading his guns. He is not paying attention to the shooter on the firing line. He will end up with a procedural." Sure as heck, when this fella started shooting he quickly reversed the shooting sequence and ended with a 10 second procedural penalty. Her message was clear–when on deck watch the shooter actively shooting, and be certain you know the proper sequence of guns and targets.

The next shooter walked to the firing line with a swagger. Sue whispers, "This guy is a Gamer but also a bit arrogant. He will end up with a miss and then argue with the spotters that he did not have a miss." Sure as shooting, it happened just as Sue had predicted. Unfortunately, now the RO had this guy's number.

The next shooter had a unique costume. Sue explained, "he is dressed as a Dandy. A city boy well dressed with the fashion of the times. A lady with similar high fashion would be called a Topper."

The next shooter was dressed like Palladin from the TV series. "A palladin is a person trying to rid the world of evil ones. You will see more of these TV personalities and popular ones are: the Lone Ranger, Roy Rogers & Dale Evans, and Gene Autry."

Butcher Blok was next to shoot. Sue refers to his double suspenders. "A portly shooter needs a second suspender. One is to hold up his pants, the other is to hold up his gun rig. Otherwise, when he lifts up his rifle to shoot, his gun rig will likely fall to the ground!"

A shooter was next to the loading table. He looked like the TV actor, Sam Elliot. Sue said, "I know this cowboy well. He has the proper moustache, growly voice, real white hair and proper physique. Watch him step up to the loading table. The other person loading ahead of him is a woman, he will doff his hat to her–meaning he will touch the brim of his hat and nod his head. A gentlemen's polite gesture common in the 1800's era."

"Look, this next contestant is twirling his pistol as he is getting his gear ready. If he does this on any firing line he will get a Stage D/Q, because when twirling, you break the 170 rule or sweep someone. This is the type of guy that rules are for the meek." Unbelievably, at the loading station, he closes the rifle lever and instead of slowly releasing the hammer, he dry fires the rifle to drop the hammer–a Stage D/Q.

Next in line was a lady shooter by the name of Blondie Quickstep. Sue knew this shooter. "She is fast on her feet and can hustle a hustler. This shooting sequence starts sitting down. At the buzzer she has to jump up, take three steps, draw and start shooting." At the buzzer she hops up, takes two steps and collapses to her knees in pain with a terrible leg cramp. *Wow, it pays to slow down a bit.*

The last shooter on this posse was Smokemeat. Sue warns me that he is a trickster. He begins his shooting string and did a fine job with the pistols and shotguns. When he fired the shotgun, he had loaded the shells with black powder which produced much smoke–but the smoke was a mixture of red, white and blue hues. *Guess he lived up to his alias and his personality trait.*

After the RO processed the remaining shooters, they moved to the next stage. We also moved along to watch another posse in action. This next stage had a real carousel horse that you had to shoot from. There was a box that acted as a step to get up on the saddle. We noted that several of the posse members did not feel the box was stable as a step. The RO overruled, and the first shooter was called down. Her name was Stormin Sandraw-Jene.

Sue exclaimed, "oh boy, this is not going to be pretty!" The buzzer went off, and there goes Stormin Sandraw-Jene on a fast run. She places one foot on the box, it rolled and she went flying on the ground, on her back! The appearance was worth a hundred words. The box was modified and stabilized. Stormin Sandraw-Jene was given a reshoot. The RO was white as a ghost, apologized repeatedly, and had a substitute RO run this stage. Stormin Sandraw-Jene came right back for her reshoot. At the buzzer she took off and this time jumped onto the saddle without even touching the box. Cowboys were still laughing when she finished shooting.

The remainder of this stage had a bunch of serious shooters. There were no other bloopers or penalties. I saw some high end costumes and saw a doctor's costume that was a perfect match for my costume–but his hat was a High Topper instead of a Derby. The last shooter was a lady by the name of Lucky Lady. She started shooting with her pistols, the first shot of her second pistol had a surprise. With the shot fired, the base pin holding the cylinder came flying out and fell to the ground–thereby locking the pistol. Someone commented, "oops, guess she is not lucky today." Sue took this opportunity to say, "I had forgotten to mention this to you. Even with the extra strong base pin spring you installed, when you are ready to load each pistol, take a moment to verify that your base pin is clicked in the retaining notch."

We then moved to another stage. This stage was loaded with targets made to slow down everyone, especially Gamers. It had the Texas Star, as a rifle target, and knockdown pistol targets. All of Sue's instructions were well founded.

Lunch was called at noon. The menu was homemade beans covered with a sweet mole sauce(pronounced molay) and a dessert of fry bread. After getting our food and sitting down, she explained, "Sweet mole is a Mexican sauce containing a fruit, chile pepper, cinnamon, comin and black pepper. The fry bread is a Native American flat dough bread fried in oil and served with a topping of jam." *Actually, both were delicious.*

During lunch, our table's topic was the currency during the Old West circa 1850's. One cowboy seemed to be the local expert. "Does any one know what is meant by a charge for a drink of 2 bits?" With no answers he started, "Two bits was 25 cents since one bit was 12.5 cents per Spanish tradition. A bottle of liquor cost $1 to $2 depending on how diluted it was with water. These charges were relative to the cost of other items of the times. Examples are: a box of fifty 45 caliber ammo was $1, a Colt 45 pistol was $15, flour was 4cents a pound or $3 per barrel, sugar 7 cents a pound, coffee 12 cents a pound, wages were $1 per day, a horse cost $40, a cow cost $30, a saddle cost $40, a 16X20 two room house cost $300 and a 32X40 four room house cost $700."

Wow, speaking of old style trivia, I commented to Sue, "with inflation during the past 100 years, I still cannot believe that inflation brought the price of coffee to $4 per pound and a 4 room house to $200,000. I wonder who was better off, the old Cowboys in the 19th century or us in the 21st century?"

After lunch, Sue reminded me of Jack's comments on Day 1. "Shooters are logy and not as alert after lunch. We are going to see several bloopers." The first stage we watched was another one of the slow down stages. The pistol targets were very small. You had to shoot 4 rounds at target one and one round at target 2. Target 2 had a half dollar hole in the center. If you put a bullet in the hole, the replaceable cardboard insert would bear the proof. The second pistol had a similar sequence. Four rounds on target 4 and one round on target 3 with the hole. Any bullet hole in the cardboard was a 15 second bonus off your stage score. To my surprise, several shooters hit that cardboard.

Then the bloopers started. A shooter named Cluts was holding a doll on the Soiled Dove stage. At the buzzer he had to drop the doll, step forward three steps and start shooting. Well he dropped the doll but he then tripped on it and nearly fell on his face. Prop failure gave Cluts a reshoot. Dufus had staged his pistols in the back of a buggy. He had to get off a horse and get his pistols to start shooting. Well he forgot where his pistols were when the time came, so he skipped them and shot the rifle staged on a nearby table. He got 10 misses. Not a good day for Dufus!

Digger was shooting his rifle when his front sight literally fell off. He managed to get at least 7 hits. At the end of his string, he puts his rifle on the table, bends down to pick up the sight, and unceremoniously places it in his pocket. He then picks up his long guns and proceeds to the unloading table as if nothing had happened.

Gerry Rigger was shooting his shotgun when the wind picked up and caught his hat. Airborne and in the path of the shotgun target, his hat got pulverized! Gerry's words, "I can't believe I did that" Since he hit the target he did not get a miss or penalty.

The last blooper we saw was a winner. Captain Mayhem stepped to the firing line and performed what Sue called a cascading meltdown, or one error leads to another. He missed a target and was clearly upset. This was a set up–he then reversed a target sequence. Now he had a procedural to boot. With a red face and an adrenaline surge, he slipped the hammer and had to go around the cylinder. To add insult to injury he then misses a shotgun knockdown. He reloads two shell and again misses both times. *I thought he was going to throw his shotgun at the target*–but he reloaded and got it done. Every one felt so bad that you could have heard a pin drop.

As we walked away Sue added, "that was a perfect lesson for you and the best one of the day. Never let a miss or any penalty rattle you.

Let it go and move on." It was almost 5 PM and we had a long ride home, so we decided to head back.

The ride home was relaxing. We were both tired from standing in the sun all day and we held hands without talking. We got home after dark. On pulling in Sue's driveway, I saw a frightful sight, that black jeep Cherokee was parked a ways down the street. That is when I made a quick decision. "Go on in and we will meet in the AM for range practice. I will pick you up at 7 am and will go for breakfast. Sunday nights, I call my kids and catch up so it is best that I not come in." Sue understood, we kissed and I waited till she entered her house. I then drove to my house very quickly, went in the garage to pick up my 2 inch thick walking cane and my concealed 38 special revolver. I then ran back to Sue's house as fast as I could.

When I got to her house, I stopped on the sidewalk to catch my breath. Sue did not have her blinds tightly closed and that is when I saw movement to the left of the window. Within seconds I heard Sue scream out in total horror. Without thinking I went to her front door, it was locked. I picked up the key under the brick and entered. I heard Sue scream out, "what are you doing here and how did you get in."

I looked up in time to spot them both at the foot of the bed. I then saw Ernie punch her hard in the face. She fell backwards onto the bed. He then bent forward and ripped the front of her pajama top open and started pulling at her pajama bottom as he was unzipping his jeans. She fought back, got her feet clear of the pajamas and managed to kick him in the groin. He then pulled out a knife and told Sue not to hit him again or he was going to cut her. Sue then spotted me entering the bedroom. At the movement of her eyes towards me, Ernie turned to look in the same direction. When he saw me he pulled up his top lip and hissed at me like a mad dog. That is when I swung my cane like a baseball bat and smacked him hard in the mouth. Blood and teeth were flying everywhere. He then pointed the knife at me and was poised to attack. This time I hit him in the forehead and nose with a bouncing blow. He collapsed to the floor totally knocked out.

I then asked Sue for a lamp's extension cord, and I rolled Ernie over and bound his wrists tightly in a figure of eight pattern. I then asked Sue to call 911. As I was now watching Ernie with my revolver, I heard Sue saying, "HELP, I just had a home invasion by a man who attacked me and attempted to rape me. My neighbor fortunately subdued the attacker and is holding him at gun point. My address is......... I need the police. Please hurry. The dispatch came back and said the police were on their way. She also asked that the neighbor put his gun away as the police are entering your home, that way there would not be any threat to the police or errors in identity.

After Sue hung up the phone, I asked her to put some clothes on before the police arrived. That moment is when she realized that her chest was totally exposed and she was only wearing her panties. She quickly put on some sweat pants and shirt. The police arrived and entered the house at gun point. When they saw Ernie with his pants down to his knees, hands tied behind his back and still spitting teeth and blood out of his mouth–they relaxed and smiled. One officer asked Sue if this was the man who attacked her. She nodded her head–yes. That same officer asked her if she would be pressing charges. She quickly blurted out, "YES".

One officer got a call on the radio. The detective on duty was on his way and asked us to not change the crime scene. The detective arrived, Lieutenant Shaun O'Brien walked in, looked at Wil and said, "damn it Doc, I really have missed you since you retired." "Hi Shaun, I am really glad you are here!"

The detective did a careful investigation with many questions for Sue and me. He then summarized by saying that Sue was lucky that the Doc arrived in time. He then said, "why were you here anyways, Doc?" I tried to explain that since my retirement I walked up here every evening. Shaun looked at me and said, "Try again with a better story." I then confessed that Sue was my girlfriend and I had suspected that this dude was stalking her recently. The remainder of the true story was spilled out in detail.

Detective O'Brien said to the officer, take this piece of crap and book him on the following charges: 1. Illegal entry-house invasion. 2. Aggravated assault with a weapon. 3. Sexual assault with a weapon. 4. Attempted rape with a weapon. 5. Stalking. He then directed the officer to collect the knife, Sue's pajama, the extension cord and all his teeth on the rug, a sample of the blood on the rug and bag them as evidence.

He then wanted to know if she wished medical attention or a police officer for the evening. I answered that I would carefully do a neurological exam and that she would be staying with me tonight, so I could check on her every two hours. The detective was then informed that the officers had checked the entire condo. They had found the guest bedroom window unlocked, and fresh grass mower clippings on that rug that matched the suspect's shoe tread content. The shoes were then bagged as more evidence, along with grass mower clippings from the guest bedroom rug. The CSI team was lifting finger prints off the guest bedroom window, guest bedroom door nob and front door nob.

The officers picked up the piece of crap and the detective said to him. "Too bad you did not use your head for something other than a place to hang your hat. Now you are heading to jail for a long time. Take him away."

We agreed we would be at the precinct in the AM to file charges. Four charges for Sue and one for me. I was to file the stalking charge since Sue knew nothing about that.

Detective O'Brien got a call. He asked me to perform that neurological exam on Sue because the EMT's were still waiting to be called off the case. I took Sue to the living room and performed a very detailed cranial nerve exam, mental status and peripheral motor, sensory and equilibrium exam. The only abnormality was the red bruise on her cheek where she was hit. A bag of frozen peas was applied to minimize the cosmetic damage. We then released the EMT's.

Detective O'Brien's last request was a surprise. He said, "the victims protective group called Victim will come in this house withing 24 hours to clean this rug of blood stains and replace all the bloody sheets. Call this number tomorrow and have someone here to unlock the door. This is a free service paid by the taxpayers."

The police left after they had Ernie's car towed, I then asked Sue to pack a suitcase of sleep-wear, toiletries, meds and street clothing. When she asked why I said, "after tonight's activities, there is no way you are spending the night here alone. You are spending the night with me at my house." She slowly moved up to my face and whispered, "since I am now your girlfriend, I guess that's OK." I just held her until she stopped crying. We then took her car and headed to my house with her suitcase, my cane and my revolver.

Once home, Sue was very insecure. She would not leave my side and wanted to hold hands continuously. We had a glass of wine and this seemed to help both of us. I put some relaxing music on, and we sat in each other's arms for the next two hours. I then performed the second neurological exam and all was normal. It was close to 1 AM and I suggested we get ready for bed. Sue came back in the living room in her pajamas and said she was afraid to sleep in the guest bedroom. I went in her room and verified that the closet was empty and the window was locked. She agreed to try it.

Within 10 minutes she was at my bedroom door, saying she heard some strange noises etc etc etc. She wanted to sleep on my bedroom floor, I lifted the sheets next to me and within seconds she was in my bed. She slowly scooted her back toward me, I placed my arm around her waist and she snugged in a semi fetal position and fell asleep.

From that moment on, I knew that both our lives would change forever–and for the better.

CHAPTER 6

Recovery

Monday day 9. "Good morning, you slept well, I kissed her on the earlobe. How do you feel?" "Much better and thanks for the personal security last night." As she got up and turned around she started laughing and said, "Wow, what a bed head!" "Heh, you have an impressive bed head of your own!" *What I did not add was the fact that her facial bruise was at its peak. I figured she would notice when she washed up, too early to bring this issue up!*

We got up and headed to separate bathrooms to wash up and get dressed. We met in the kitchen where I handed her a cup of coffee and a plate of pastries. She looked at the pastries and exclaimed, "where did you find bearpaws and how do you know about these." "I was at the local bake shop looking for fresh donuts to share with Jack and saw these strange shaped pastries with three toes. The lady explained that these pastries were a precursor to the donut before donut molds were widely available.

The taste is unique and made from the recipes of the early 1800's with a top sprinkling of powdered sugar. Their shape today is attributable to the modern molds that form a bear's paw and three toes! So I bought a dozen and froze six which we are going to share this morning–three a piece."

During breakfast Sue asked, "how did you keep Ernie so quiet when I was on the phone with the 911 operator." I said, "I whispered in his ear that I was not a man of much humor in the best of times, and this was not the best of times. I also said that if he tried to get up, that I would shoot him in the foot. If that failed I would take out his knee cap or his personal tool."

"He was on his belly and never moved but kept groaning. When the police arrived they got a moon shot since his pants were down. Later when they removed the extension cord to handcuff him, they rolled him on his back. That is when I realized why he was groaning so much, his scrotum was blue and the size of a grapefruit–the result of your well placed kick!"

Suddenly the door bell chimed. Jack came in, looked shocked and said, "I just saw the local news, Sue are you OK?" She got up to hug Jack and said that she was fine. That is when Jack said, "where did you spend the night?" That is when a switch snapped in Jack's head. He looked at both of us repeatedly and said, "You and him, you and her?" We both shook our heads in unison and nodded, Yes.

Jack started laughing and hugged Sue saying, "Good for you" and shook my hand saying, "nice going, I never saw this coming and would never have predicted this, knowing you were both a long standing bachelor and bachelorette. I am so happy for both of you."

Shortly thereafter, the local police station called to say that the complaints were ready for our signatures. That is when I asked Jack if he would unlock Sue's condo so the cleaning service could come and clean the room of Eddie's blood. He agreed and I called the number on the card. They said they would be there at 11 AM. I told them that Jack would be there for them.

When we got to the precinct, Lieutenant O'Brien met us and asked if we knew any of Blackwell's friends. He explained, "many stalkers share their escapades with someone as a bragging thing. Do you know anyone that might fit that spot?" I asked why, "because we might be able to prove premeditated stalking, which would promote a plea deal. That would free both of you from testifying at a trial." I then presented what I knew about Stan Winslow and suggested he be interviewed.

The lieutenant looked at officer Greene, the unit secretary, and she started typing on her computer. The CSI then came to get Sue for comparative photographs and victim's finger-prints. That is when I asked, "could you give her a certified hard copy of her prints?" "Sure can and will be happy to do so." "I did not know that photographs were taken last night, it must have happened when you and I were talking. That was a good move lieutenant!"

We sat down to read the complaints and we both signed our names. Officer Greene had a face on the screen, I looked and confirmed that this was Stan. The lieutenant wrote down his address and phone number. The last thing the lieutenant said as we were leaving was, "I will call you when we have a disposition on the case. If you plan to leave town for an extended period, better call me before you do, so I can reach you if necessary!"

"Oh, and by the way, Ernie spent most of the night in the ER getting: more extractions of loose teeth that were a hazard for aspiration, several oral stitches, surgical exploration of a torn artery on his forehead, and a surgical decompression of his scrotum to save his testicles. He is a mess this morning and is still groaning–have a nice day!"

As we were leaving the station, Sue asked what was next on the agenda. I said, "we are going to Sam's gun shop and range to buy you a small concealed handgun, and apply for a concealed weapons licence–a CWL. Both are available at Sam's since he specializes in concealed handguns and has a certified instructor in the shop for issuing a CWL. This is where I bought my revolver and got a CWL. If everything goes well we will be home by 1 PM.

Arriving at Sam's, a salesman was showing a handgun to a customer and the owner stepped up to us. "May I help you?" Sue said, "I would like to buy a small handgun and apply for a CWL." The owner replied, "we can provide both except for a fingerprint card." Sue pulled out her fingerprint card and handed it to the owner. He looked at it and said, "This will work. Do you want a revolver or an automatic?" Sue responded that she wanted a light weight snub-nose revolver.

He then moved to the display case where there were 20 choices. He pulled out three models in 38 special rated for +P self defense ammo. "This is the popular Smith and Wesson ladies choice without a hammer–which prevents the hammer from snagging in a pocket or a purse." Without hesitation, she placed it in her hands and quickly added, "This is perfect." She then chose a soft swede holster for her purse/pocket, a flexible leather holster for her belt and a box of +P self defense ammo.

The owner then said, "that will be $650 for the gun, $125 for the holsters, $100 for the CWL course and the box of ammo is included." Sue pulled out her credit card and I said, "put that away, this is my gift to you!" The owner smiled and added, "don't I know you sir," when he saw my name on the card. I explained that I had been a customer for the same purchase some two years ago. After a call to pass the Brady bill federal check, the payment was made. The owner then said, "have a seat or shop around, the instructor will be with you shortly and it looks like he will have two students for the course, as he nodded to the other customer."

The course was nearly an hour long and worth taking. We then went to the range and the instructor was informed that Sue was a Cowboy Shooter and the other customer was a USPSA/IPSC Shooter. The range time was very short. The instructor filled out the course certification and told the other student that he had to get fingerprinted at the local police station. He also informed both, "stop at a Walgreen with a photo shop and get two passport photographs. Sign one and mail the application with a $200 check to the Division of Licensing. A laminated card with your photo will arrive within a few weeks".

On our way home Sue said, "thank you for the gift and your personal consideration for my security." After a pause, she asked what was planned for the afternoon. I answered, "we are going home to practice dancing–all the turns I need to learn." Sue commented, you are behaving like a Red Cross worker, keep someone occupied in the face of personal strife. I just smiled and said, "yes, and I hope it's working!" She responded by holding my hand.

The afternoon was a real pleasure. We put on CD's by George Strait, Alan Jackson, and Brooks & Dunn for two-steps and waltzes. The ten turns we practiced included: simple outside and inside turns, push out, sweetheart and promenade, around the world, around the man, under the arch, cuddles wrap, the pull through and the triple R. After I had mastered these turns with a two-step, we repeated all of them with a waltz.

Four hours later we were both bushed. We rested with a glass of wine and Sue then prepared dinner. A delicious chili recipe on a bed of rice and ice cream for desert. In the evening we watched a movie–a comedy. It was nice to hear Sue laugh.

After the movie, the conversation centered on Sue going back home. Sue's argument was sound. "I have to go back sometime to my condo. I now have a weapon that I can carry on me or place in my night stand. Don't worry, I will be OK and I will be careful. Retrospectively, there was no reason for that guest bedroom window to be unlocked. I won't ever take my surroundings for granted like I did last night." She had a convincing strong argument difficult to negate. So I agreed.

"OK, let's take your car back to your house. I will do a sweep of your house, with you, and then I will walk back home. After she got ready, as I opened the front door, I softly said, "STOP." "I can't do it, no, I don't want to do it!" "But Wil, you agreed that I had a realistic strong argument." "Strong argument, Yes, impossible alternative, No!" "Come and sit with me and hear me out."

"When I left the hospital after my near death event, I promised myself several changes in my life. The one thing that is apropos now, is the idea that I would never again do anything that was wrong for me, or that I did not want to do. The night of the home invasion was a reality check for me, I could have lost you." Sue then said, "Will, you have me confused, what are you saying?"

"Sue, I don't want you to leave. Please, would you stay with me as my significant other OR can I be your significant other? It is clear to me that I am falling in love with you." Sue suddenly placed her hand on my mouth, she snuggled up close and said, "Oh Wil, I knew I was falling in love with you when I woke up this morning in your arms." "Sue, I am ready to commit to you. I want you in my bed again but this time as lovers."

She gave me a warm and affectionate kiss, got up and took my hand, and walked me to the bedroom. At the bedroom door, she said, "I know we are rusty, but two caring people can figure it out." The door closed and nature took its course............................!

Tuesday day 10. In the AM we started stirring and both awoke at the same time. Sue softly said, "Wow, I had forgotten how pleasant intimacy, between two people who care for each other, can be." No one was speaking and finally Sue wanted to know how I felt. I answered, "I think we had periods when we slept." Sue said, "Will, be serious." "So I came back with, "what happened in this room stays in this room." That is when she jumped out of bed, standing in her birthday suit with her hands akimbo, and that look that I knew I was not going to fare well with. She said, "Wil Summer you are exasperating this morning." So I came back with a more real statement, "At this exact moment, I can certify that you are a natural blonde." It was instantaneous, she jumped astride on me, and repeatedly punched me in the chest. I was laughing so loud that she started laughing as well. Then I pulled her face close to mine and said, "we both lost many years, but this night made up for those lost years." I could tell Sue was thinking, she eventually spoke up. "We are going to have more nights like tonight, but a bit more sleep at our age is a good idea."

We both woke up famished and so we made a replenishing breakfast. During our meal, I brought up the idea that Sue's personal belongings needed to be moved to #24. Sue even suggested that we move her brand new Lazy Boy rocker/loungers and sofa to replace my worn out living-room furniture. I asked, "what about other furniture?" She replied, "you have all beautiful Ethan Allen furniture, I have nothing that can even come close to these pieces." So after more discussion we made a list of everything we wanted to move today.

1. Livingroom chairs and sofa.
2. All refrigerator/freezer contents.
3. All food and cooking ingredients.
4. A few of Sue's favorite cooking utensils and pans.
5. All of Sue's spring and summer clothing.

6. Electronics–laptop, tablet, iPhone and printer.
7. Gun safe and cowboy guns.
8. All reloading tools and components.
9. All shooting materials, including cowboy clothing.
10. Medications, make-up and toiletries.
11. Financial and communication files.
12. Miscellaneous items we spot while moving.

We looked at the list again and we were both satisfied that this covered the basics. We realized that we would periodically have to return to #97 for more needed items. While Sue was doing the dishes, I called Jack to request his help and his truck for moving. He said he would be right over for coffee.

We had more coffee while waiting for Jack. I noticed Sue still had a facial glow which was not part of the traumatic bruise. When Sue realized what this glow reflected, she got up to apply some more make-up but was intercepted by Jack entering the house. As Jack spotted Sue he exclaimed, "WHOA, I need sun shades or a baseball cap to neutralize the brightness of your face. Should I leave and come back later?" Jack and I started laughing. Sue interjected, "you men, never forget that this facial complexion reflects a beautiful thing, not a joke–with a smile of contentment." "OK, Jack, it's time to load furniture."

With my livingroom furniture in Jack's truck, we headed to #97. We then loaded her new Lazy Boy pieces and brought them to #24 while Sue was beginning to box her personal items. The next load covered everything on our list. While Jack and I were loading up, Sue was vacuuming. We turned the refrigerator and freezer off, washed the inside of both and left the doors open to prevent mildew. We set the AC to 90 degrees and the humid-a-stat to 55 %. Picked up all the photographs throughout. We all looked around and all agreed that there was nothing of sentimental value left in place. What was left behind was all replaceable.

Jack asks Sue, "any second thoughts or regrets?" "Absolutely not, I have a new home and a companion," as she grabs my arm and escorts me out of the house. I heard Jack mutter, "looks to me like more than a companion, heh!"

After unloading the vehicles and placing everything away, we had a light lunch. Verifying that I had nothing on the agenda, she then suggested that we go to the range and finish my training.

On the way to Dusty's, Sue brought up the topic of shooting practices. "First is the physiological basis of shooting." I thought, *she is going to explain to an MD all about physiology, this should be interesting.* "The body's mechanism that promotes shooting is based on the physiology of muscle memory, and the brain's electrical system of cellular synapses." *So far, so good!"*

"These two systems can be 'trained' to function at their maximum capacity. With the muscle system, you train two types of muscles, slow and fast. Holding a pistol uses slow muscles and pulling the trigger uses fast muscles. Another example, drawing a pistol to shoot uses slow muscles initially but quickly progresses to fast muscles. Both types of muscles can be trained by repetition–meaning repeated practices."

"The neurological system can also be activated so you can enter the "zone" of shooting. This is a mental state that allows you to focus on the shooting sequence, and blot out any thoughts that could interfere in it's completion. In other words, your brain can be trained to be astute, fast and proficient!" She adds, "the time to enter the "zone" is when you are on the firing line and the RO asks if you are ready. If you are not ready, concentrate and delay the RO–the RO will understand."

"The other issue is the natural talent. This is actually a genetic inheritance of more slow and fast muscles, as well as more brain cells with better synapses. Despite this anatomical advantage, all natural talents need to practice to maximize their potential. When you are a natural talent, your learning curve is shorter than most shooters."

"The last point is the dedicated practice. As a beginner, don't go to the range just to shoot one stage after another. If you have a move that you're having trouble with, practice it repeatedly until you feel you're getting it. As an example, if your draw is still clumsy, spend the time to smooth it out. Another example, practice loading the shotgun with two shells at a time, without fumbling. The key to a successful dedicated practice is the mastery of a problematic issue."

"In summary, a beginner should practice, practice, and practice. Training your muscles and brain will eventually become second nature. Eventually, you will become experienced to the point that practicing will not be as crucial. I still practice because I enjoy shooting so much. Plus, I always try to practice, as a primer, before a Cowboy Shoot. This primer just seems to rejuvenate my abilities and I always have better results at the shoot."

"As after thoughts, always use a timer as your start/stop. That way you can determine where you need extra help. And last, when you get tired and no longer care how you are doing, STOP, before you develop bad habits. *Wow, what a nice job she did with this subject.*

The practice went well and as Sue suggested, I did practice my draw and loading the shotgun. Then I ran scenario/shooting sequences one after the other. At first my stage time was +-52 seconds, but at the end of the practice, I was down to +-48 seconds. Sue pointed out that with one more practice, I might shave off a few more seconds. She was very vehement when she said, "at your first shoot on Saturday, do not try to go faster than 48 seconds. As a well trained and practiced beginner, this is presently a smooth and effective stage time for you."

When I got tired, I said to Sue, "let's go home–our home." She put her arm around my shoulder and walked me to the car. I noticed she had that other look on her face, the one that I fare well with, compared to the look she gave me this morning.

After loading my gear, I asked Sue, "now that my training has come to an end, are we done with the business mode? *Thinking she was coming back with a permanent social mode.* She surprised me and said, "we are now leaving the business and social mode and we are finally entering the reality mode."

Tuesday evening day 10. This was our first non pressured evening at home as a couple. The first thing she did was call her two daughters, and told each one that she was shacking up. Actually these conversations went well and both daughters were obviously happy for their mother. Sunday night I would call my kids and inform them of the same.

We then had a relaxing dinner of London Broil, baked potato and broccoli with red wine. We then watched the evening news followed by a one hour TV show. We then read for the remainder of the evening. Sue was reading a romance/novel and I was continuing my reloading book, Reloading–A Practical Hobby.

The evening was certainly peaceful and relaxing but I kept glancing at Sue and occasionally caught her doing the same. Finally I could not wait any longer and said, "I am ready for bed." Sue put her book down, got up, took my hand, and guided me to the bedroom. She added, "and we agreed that we would get more periods of sleep."

Wednesday day 11. After a replenishing breakfast, Sue asked what I wanted to do today. I said, "tomorrow I have a special day planned, and Friday would be our day to practice our primer before Saturday's shoot. I still have the willies about my solo shoot, and an extra day at the range would help calm down my nerves." Sue did not miss a step, she said, "load up while I prepare a casserole for dinner and we'll get going."

En route to Dusty's, she brought up some quick subjects. These included:

1. "Take the RO-1 class as soon as one is available. Our range master, Ranger Rooster, is planning to give one soon. You are going to learn so much, especially in running a stage. With an RO-1 certification, you wear the group's pin on your hat. When an RO needs an assistant, you may be

asked to take over the posse. This has happened to me several times in the past year."

2. "Posse members do not confront other posse members. If there is a problem or safety violation, take the issue to the RO. Actually a confrontational shooter can be charged with a 30 second Spirit of the Game penalty. Only the RO or the Match Director can resolve a dispute. The reverse is also true, if you are confronted, immediately take your counter-point to the RO. It is unfortunate, but some people like to run their mouth, and it is their mouth that gets them in trouble. Just remember you are there to shoot safely and have a good time."
3. "During your training sessions, I have mentioned sporadically some examples of Stage or Match D/Q's. Tonight I have prepared a handout on all these unfortunate occurrences. We will review these and then you can carry your copy in your cart."
4. "If you ever come to the range without me, place the timer on your gun belt and use it. As I have said, it is a great way of training your brain to avoid a fruit salad syndrome."

At this practice session, Sue had brought her guns and she placed them in my gun cart. I appreciated that the upright portion held four guns in their separate slots. We established a pattern of me shooting several stages, and then Sue would shoot a couple. It was easy to see that Sue really enjoyed shooting. On a break, She confided in me and said, "a CAS event is the kind of day I live for. The more I participate in this sport, the less I am bothered by the upper class's disdain of this fantasy and shooting sport." I quickly added, "ditto, and I also despise the "gun haters" who are trying to take our guns away and ruin such a marvelous sport."

We continued shooting in turns. Every time Sue was on the firing line, watching her was seeing a master at work. Without a doubt, two revelations came to me. The first was that practice was the quick road to "owning" this sport. The second was that this was a hobby we could share–a help in maintaining a healthy relationship.

We had brought Italian grinders for lunch to save time, but by 2 PM we were out of ammo. Two people shooting can eat up ammo very quickly. Plus, Sue was such a prolific shooter that she could send "mucho" lead downrange in a short time. So we loaded up and headed to our gun room.

Since we had already moved her Dillon Square Deal B press over to #24, we quickly set it up on the bench next to mine. Within a short time we were both reloading. At 6 PM we took a break for dinner. A chop suey dish she had prepared before going to the range. After dinner we went back to reloading. Suddenly I thought, *Here we are, we shoot together, reload together, dance together and now live together. Is this what is called a multifaceted companion or is it a lot more?* At 11PM we were tired but we had many thousands of loaded 38 special rounds, and several hundred shotgun shells for future use. We were too tired to review her handout on D/Q's and put it off to some other time.

We went straight to bed and skipped all other activities for the first time–but we promised to catch up in the morning.

Thursday day 12. After catching up on extracurricular activities, we had another replenishing full breakfast. After doing the dishes, I said to Sue, "today I have a special day planned for us. My dream for the summer is to travel out West. I have always wanted to do this, but it was never practical to leave my practice for long periods of time. I want to visit some of our national parks and monuments, see the western landscape and visit western historical sites and towns. Now I can add, shoot CAS in different states to see how they do it differently than we do in Missouri."

"Let me show you on a map what I am proposing. My goal is to set up 5 bases of operations from which we would spend +-2 weeks to visit the sites and do some Cowboy Shooting. Leaving by the end of May means that we need to head south to warm weather. We would go through Oklahoma and Texas to our first base of operations in Deming, New Mexico. After that we would head to our second base in Albuquerque, New Mexico, putting us next to Edgewood for the SASS national championship at Founders Ranch. There are many great sites to visit in Albuquerque as well."

"Our next stop heading north is Durango, Colorado. This is home to the popular Mesa Verde cliff dwellings and many other great locations to visit. Colorado has many CAS clubs for us to visit or compete. If we stick to our schedule of two weeks per base, which includes traveling, that would put us in our fourth base–Cody Wyoming by the middle of July."

"The next and last base would be heading east to Hill City, South Dakota. These last two bases of operations have many tourist attractions. We might spend more time in these two locations. In any event, we will be heading south by September 1. We will then go through Kansas and Nebraska on our way home. These two states have plenty of historical locations and even tourist attractions, related to television shows such as old Dodge City of Gunsmoke. We would travel and visit these last two states by stopping for a few days at areas that appeal to us."

"In any event, this circuitous route should bring us back home by the middle of September. That means some four months on the road." I could tell that Sue was totally enthralled with the prospects of seeing some of America and shooting at different locations, but I also detected some hesitation on her face.

Sue finally spoke up, "This is certainly anyone's dream, especially when you throw in SASS headquarters at Founders ranch, but I cannot afford my portion on my retirement income."

"Sue, you don't have a portion, and I can afford it." I handed her my money market check book. "These are my liquid funds that are not tied to my IRA, Keogh, 401 K, market investments or the Social Security that I will get this year." She looks at the balance amount and her eyes seemed to pop out of her head. She adds, "I stand corrected, you can afford it."

To put the topping on the cake I added, "we would do this with a truck and a camper, the best way to be on the road for four months." I then asked Sue, "if you approve, would you do this trip with me?" Without hesitation and a smile from ear to ear she says, "of course, you are not going anywhere without me and you know that!"

"GREAT, let's go buy a truck and a tag-along camper."

Arriving at the Dodge dealership, we were lucky to find all the sales personnel busy with customers. This allowed us to look at the trucks without the annoyance of a tail. We first established that we wanted a white truck, so we looked for this color and found five. Three were the 2500 series(3/4 ton) with four doors. We read the window specs of all three and then headed to the showroom.

A woman sales person greeted us at the door, informed us her name was Gail, and she was the head sales person for trucks. She escorted us to her office and I proceeded to give her my list of what I wanted in a truck:

- White Ram 2500 four door two wheel drive.
- Automatic transmission/gasoline engine.
- All the bells and whistles and all power accessories.
- AC, cloth seats and full running boards.
- Complete tow package for camper with transmission cooler.
- Front end tow hooks.
- On board computer with hands free phone, GPS, U-Connect Access and 3 G WI-FI hot spot.
- Hard top white bed cover with right and left entry panels.
- E-rated 10 ply tires.
- Rear Back Up viewing screen.
- Upscale mud flaps and floor mats.
- Extended exterior mirrors.

She made several entries in her computer and made a photo copy of my list. She took the list to the parts manager who confirmed that all accessories were in their inventory. I said we were trading my Nissan Rogue SUV and that I would be paying cash. Gail then sent a man to check out my SUV and provide her a value for the vehicle.

We did some haggling over the trading price and I summarized by saying, "this is the figure I would be willing to pay by check." Gail said, "let me take it to the owner, my dad." In a short time, Gail came back with an older well dressed man who extended his hand and said, "congratulations sir, you just bought yourself a great truck."

After some small talk, Gail asked when I wanted to pick up this truck. I said, "I want this vehicle road ready at 9 AM Monday morning." When she assured me that it would be ready along with the paper work, I then gave her a $5000 deposit to cover the accessories I requested.

On route to the RV dealership, we stopped for a quick lunch at a truck stop and sat at the counter for soup, sandwich and coffee. Arriving at the dealership we noticed that there were hundreds of tag-along campers or fifth-wheels–but no motorized RV's. A middle aged salesman greeted us outdoors as I said, "We are looking for a tag-along camper and here is my list of requirements and accessories." Looking at the list he responded, "It appears you have had a camper in the past, so let's go into my office and go over this list which includes:"

- A road worthy high end unit made for extended road trips.
- 32 foot lite or ultra-lite model with a TW of +-5000 pounds and a carrying capacity of +-2000 pounds.
- An 8 foot "empty" bunk-room at one end and a master bedroom with a queen size bed at the other end.
- One electrical and manual push-out in the center to include dining table and living room.
- Dining table is an actual table with four chairs and the living room has two rocker/recliners for tall people. NO dinettes.
- Microwave and convection oven.
- Refrigerator with propane conversion.
- A free standing shower room, separate from the toilet room.
- 32 or 40 inch living room TV that rotates 180 degrees to face the bedroom.
- Reese hitch, leveling bars, sway control kit, electric brakes, and remote tire monitoring system with steel valve stems on each camper tire.
- Automatic awning with manual controls if needed.
- Power leveling jacks including a drill adapter for manual use.
- Electrical connectors for 30 and 50 amp service.
- Extra ply camper tires–? 8 ply or what you recommend.
- The usual plumbing accessories for outside use.

- Plastic leveling block kit with wheel chucks.
- Flooring–carpet in bedroom and linoleum everywhere else.
- Standard electronics plus HD antenna with booster, WIFI booster and outside cable access.
- Exterior propane stove for outside cooking.
- Two 50 pound propane tanks if possible.

The salesman finally said, "my name is Greg and I will be happy to assist you. Let's start with scanning your list and enter it in the computer. We have 50 tag-along campers and I know that at least 20 or more are the popular size of 32 feet. The only item I know we don't carry are power leveling jacks, that is why we give you a drill adapter instead of the manual crank alternative. Of course my big question is why you want an 'empty' bunk-room?" We gave him a full explanation and moved on.

After a few minutes, the computer beeped. Greg looked at his screen and said, "we have three units that match almost 80% of your requirements and the computer also states that the other 20% are available in out parts/accessories department." "Great, let's go check them out."

On our walk through the yard, Greg added, "I hope you choose the unit with the highest price tag because it is well made, has a more fancy interior and is more road durable than the other two." Greg was certainly an experienced salesman, he first showed us the low end model followed by the mid level unit, and finally the high end model. The exteriors had all the same features, but the interiors were clearly different. It was clear to both of us that this high end unit had much better furniture, fine finishes to walls, better quality kitchen cabinets and most important, the largest kitchen counter space and storage pantry of all three units. Sue really checked out the kitchen in every detail. She expressed total satisfaction and said, "if it's ok with you, I prefer this unit." I looked at Greg and said, "lets do the paperwork."

Greg assured me that this unit would be ready Monday AM. "On arrival, the mechanics will install the electric brakes, match the wiring harness to the camper and perform whatever else needs to be done. The paper work will be ready." With a look of doubt on his face, Greg added, "Are you sure you wish to pay this cash? We have several long term mortgage plans with low interest rates!" "There is no doubt in my mind, and to seal the deal, I will give you a $5000 deposit."

On our way home, Sue said, "I didn't know you had once had a camper." "Years ago when we were first married, we had a small camper. When the babies came along and my practice got busy, we sold the unit. We always had plans to return to camping, but that never came to pass." "Well I guess that there are many things about each other that we will eventually discover." "Yes, but that is in our past! You and I are in the present–that's all that matters now."

To change the subject, Sue asked, "Do you have second thoughts, today you managed to spend $100,000. I answered, "best money I ever spent, no actually, the only money I spent in the past decade. Sue, we are going to have a trip of a lifetime and see some of this great country. Plus we are going to do it in some comfort and not have to live out of luggage and motels."

Thursday evening day 12. After dinner, Sue reviewed her handout on penalties, Stage and Match D/Q's. She points out, "I wrote most of them down for you to keep in our gun cart." I took the list and went over each one:

<u>5 second penalty</u>

- Each miss or unfired round.

<u>10 second penalty</u>

- Procedural.
- Minor safety violation. There are three. Leaving an empty or live round on the rifle carrier or in the magazine. An open but empty rifle that falls but does not break the 170 rule, and cocking a pistol before 5 feet away from the shooter.

STAGE D/Q

- Shooting on the move.
- Dropped unloaded gun on firing line.
- Violation of the 170 degree rule.
- Any discharge within 5–10 feet of the shooter.
- Holstering a pistol with the hammer cocked.
- A cocked gun leaving the shooter's hand.
- A live round in the rifle chamber.
- Changing location with a cocked gun.
- Unsafe handling of a firearm.
- Using an illegally modified firearm.
- Sweeping someone with an unloaded gun.
- Dry firing a gun at the loading or unloading table.
- Arriving at a loading table with a loaded gun.

"So far I understand every one except the last one. What is this about arriving at the loading table with a loaded gun?" "Well it is very common for people to use their cowboy guns in open carry states. They just forget that their pistol is loaded when they get to the cowboy range, and place their pistol in their holster! Heck, I am told that it also happens in concealed carry states!" "Very good explanation."

SPIRIT OF THE GAM–30 SECOND PENALTY

- Shooting a stage differently to gain a competitive edge.
- Shooting ammo below a minimum or above a maximum power factor.
- Failure to perform non shooting activities as is required in the fantasy scenario.
- Confrontation with another shooter.
- Two of these leads to a MATCH D/Q.

MATCH D/Q

- Two STAGE D/Q'S or two SPIRIT OF THE GAME penalty.
- Belligerent or un-sportsmanlike behavior.
- Failure to cease fire on a STOP order.
- Shooting under the influence of alcohol or drugs.
- Dropping a loaded gun.
- Firearm discharge less than 5 feet.
- Sweeping someone with a loaded gun.
- Serious interpersonal conflicts between shooters.

Sue adds, "these are the one's I remember from my RO1 course and are all SASS rules. I am sure there may be more. You have to refer to the current SASS handbook for a more detailed list and current changes. You will be getting a handbook with your SASS membership."

Sue then laid out the agenda for the next two days. "A pre shoot primer tomorrow AM, something special tomorrow afternoon, dancing tomorrow night and your solo shoot on Saturday. So let's get some sleep." "You mean some periods of sleep, heh?"

CHAPTER 7

Primer and Solo Shoot

Friday day 13. Sue again emphasized the importance of a pre shoot practice the day before a competition–a primer. She then informed me that she was not going to be a shooter on Saturday. She would register as my coach and would be allowed to mingle with the posse. This would allow her to be available for suggestions or answer any of my questions. She also had a good point, "you will likely not need my help, but knowing that a newbie has a coach, other posse members will relax. They will all know that I will be your watch-dog, and they will not have to watch you or worry about you. It is a great practice that everyone follows with newbies."

Once on the firing line, I shot my first stage without misses or penalties, and a shooting time of 48 seconds. Sue commented, "that was better than expected on the first stage. Most shooters have the shooter's willies on their first stage which can lead to misses, procedurals or long shooting times. You did well because you kept your cool and you were likely in the zone."

The second stage was a skip sweep,2-4-5-1-3. I started shooting, 2-4 and paused. Sue chimed in, "5-1-3." I then finished the stage with a time of 52 seconds. Sue then added, "the RO is not here hoping that you will fumble or blunder, he is here to help you, that is why I said 5-1-3. The RO not only counts your shots and keeps you safe, he will help any shooter that forgets the sequence as you did."

The next stage I found myself speeding up. I consequently jacked a live round out–without realizing it. Sue yells out, "one more." I hesitated and almost questioned her call, but I reloaded one round and continued the stage. Time again 52 seconds. Sue explained, "if an RO makes that call, don't hesitate and loose seconds, just reload one round and continue. If it is found that the RO made a mistake, you will get a reshoot. Bottom line, believe the RO's calls while on the firing line."

The next two stages were clean shoots with a time of 48 and 49 seconds. Although Sue had discussed this issue during my training, she reiterated, "you looked great with a secure stage presence. Keep this tempo during your solo shoot. Later you can work on shaving seconds off your time."

Despite what Sue had just said, the next stage was easier than most with a Nevada sweep for the pistols and rifle. Plus there were only two shotgun fixed targets.

With this in mind, I thought I might break my 48 second plateau. The pistol and rifle targets were a breeze, when I got to the shotgun, I fumbled the loading and one shell hit the ground. I reloaded a single shell and lost several seconds. My time still 49 seconds. Sue jumped right in and said, "I know you expected a better time on such an easy stage. First of all, never predict your stage outcome, and secondly there is no such thing as an easy stage!" *Boy, that woman is beginning to read my mind.*

"By the way, you nicely recovered from that shotgun shell fumble. Speaking of recoveries, anytime you have a slipped hammer, a jacked rifle round, or many other fumbles, try to recover by using a smooth systematic process to undo the fumble. If you do so, you will hear, 'nice recovery' from the RO, or spotters, or unloading table official, or even one of your posse members. We all fumble, but some of us get so flustered by the adrenaline surge that we don't all recover gracefully. In short, everyone respects a well done recovery."

On the next three stages, I started missing rifle targets. Finally Sue said, I have been watching and I am now convinced that you have developed a bad habit. Occasionally you peek over your sights as you are pulling the trigger. Every time you do this, you miss. The cure, keep your head down and your sights in your line of vision."

"In addition, a bad habit is a freak event that develops insidiously, and is hard to detect by yourself. That is why during our practices, I will watch you and you will watch me." I loaded the rifle several times and proved to myself that she was right.

I shot the last two stages and then Sue said, "Wil, it is lunch time and I really feel you are ready to face the music. Stay cool, get in the zone and rely on your abilities. You will do well tomorrow. In addition, not to inflate your ego, I believe you have a natural shooting talent. Even more important, you have the drive to be very good at what you do." I stopped her, touched her hand and said, "I feel the same way about you."

We went to the usual diner next to Dusty's. During lunch she suggested that we take the afternoon off. To keep my mind off tomorrow, let's go to an inside water park for relaxation. Tonight we go dancing for our usual Friday evening event at the Country Roadhouse."

After getting home, we loaded my SUV with all the gear and guns for tomorrow's shoot–according to my check list. We then changed into our swimsuits. Sue came out of the bedroom wearing a bright orange mini bikini. This was a super revealing two piece, she was overflowing at the top and barely covering her bottom. Sue saw my facial expression and said, "not enough material, huh? "Well, if we were going to a Florida beach, you would fit in. However, we are going to a family water park." "OK,

I have the parent orange one piece suit, a generic form of a Miss America suit with an open back. Think I should change, huh?" "Yes, you would feel more comfortable with kids around." *I really like this two piece suit, Sue looks like a super model on a runway. I will keep searching for a more appropriate locale where she can display her bikini and endowments.*

Sue came out of the bedroom, rotating and modeling, and asked, "what do you think?" "Lady, you would look good to me even if you were wearing barn overalls, but yes, you look gorgeous and fantastic. Every day I see more evidence that fits your name, Lady Slipper."

The water-park was an uplifting venue. I certainly did not have time to think of the Cowboy Shoot. Actually, we found ourselves acting much younger than our ages. We started with the wave pool, and before we saw the big wave, we found ourselves on out butts. We went to the rain pool–as we walked down a path, rain water starts coming down in buckets. So much rain water in sudden large volumes that Sue almost lost the top of her generic suit.

From there we went to the water slide. We enjoyed this one more than the others. We went down the slide several times. The last time, we sat astride and held on to each other, with the added weight we doubled our speed.

After doing all the water antics we cared for, we retired to the adult pool. The water temperature was 86 degrees. We swam in the deep end and then floated on noodles.

Finally, we relaxed in the lounging chairs till we dried off. *As we laid in the sun, I thought how pleasant it was to enjoy life with such a companion.*

On our way home, Sue made reservations at the Country Roadhouse. When we got home, we had just enough time to change into dancing clothes and head out.

While driving I asked Sue, "since your facial bruise still shows, how do you want to deal with this?" "I tried to cover it up with extra make-up but it didn't completely hide it and actually made it more conspicuous. I decided to go 'au naturel'. I figured that there were no secrets with all the TV newscasts, so might as well get it over with."

Friday evening day 13. As we entered the Roadhouse, the patrons acted as if they had all been struck by a lightning bolt. It was dead quiet as we walked to our table, holding hands. Everyone stopped talking and watched us. The only sound heard was the tapping of our heels on the hardwood floor.

Once we were sitting down, the hall came alive. Everyone came up to us, the women were hugging Sue and the men were shaking my hand. All their comments centered around two points. The ladies were relieved that Sue was OK, and the men were glad that I had arrived in time to bring an end to the attack.

There was one element of sadness that many expressed. It was a shame that such a vile thing had to be done by one of their own dancers. Many added, "Ernie did not represent 99% of patrons who dance in this club. He was a solo individual, with a hidden psychopathic paranoid personality, that no one could detect."

As the people dissipated, the owner came to our table and said, "Thank you for coming tonight. That took a lot of courage Sue, and it attests to your character." Then, Stan shows up and asks if he could join us. "Of course, what is on your mind?" "Detective O'Brien looked me up. I told him that Ernie wanted to know your address. When I refused, he told me that he was going to follow you home, to find out where you lived. I told him that such activity was illegal, and he could be charged with stalking. I did assume that he would cease and desist–and would back off."

"I am sorry that I was wrong and did not pursue the matter further. So to make a long story short, I went to the police station and signed a prepared statement of my involvement. Detective O'Brien mentioned that this evidence of premeditation could lead to an out of court pre trial settlement–this would be good for all involved." Sue got up and gave Stan a hug and said, "thank you for your honesty and help."

We then had a light dinner of soup and salad. A mixed salad with poppy seed dressing and clam chowder. We finished dinner as the dance was started at 9 PM. We knew we had an hour before the DJ reintroduced the Blue Rose. So we danced and did all our ten turns to several two-steps and waltzes. Sue even did several line dances. At 10 PM the DJ surprised everyone.

"Due to popular demand, we have decided to teach a new two-step/waltz 'turn' every Friday night and continue with a new partner dance every Saturday night. To start the series of new turns are other instructors from the Sugarhouse Dancers, Richard and Claudette. The music started and the instructors demonstrated the Hammer Lock. A tricky move to put the lady in reverse and in cross arms. The comments on the floor included: "no way in this lifetime, or I'll break her arm!"

Well the instructors prevailed. Actually they fooled everyone, because it was simpler than it looked. One dancer was heard saying, "I cannot believe that I learned this twisted deviation from natural body mechanics. I really like it because the woman has to travel backwards, and has to do the twisting in and out of the lock!" *I recalled, the woman does all the work, but she is the one that gets all the praise!*

After everyone seemed to be capable of performing the turn, the DJ started the music. Dancing couples of all genders were performing the Hammer Lock. Eventually the smiles started appearing, and when the music stopped, the applause guaranteed that this would be a "keeper" turn The DJ adds, "Practice it tonight, while it is fresh in your mind."

The next dance was a slow dance, Never Again, Again by LeeAnn Womack. Having Sue in my arms felt as good as it did the first time a week ago. *I thought, so much has happened in the past week. All good, even the home invasion had a good ending. I wonder what the next weeks have in store for us?* We then danced till 11 PM and went home–straight to bed by Midnight.

Saturday day 14. On the road by 6 AM to the Desperado Club, Sue probably noticed that I appeared tense or pensive. She broke my thoughts by asking, "I hope you did not forget anything?" "Oh darn, I forgot my guns." "Bull-ticky, I doubt it, I helped you load them last night. And besides, you claim that your check list has never failed you!" "OK, you win, I needed something to break my trend of thought." Sue then turned towards me and said, "Will, stop worrying, you are going to enjoy yourself–trust me!"

On arrival at the club, we unloaded my gear, and headed to the food wagon. We each had an egg/cheese sandwich with coffee. We then headed to the registration desk and I paid the shooting fee of $25. I signed up in the senior class and Sue chose the white posse.

As we were walking away, Ranger Rooster intercepted us. "I was told that you were prepped and trained by P–Shooter and Lady Slipper." Sue naturally takes my hand

and of course Ranger Rooster never missed a trick–he winked at me! I volunteered, "actually, her training was more like a shanghai"–*she started squeezing my fingers.* But I am happy with the training results."–*her grip loosened up.* "Well, welcome to your solo shoot and enjoy your day."

"As punishment for your shanghai claim, you are going to purchase a one year membership to this club. The cost of $50 will go towards the purchase of materials to finish the last seven facades of our 10 stages. We hope to finish these 7 stages in the next 6 months. The work is being done by the members and we will be notified when our stage facade comes up. This will satisfy our volunteer work day."

While waiting for the mandatory Shooter's Meeting, Sue says, "Ranger Rooster will mention three issues: The shooting order, brass picker's clearance, and posse makeup and details" Suddenly a loud cannon blast gets everyone's attention–a meeting call.

Our match director starts the meeting with the "Pledge Allegiance to the Flag." The standard convention rules are read as they are at all shoots. The subject goes to brass pickers. "Please give the RO and the shooter ample room to exit the firing line before stepping in to pick up brass." He then moves to the second subject, "the shooting order will be the random order of each posse established by your RO. This method has now become this club's standard. The last item is the makeup of our posses. Of note is that we have 60 shooters today and each posse is assigned 15 shooters. The four posses are: red, white, blue, and gold. The posse's starting stage and members are posted on the bulletin board"

Ranger Rooster asked if there were any announcements or questions. Looked like there was none, then suddenly one shooter raised his hand. "Why is our club not a SASS affiliated club?" Ranger Rooster answered, "We are a young and small club. Our prime directive at this point is to find more new shooters–like we have two newbies today. Our next goal will be to get these new shooters to join our club. The last goal will be for all our club members to join SASS. Once the third goal is achieved we then can have SASS shoots where only SASS members can participate or we can hold open shoots and just follow SASS rules." With no other comments, we all proceeded to our starting stage.

The RO, aka Bill Buck, welcomed everyone to Stage 5. He then shuffled the score cards and said, "I will call the random order. Please sound out that you are here, and note who is shooting ahead of you. We want you to step to the loading table, without the scorekeeper having to find you or to call your name."

My name came up #7. Sue said, "that is a good spot. Pickup brass for the first five shooters, then step to your cart and get yourself ready." I had memorized the shooting sequence, but it was reassuring to watch the five shooters before I picked up their brass. Finally my turn came up, and I was on the firing line. I loosened the pistols in their holsters. I heard, "do you understand the course of fire?"–I say yes, "is the shooter ready?"–I say yes, "STAND BY", a pause and the buzzer goes off. No fruit salad syndrome. I proudly did everything correctly without a miss.

As I followed the RO off the firing line, I saw him give Sue a strong thumbs up sign. The RO then informs the scorekeeper, "time 49 seconds, a clean shoot and no penalties." I know I had a smile on my face, but Sue had me beat, she was wearing a million dollar smile. I got to the unloading table and the official added, "congratulations, for a newbie, that was an excellent job comparable to many shooters on your posse." Sue added, "good for you, now the rest of the day will be a piece of cake!"

The remainder of the morning generally went well for most of the shooters–including myself. The last stage before lunch saw quite a few misses. The targets were very small, the shooters were getting tired or getting hungry. I went to the lunch line with one miss on my card.

Lunch menu was enchiladas and refried beans. I softly mumbled to Sue, "Tex-mex food again, what is wrong with an American burger or hot dog?" After I tasted the meal, I stopped complaining, the food was delicious.

During lunch, Jack showed up. He explained, "I had problems with my sick elderly mother who needed hospitalization. She is now stable." Sue explained, "this shoot consists of eight stages. We have three left and you will get to observe our student–trust me Jack, Doc Derby is making us proud."

After lunch, with the shooters still in the clubhouse, Ranger Rooster made an announcement. "Next weekend is the yearly Cowboy Shoot at the Bar W Ranch located 400 miles from here, in the Texas panhandle. The shooting starts Thursday noon and finishes Saturday afternoon. Saturday evening is dinner and dancing. Sunday morning is the awards and closing ceremony. It is a long trip, but well worth it."

"For those of you who have not reserved a camping or shooting spot, please call ASAP to do a tentative phone reservation. They have 100 camping sites with complete hookups, and will only accept 100 shooters of CAS clubs for the main match. For those of you who have never attended this event, you are missing one heck of a good time. The most popular portion of this event is the side shoots, which all shooters join, including the local people who do not shoot the main CAS match"

Jack then informs Sue, "I have made reservations at the Lazy Nights motel in the adjacent town." "We have other plans but we will see you there" I interjected, "we have other plans?" "I will tell you all about it when we get home."

After lunch, something incredible and funny happened. The RO gathered the shooters, read the scenario and shooting sequence, for Stage 2. No one realized that shooter #3 (Tru-fak) was in the bathroom and missed the stage directions. Tru-fak arrived on a run, grabbed his guns and ammo, and stepped to the loading table. He grabbed the booklet of stage directions, read the stage, and said, "that's an easy stage, I am good!" On the firing line, he did well with 38 seconds and clean. The RO looks at the spotters who all had their hands down in a state of confusion. Tru-fak asks the RO what the problem was. Bill Buck looks at the shooter and says, "that was a fine job you did with this stage, the problem is that you shot the shooting sequence of Stage 3, but this is Stage 2!"

The entire posse erupted in laughter and many tapped Tru-fak on the shoulder and said, "nice job you old coot." No one knew how to score this stage, so the match director decided to give Tru-fak a reshoot.

The last three stages were a pleasure for me. I left the range with two misses for the day, but no procedurals or safety violations. While putting my gear away, I told Sue and Jack, "it feels good knowing I have made my bones."

My posse was first to finish shooting, and we gathered at the clubhouse for the awards ceremony. Sue took this opportunity to introduce me to all the "white posse" members. I did not know that Sue always shoots on the "white posse" and that the posse members were all her friends. Her introductions were semi formal but with a subtle personal touch–everyone noticed that Sue never let go of my hand.

The awards ceremony began. The first award was the Iron Man certificate for a clean shoot. There were five, Sue explained, "some shooters don't do speed and they slow down with every intent of going for the clean shoot award. There is nothing wrong with this, it's everyone's prerogative to do so."

The next award was the ladies division. There were 10 shooters out of 60. Because of the many categories, sometimes there was only one shooter per category, and of course they got the first place award. The senior class had 5 shooters and Sue added, "these are all good shooters and my serious competitors." I looked at Sue and asked, "do you regret being my coach, you likely would have beat some of these five shooters." "Never regretted a moment, this was your day, and in the future I will have many opportunities to rattle these five ladies."

Next came the men's categories to include the 50 shooters. I had forgotten the many categories possible: Cowboy, Duelist, Gunfighter, Frontier Cartridge, 49er, Wrangler, Classic Cowboy, Senior, Silver Senior and Elder Statesman. Today's shoot had six of these categories represented. The awards were given and my class was last on the agenda.

The Senior group was very popular. Probably because this was the age of retirement, 60-64. We were 12 shooters and three awards were to be given. Suddenly, Ranger Rooster made an announcement. "In the third place is a newbie, Doc Derby. Prepped, trained and coached by

P–Shooter and Lady Slipper. Nice job the three of you!" As I was getting my award, every shooter got up and gave me a standing ovation. *I knew that I had just experienced a memorable once in a lifetime event.*

Sue drove all the way home. She asked, "I know I have never asked you your thoughts about CAS and the past two weeks, I would love to hear your assessment?" "Here is what I think:"

1. "I enjoy the fantasy scenarios: shooting at Indians circling a wagon train, outlaws robbing a bank, crooked card players and other fantasies from our stage writer's creative minds."
2. "Like you, I enjoy shooting. Practices are welcomed times where I can shoot three guns, and shoot as much as I want to. The competition shoots are great times that allow us to test our abilities."
3. "The shooting and reloading now gives me two hobbies that I can do any day I want to."
4. "Cowboy shooters are a great bunch of people who are a joy to meet."
5. "This sport has renewed my interest in American history of the 1800's. I want to read more on Oregon Trail wagon trains, pioneer living, the buffalo harvest, cattle drives and Old West historical towns."
6. "I look forward to start reading Western fiction and historical fiction from such authors; Gary

McCarthy, John Legg, LJ Martin, William Johnstone and more. My first read will be the historical fiction series on the national parks by Gary McCarthy."

7. "Now, I am looking forward to traveling out west–where the Cowboy history all started."
8. "The most important byproduct of all this is you. I have met and hooked up with the most wonderful companion any man could have. Thank You so much."

CHAPTER 8

Our First Trip

Saturday evening day 14. After unloading my gear, we had time to relax before heading to the Country Roadhouse. We were sharing a bottle of wine when I addressed Sue, "So now, tell me about those other plans we supposedly have." "Well, when you were finalizing your purchase of the camper, I took the opportunity to call the Bar W Ranch, and scheduled our first trip with the truck and camper. I reserved a site for the camper and did a tentative registration for both of us–for the main match and all the side shoots. That is why I pushed you to take a membership in the Desperado club. Only Cowboy club members can shoot in the main match."

"Since we need to be at the Bar W Ranch by noon Thursday, what is a tentative agenda to get there by noon?" She was prepared, "we are going to have three busy days. Sunday we go shopping for lumber, food and many things we need in the camper. Monday we pick up the truck and camper. Monday evening we start building the gun room in the bunk room. Tuesday we finish the gun room, load the camper with all the necessary items, and hitch the camper to the truck."

"What about Wednesday, we don't need to be at the ranch before Thursday noon." "Well, if you agree, I thought we would travel 300 miles, stop at a camping area to try out this thing called camping! That would leave us only 100 miles to travel on Thursday."

There was silence and I finally said, "you know, I really lucked out when you pulled me out of the swamp." "That's OK, you can properly thank me later tonight. Right now we need to get ready to go to the Roadhouse for dancing." "Well, I don't know if we should spend all that energy at dancing and other activities, we have a heavy schedule ahead." "Not to worry, we can leave the Roadhouse early to save energy for other activities."

We arrived at the Country Roadhouse in time for drinks before dinner. We had a light dinner of turkey burgers and salad. As usual the dance started at 9 PM. Several line dances followed by two-steps and waltzes. The DJ then invited dancers to do the Blue Rose to Toby Keith's, Who's Your Daddy. It was well attended with most of the patrons present. Everyone was then encouraged to do a two-step and perform the Hammer Lock. It was clear that there was a general commitment amongst patrons to learn new moves, turns, and dances.

After several more dances, the DJ announced the "teach" of the night. "The instructors, Jerry and Lynn, will perform and teach the El Paso." The music started and a flawless El Paso was demonstrated. These instructors followed the same standards of the Sugarhouse Dancers–teaching 4 to 8 steps at a time and not progressing till everyone could do the steps. In no time the dance was picked up. Jerry pointed out that, "the Blue Rose had vines. pivots and shuffles. The El Paso has rock steps, turn steps, triple steps, sway backs and shuffles. The point being that partner dances often share similar moves. In this case the shuffles are the shared moves."

Finally the DJ started the music with a song by Brooks and Dunn, Neon Moon. Everyone was in step, and it was easy to see that we all enjoyed this dance. The DJ then announced next week's lessons. "The Friday new turn will be Around the World by Curt and Sandy, and the Saturday partner dance will be the Texas Waltz by Charlie and Jeanne." Sue commented, "next weekend we will be gone to the Bar W Ranch. We already know Around the World, and I have performed the Texas Waltz as a line dance. I will show you how to perform it as a couple, at a later time."

We danced until 11 PM when Sue said, "maybe we should head home and conserve some energy–for that thank you I was promised." "Good idea, and not to worry, that thank you is utmost on my mind."

Sunday day 15. One thing led to another, and somehow we did not get to sleep till 1 AM. We slept later than usual but awoke by 9 AM.

We then cooked another replenishing breakfast. By 10 AM Sue reminded me that this was our shopping day and suggested that we make a list of needed items before hitting the stores. We quickly had to break down the master list into different categories for different stores. Here is the result:

A. Collect free items at #97 Derby Lane.

- Bed sheets, bedspread, and pillows.
- Cleaning supplies for kitchen, bathroom and linoleum.
- Broom/pan, wet and dry swifter, Dyson portable hand held vacuum.
- Bathroom towels.
- Emergency supplies for the medicine cabinet.

B. Clothing transfer from the house.

- Casual, dress-up and Western wardrobe for dances or other gala events. CAS costumes, Cowboy boots and hats for all occasions.
- Footwear. Snake proof hiking boots, and sneakers.
- Cold weather clothing and gear.
- Rain gear.

C. Shopping list–hardware.

- Lumber to build the gun room. I had already made a separate list of these items to include assorted hardware and locks.
- Two end kitchen cabinets with drawers.
- A lightweight steel gun safe, like a gym locker.
- A lightweight steel wardrobe with one drawer and a shelf for footwear. I had already found this item in the tool section as a cabinet to store tools–easily convertible into a wardrobe.
- Two utility stools.
- Tool box with assorted tools.
- Ryobi kit–drill, saws-all, light and drills/tips.
- Four lawn chairs.
- Flashlights/batteries.
- Hand axe.
- Fire poker with sleeve.
- LED table lamp for power outage.
- Bug repellent.
- Heavy duty extension cord.

D. Shopping list–gun shop.

- Pepper and bear spray.
- Heavy duty cattle cane.
- Kevlar full length snake chaps.
- 357 mag snake loads.
- 12 gauge OO buckshot and 1 oz. slugs–for bears.

E. Shopping list for drug store.

- Standard medications to include pills, ointments and sun-screen.
- Toiletries, toilet paper, makeup and hair care.

I thought of adding, "don't forget your birth control pills," but I knew I would get that look–the one I don't fare well with. So I just moved on to groceries.

F. Shopping list for groceries.

- Basics–mustard, ketchup, salt, pepper, pickles, mayo, sugar, splenda, butter, coffee and half & half.
- Three meals per day for four days.
- Water, coke, 7up, and OJ.
- Vodka, red and white wine.
- Salad dressing–Italian and poppy seed.
- Assorted cheeses and crackers.

As I perused these lists, I thought, *It was a real good idea that the camper had a large pantry next to the kitchen. We would certainly fill it up.*

Normally, I despise shopping, however this was not just shopping, it was a mission to find everything on our lists. The first load was the lumber and general hardware items. Both our SUV's were full, even with the plywood being precut. We went to unload and the next load was done with one SUV, to include the gun shop, drug store and grocery store items.

The drug store and gun shop shopping were a quick in and out. The grocery store was something else. We covered every isle, but we found everything and some extras. On returning home, the refrigerated items were placed in my 36 inch wide refrigerator. Everything else was placed in my gun room, next to the overhead doors.

Sunday evening day 15. When shopping, Sue picked up a whole chicken coming out of the oven. We enhanced that with Stove Top dressing, cranberry sauce and wine–a hardy meal for two famished workers. After dinner we decided to do more prep work. Sue would tackle the un-boxing of the end cabinets/drawers, the wardrobe cabinet, the gun safe and all other hardware items/tools. I would start precutting the lumber for the reloading bench and other wood accessories.

We started our tasks, and to our surprise, it took us two hours to complete the jobs. The last thing we did was to go to #97 and get those items we had planned for. The end of the day finally arrived. We were both tired but it was a good fatigue. Sue was first to head for the shower, while I took the opportunity to call my three kids as planned.

With all three of my children, I said the same line, "well this old man has taken a big leap into the future,

I am shacking up with a blonde bombshell, and we are going to travel the West in a truck/camper!" It is amazing how silence on the phone can be interpreted as shock and awe. *Retrospectively, I wished I had made the calls on skype–just to see their faces.*

Actually the discussions were very congenial. All three wanted to meet Sue before we headed out on our summer trip, and I agreed that we would arrange a family meeting, and include Sue's two daughters. Sue came out of the shower as I was finishing my calls. I told Sue of the need for a double family meeting to include her daughters. Sue started calling her daughters as I headed to the shower.

After showers and family calls, we simply went to bed. Looking forward to our big day tomorrow.

Monday day 16. We were on the road rather early, to arrive when the Dodge dealership opened at 8:00 AM. My SUV was cleaned out of personal belongings, ready to trade for the truck. We had planned to use Sue's brand new Toyota SUV for local use. Whereas the truck was reserved for large loads, cowboy shooting and hauling the camper across the country.

When we arrived at the Dodge dealership, our truck was in front of the showroom. We went over the exterior and interior carefully and quickly accepted the results. As we stepped into the showroom, Gail greeted us and said, "your truck is basically ready, we have added all the requested accessories. If you give me your phones, our tech service will program them into the computer to give you hand's free phone service, and the simultaneous use of both your phones."

Gail added, "otherwise, all that is left is paper work, insurance and payment. You are likely aware that 99% of our business is dealing with banks issuing vehicle loans. A cash purchase is very rare. Because of the large amount, our office accountant went to the bank to cash your check. Without revealing personal information, the bank manager assured her that there was plenty of funds in your account to buy several trucks."

The paper work and payment was completed. The technician then showed us how to operate our phones, and showed us how to remove the bed cover–as a two man operation. The technician also pointed out that, despite our being shown how to use all the bells and whistles, we will have to use our owner's manual until we master them. Our departure was delayed because the insurance company did not open their doors till 9:00 AM. When we left, my insurance had been transferred, and everyone involved were guaranteed that we had bonded insurance with a confirmation number.

By 10 AM we were heading to the camper dealership, an hour's drive away. We both drove to get familiar with a truck compared to an SUV. We were expecting a stiff ride from a 3/4 ton vehicle, but the ride was smooth and comfortable. The steering was responsive and there was no feeling of sitting in a boat. All in all, we were both happy with this purchase.

We arrived at the camper dealership shortly after 11 AM. On arrival, our salesman, Gregg, sent the truck to the shop for modifications: installing electric brakes, matching the electrical adapters to the camper and installing the camper tire monitoring system into our on board computer. We then told Gregg that we were going across the road to that family restaurant for lunch. "When you return the camper will be up front, since it is road ready, with all your add-ons."

As a family restaurant, we were not surprised to see their special of the day–meatloaf, mashed potatoes, carrots and gravy. Sue commented, "usually a special of the day is a good meal." We both ordered the special–it came smothered in gravy and was delicious. With coffee, our bill was less than $20.

On our return to the dealership, our unit was parked out front. I took out my list of add ons and we went to work. We checked and scrutinized all the outside accessories. Gregg and a technician joined us. They showed us how to: operate the push-out and awning both electrically and manually, and the manual operation of the stabilizing jacks and exterior propane stove.

We then went inside, and the first place we both headed for was the bunk room. It had been stripped 100%. Every piece of furniture gone, and ready for building our gun room. We then followed the technician's systematic presentation. He explained how to operate the hot water, furnace, refrigerator conversion to propane, and the cooking gas stove and convection oven. Afterwards, Greg and the technician sat at the table and let us go through the entire unit. They answered all our questions. I finally appreciated the well built spacious pantry.

Although the bedroom closet had as much room as possible, the extra wardrobe in the gun room would come in handy. Sue was very thorough in checking out the kitchen and asked many questions. In the end she said, "This kitchen is more than adequate, I can work with this." The last item to review was the electronics. They especially explained the use of the HD antenna booster and the WIFI booster.

We all went back outside when the truck came out of the shop. The technician showed us how to hook up to the reese hitch, properly adjust the leveling bars, install the anti-sway kit and check all the camper lights. Their final adjustment was the electric brakes. We then went for a test drive with me driving. The technician gave us his final instructions, while driving on a secondary road, and verified that the electric brakes were properly adjusted.

Back at the office, we did the paper work, settled the finances, and called our insurance agent. Our insurance was bonded and we were given a confirmation number– the policy will be coming in the mail just like the truck.

The ride home was a new experience–we were pulling our home on wheels. We both drove to get acquainted with the 5000 pounds we were hauling. I said, "here we are, going down the road with a new truck, camper and all the amenities to live in comfort, with a goal of being on the road for the summer. It doesn't get any better."

Monday evening day 16. We arrived home by 3 PM. We were both anxious to begin building our gun room. In short order, we started putting together the reloading bench. An 8 foot long, 24 inch wide piece of 3/4 inch finished birch plywood was laid down on the two end cabinets with drawers. All three pieces were secured to the wall studs with angle irons and the cabinets were also secured to the floor.

A 12 inch wide shelf was secured to both end cabinets and elevated 6 inches off the floor. This low shelf had a 5 inch high lip to keep contents from falling out during traveling. The last item was an eight foot long trough on the rear portion of the bench, also with a 5 inch high lip to keep small reloading tools secured while traveling. The lower shelf and the bench trough were painted with leftover blue-gray paint. The drawers were then secured with locks to prevent opening during motion. That finished the left side of the gun room.

We then ordered a pizza, for home delivery, and started planning the right side of the gun room. After dinner, we moved the grey steel gun safe into the right side of the gun room. This was a light unit measuring 20X20 inches and 5.5 feet high. It held 6 long guns and had a bottom drawer for the pistols. We secured it to the wall studs and floor.

We then brought in the grey steel cabinet modified with a wooden dowel to hold clothing hangers. It was 24 inches wide by 20 inches deep and also 5.5 feet high. It was also secured to the wall studs, floor, and also to the gun safe using several bolts with lock nuts.

The last item was to secure the gun cart and the utility benches next to the wardrobe cabinet. We designed a reusable system of fixing these three items in place. The end result was that we were left, with a center aisle of 3+ feet, for maneuvering and working.

Thinking we were done, we stood back to view the end result, and quickly realized we had forgotten a crucial item. I went into my garage and took down a 3 foot LED silent shop light. We installed it directly over the center of the bench, where our reloaders would be located.

Tomorrow we would be loading the camper as well as the gun room. For now, we put our tools away and went straight to bed, somewhat exhausted from a full day.

Tuesday day 17. After breakfast, we brought electricity to the camper via an extension cord from the garage gun room. We decided to start loading the furthest room, the gun room. First to go in was Sue's reloaders, the Square Deal B pistol reloader, the MEC Sizemaster shotgun reloader and the RF–100 primer loader. The next items were all the accessory reloading tools placed in the trough on top of the bench. Last were the reloading components, powder, primers, hulls and wads, placed in the cabinet drawers. Lead bullets and birdshot were placed in waterproof plastic ammo boxes and stored in the truck bed against the wall to the rear seat. The lead was considered too heavy for the camper floor and too heavy for the gun room–creating a problem with balance and camper tongue weight.

We then brought our cowboy guns and secured the long guns in the gun safe with leather straps, extra velcro strapping and ample padding. The cowboy pistols were placed in their original padded plastic boxes and stored in the bottom drawer. Door and drawer closed and locked. Loaded ammo was kept in the low shelf under the reloading bench, secured behind the shelf's high lip. Other shooting stuff was added to the unused reloading bench's drawers.

The wardrobe was filled with our CAS outfits, rain gear, and boots. We also included dressed up western outfits for dancing and special events. Our Cowboy hats went on the top shelf. In the bottom compartment we stored our leather rigs, slides, loading blocks and extra belts. Both doors were then secured with locks for traveling.

The next items went outside. There were two large storage compartments with locks and one unlocked small compartment. In the large compartments we stored the lawn chairs, water hose, tool box and all the small items bought at the hardware store. The sewage pipe had its own storage slot. We got everything in but any new acquisitions would have to go in the truck's bed, or move the lawn chairs into the truck's bed to make more room in the storage compartments.

The small unlocked compartment had a secure closure and was used for the leveling blocks and the wheel chucks. Before they went in I showed Sue how to slide the floor forward and lift it up. This exposed a compartment for spare keys. It was a tricky maneuver to lift the false floor, and therefore a secure place for our spare truck and camper keys. Sue wondered how she missed this info, "when you were investigating the kitchen, Gregg showed me the hidden compartment."

The next items to be moved in was the food and drinks. Thanks for the extra refrigerator size and the pantry, we got all the food and drinks in place. The toiletries and medications were next, the last items were the towels distributed between the toilet/sink room and the separate shower room.

The moving was complete by 3 PM. We then made the bed up with Sue's sheets, bedspread and pillows. Suddenly Sue was all over me with kisses, hugging and unbuttoning my shirt. Finally I said, "woman, what is your problem?" "You are my problem and only you can solve it." "But it's in the middle of the afternoon." "So close the curtains, lock the door and we'll pretend it's the middle of the night. Then we can initiate this camper and bedroom properly." *I thought, how can any man resist?..........................!*

After our passions were spent, the bedroom was quiet, the only sound was us regaining our breaths. Sue was first to speak in a low choppy voice, "Wil, you were right, what happens in this room stays in this room!" After my old line registered, I added, "can you imagine, if our children only knew!" We both broke out in laughter. Eventually Sue says, "please, say no more, come around the bed and help me up!"

After another replenishing dinner, I said, "your original idea of taking off tomorrow and going camping was a good plan. If you are game, let's do that tomorrow morning." "Yes, I am ready and looking forward to our escapade."

We then watched the local and national news, followed by some relaxing reading. We both started reading a national parks historical fiction by Gary McCarthy, Grand Canyon Thunder. Two hours later, Sue suggested we get some extra sleep time and added, "plus we never know what else can happen." "Twice the same day, we are too old for that." "Never too old, besides, we need to catch up on nights we were too tired to function...!"

Wednesday day 18. After another replenishing breakfast, we hooked up the truck to the camper. Jack showed up to see what we were up to. "I came yesterday, but when I found the door locked and the camper rocking, I decided it was best to return at a better time. Next time, put your stabilizing jacks up!"

Sue never missed a step, she added, "well Jack you need to see our camper and especially the gun room." Jack came in and examined our gun room in great detail. "Wow what a nice user friendly reloading center. I love the way your camper is arranged. What are your plans for the summer?"

I went into details about our circuitous route over several western states for visiting and cowboy shooting. "Today we are heading out to the Bar W Ranch. We have a campsite reserved at the ranch, and tonight we will be camping three quarters of the way to the ranch. We will meet you Thursday noon at the Bar W."

With coffee in hand, and Willie Nelson's On The Road Again. we took off for Texas. Sue set the GPS for the Bar W's address, and a new experience had just begun.

We both drove and it was amazing how well this truck could handle a fully loaded camper. As soon as we arrived in Western Oklahoma, the scenery changed. Large prairies and desert terrain scattered with Black Angus, Herefords, and Short Horn cattle. We did see many crossbreed cattle. It was clear that the terrain needed many acres to support one head of cattle. The ranches were few and far apart. Their location was marked by a high entrance gate with their ranch brand on the gate. This land had a historical culture of its own.

Driving along, we came up to a small scenic town. It had a touch of Old West design as well as modern facilities and shops. We drove through and came up on a camping area. The campground was clean and at 1 PM it was already 50% occupied. Since we were about three quarters of the way, we stopped to inquire. It cost $35 per night for full hook ups and free firewood. The only amenity was an in-ground pool set at 88 degrees, to compensate for the outside temperature of 72 degrees. They were expecting 100% occupancy by 7 PM, because of a big Cowboy Shoot down the road–the Bar W Ranch. We registered and went to our designated campsite.

We set up our campsite for the first time. We unhitched the camper, leveled it, chucked the wheels, set out the power, sewer hose and water hose. Took out two lawn chairs and made a quick sandwich lunch. We then changed in our swimsuits. Sue put on her one piece generic Miss America suit saying, "I suspect that this pool is a family location, and my mini bikini will stay in the drawer again." "Sadly, you are right." *I thought, I can't wait for an adult location where she can wear this revealing mini!*

The pool was comfortable despite the cool air. The deep end was clogged up with adults bobbing on noodles. People were friendly, after introductions, we joined in the conversations. The major topic was the upcoming shooting event at the Bar W. Many of the people in the pool were going as CAS shooters. The ones who had been there in past years described the event.

"Other than the CAS event, the popular side shoots are the most attended by both CAS members, local cowboys and general public from nearby towns. The popular side events are the aerial shots and the fast draw with wax bullets, but there are 8 more to join. There are two other venues that attract people. They have horse rides every day and the big dinner/dance on Saturday night is the epitome of a gala event."

Another person adds, "they expect 100 cowboy shooters and 100 local people for the side events. That makes 200 participants, the problem is that everyone has a spouse, friend, date, mistress or significant other. This means congestion but the organizers seem to manage things well. The only way to beat the crowds is to do as many side shoots on Thursday afternoon, finish them early Friday morning, before the local people arrive. Use Friday afternoon for horse rides, when everyone is trying to get onto the side shoots."

Their enthusiasm was infectious, making us even more eager to arrive at the ranch. It was too cool to sit by the pool so we said our goodbyes and headed to our campsite by 4 PM. Arriving at the camper, I unlocked the door and Sue asked, "Are we in the mistress or significant other category?" I paused, "Let me show you." I put my right hand on her right shoulder and the strap came down, then the same happened on her left shoulder strap. By the time Sue realized what was happening, she barely escaped in the camper, carrying the door with her. By then, her entire one piece generic suit had gone south just above her knees. I heard the click, as she locked the door, as a self preservation move. Then she started laughing and it lasted for a long time. Meanwhile, the neighbor gave me a thumbs up sign–I didn't know he was watching.

When she finally came outside, fully dressed, she acted as if nothing had happened. I looked at her and said, "is there any doubt in your mind that you are no paramour." We both started laughing as well as the adjacent neighbors. She only said, "expect some pay back of the same quality–when you least expect it."

That afternoon we sat in the shade of the awning and enjoyed some red wine. For dinner, we cooked two t-bones over an open wood fire, with a side baked potato.

It had been many years since we tasted the wood smoke on our steaks.

The evening was another experience. We sat by the fire till late. The mesmerizing effect of the fire mellowed us to complete contentment. We finally started talking about our earlier lives with our spouses and raising our children. For the first time, Sue did not express any ill feelings regarding the divorce. It was clear to me that she was moving on–hopefully because of her new life with me.

I eventually said to Sue, "well I do believe that our truck/camper has passed mustard on its maiden voyage." She added, "Something tells me that this kind of living will continue to grow on us. This has certainly been a great day."

At bedtime, Sue asked, "is there any interest in giving our bedroom a second initiation?" "Yes, certainly worth a try!.........................!

CHAPTER 9

The Bar W Ranch

Thursday day 19. We got up late and made another replenishing breakfast, of cheese/egg sandwiches, on our outside propane stove. After several cups of coffee, we decided to break camp and head out. Closing camp was simply a reverse of setting up, and in no time we were on the road. With Willie Nelson's, On the Road Again, blasting away we pulled out to the same secondary road on route to the ranch.

By 10:30 AM we arrived at the Bar W Ranch. The ranch was a site to see. Buildings on both sides of a central main thoroughfare with street lights, hitching rails, water troughs and vehicle parking spots. On the left was the main home of the Whitehouse family. Adjacent and connecting was an Olympic size swimming pool with a large deck of paver bricks, flood lights, lounging chairs, towel service, tables with umbrellas and an outside bar.

The next adjacent building was a large structure with a sign saying, MEETING AND DANCE HALL, occupancy 300 people. The next section had a corral with a sign, HORSE RIDES. We saw good looking horses with different coat colors and body sizes. Sue pointed out, "horses on a Texas ranch are Stock Horses–small to medium, agile and well trained cattle herding horses."

The corral was adjoining a large two story barn. This was a typical western barn with, a wide first floor of paddocks on each side, with an open area in the middle, and with a tack room in the rear. The second floor for hay storage, was half the size, giving the structure the typical appearance of a wide first floor and narrow second floor. The rear of the barn had a powered hay bale elevator. The right side of the barn had a single row of porta-potties, running the entire length of the barn. After an appropriate distance, the last location on the left was the camping area. Four rows of 25 campsites with full hookups, picnic tables, but no fireplaces. Open fires were not allowed because of the risk of prairie fires.

The right side of the main street started out with another private home, we were later told was for the owner's son and family. The next buildings were a row of service utilities to include: saddle and harness shop, blacksmith shop, carpenter and handyman shop, a veterinary hospital and an auto repair shop, with a large parking/carport in the rear.

Then came the large bunkhouse with the adjoining cookie shack, kitchen and dining room–located across the street from the porta-potties. The last building was the office with a sign saying, REGISTRATION. Next to this spot was a sign indicating, ROAD TO SHOOTING VENUES, located across the camping area. Just beyond the road was a large cabin. We were eventually informed that this was the home of the ranch foreman and his wife–who was also a ranch hand.

We stopped at the registration booth and were greeted at the counter by the Registrar–Mrs. Beecher. She then said, "welcome, you are an early arrival and so will have the choice of prime campsites." We chose site #5 which was on the main street row, far enough from the porta-potties but close to all activities.

Mrs. Beecher then explained, "you have a choice of partial or full passes for meals." We ended up paying for all 10 side shoots, the main match, full passes on all meals, the campsite, the variety show on Friday evening and the dinner dance on Saturday night. The awards breakfast on Sunday and the use of the pool were included. "If you choose to do horse rides, you would have to return here to pay for the length of your rides, once you make your reservations at the horse corral."

Mrs. Beecher's final directions were enlightening. "The side shoots are open to the public without reservations. They are very popular and we are expecting at least 100 local shooters along with the 100 main match shooters."

"My recommendation is to utilize this afternoon and shoot at least 6 of the 10 stages. That will leave you 4 for Friday. Between 7–8 AM you could easily shoot three of those stages and keep Stage 10, the Texas Star, for last. You will have ample time to set up your campsite, have lunch at the cookie shack and be at the side shoots by 1 PM."

We were informed that the side shoot RO's were the ranch employees, but the main match RO's were official SASS RO1 shooters. Also, some of the side shoots have scenarios, some do not. And last, Mrs. Beecher clarified that our club director, Ranger Rooster, would have to verify that we were Desperado club members–a requirement of the ranch match organizers.

We were given three brochures, one on the history of the ranch, an other on the scenarios of the main match and the last was an explanation of the monetary proceeds of this match. All funds were donated to a local Wounded Warrior Program, which supports a local residential rehab and nursing home, for these individuals.

We thanked her and moved our camper to site #5. We set up quickly, changed into cowboy clothes, loaded up our gear and headed to lunch with our cowboy cart. At the cookie shack, the menu for the entire event was displayed. We had several choices for each meal but the same choices every day. Sue commented, "with these great choices, our frozen foods will stay in the freezer." The menu included:

BREAKFAST. Biscuits and gravy, steak and eggs, oatmeal and corn bread, skillet Texas hash, and pancakes with bacon. Each choice includes toasted homemade bread, peanut butter, jelly and coffee.

LUNCH. Beef stew with vegetables, hot roast beef sandwich, beans and salt pork, an all beef burger/steak fries, and a "cattle drive" casserole with chipped beef/vegetables in a white sauce. Any of the above with sweet biscuits, a mixed bean salad, coffee and a dessert of Cowboy honey drop cookies.

DINNER. Standard 8 or 10 ounce sirloin steak. BBQ 8 or 10 ounce strip steak, Dutch-oven Swiss steak, Cowboy beef brisket or 10 ounce ribeye steak. Any of the above with a side dish of beans with green chile, and a choice of baked or mashed potatoes. Dessert choices of fresh peaches in simple syrup, Cowboy double layered chocolate cake or old fashion bread pudding.

PS. All the beef choices are a product of our own locally grown ranch stock.

When ordering we had the choice of a light or a full serving. With side shoots on the agenda this afternoon, we both chose the light serving of the hot roast beef sandwich with the Cowboy cookie dessert.

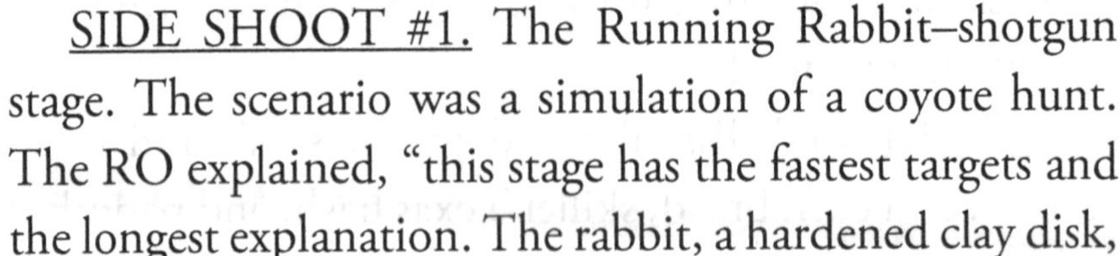

SIDE SHOOT #1. The Running Rabbit–shotgun stage. The scenario was a simulation of a coyote hunt. The RO explained, "this stage has the fastest targets and the longest explanation. The rabbit, a hardened clay disk, comes out of the box on the right and travels to the left. It will roll and hop at a fast clip until it disappears behind the berm. Take your first shot as soon as it comes out, that way you can use your second shot if you miss on the first shot. The key to a hit, lead the disk and as you fire continue swinging ahead. If you stop your swing, you will hit behind the rabbit, and miss. Remember once the rabbit is behind the berm it is too late for your second shot. A hit is when you break the disk or knock it down flat. If the disc just changes it's direction, keep shooting."

"When ready, yell OUT, and I will release the rabbit. For the next rabbit, reload quickly, and yell OUT when ready. This is a timed event and you get 5 rabbits on the clock. A hit is a 10 second bonus off your time and a missed rabbit is a 5 second penalty added to your time." The RO gave everyone a demonstration by shooting two rabbits in a row!

The two shooters ahead of us did poorly. It was clear that this would be a challenging stage. Sue went first, she missed the first two rabbits but then got the hang of it. She hit the next three rabbits, some on the first shot and some on the second shot. I missed the first rabbit but got the next four–all on the second shot. Although I had one more hit, she beat me on time because her reloads were much quicker.

<u>SIDE SHOOT #2.</u> Charging and Running Bear–rifle stage. The scenario was a simulation of a grizzly bear

attack. The RO explained, "The charging bear is a 10 inch steel plate with a painted bear's head. The running bear is a painted silhouette of a bear, 10 inches high but 30 inches long–running left to right. With a loaded rifle, you have a maximum of 10 shots to share between the two targets."

"When ready, the light will turn green and the bear starts charging. Shoot at will until the bear disappears into the receiving box. The running bear will start immediately as the charging bear arrives in its box. Continue shooting at the running bear until you are out of ammo or the running bear disappears in its receiving box."

"A hit is a 10 second bonus and a miss is also a 10 second penalty. Any live round left in the rifle is also a 10 second penalty. I will stop the timer after your 10th shot or after the running bear is in its receiving box. Past experiences have shown that, shooting beyond your speed comfort zone, will produce more misses and even an occasional jacked out round." The RO demonstrated a full cycle of both bears and he got 6 hits, 3 misses and one round left in the rifle.

I went first this time. I got 4 hits on the charging bear, 3 hits on the running bear and 3 misses. Sue went ballistic on the charging bear and got 6 hits, but was erratic on the running bear and only got one hit. She also emptied her rifle and so had 3 misses. She beat me again because her time was shorter than mine.

SIDE SHOOT #3. Dueling Tree–pistol stage. The scenario was about a gunfight. The RO and his wife explained, "the dueling tree has 6 targets, 3 reds on the left and 3 blacks on the right. The backs of each target has the opposing color. In this case, Shooter A(Doc Derby) shoots at the reds and Shooter B(Lady Slipper) shoots at the blacks. At the buzzer you shoot all 10 pistol rounds."

"Every time Shooter A hits a red target, it flips over to the right as a black target, and vice versa for Shooter B. Each shooter tries to convert his targets to the other side, and so does the other shooter. As soon as one shooter has shot his 10th round, I will stop the clock."

"At the end of the competition, any shooter with more than three targets on his or her side will be given a 10 second penalty, for each of those extra targets. The shooter with less than three targets on his or her side will be given a 10 second bonus, for each of the missing targets. In addition, any shooter shooting too slow and ending up with a live round in a pistol will also be given a 15 second penalty for each remaining unfired round." His wife adds, "a miss on a target is not given a penalty, all that matters is what is left showing at the end of the competition."

The RO gave us a demonstration, competing against his wife. At the end of the competition, each shooter had 3 targets remaining–we thought a draw. However the lady had a live round remaining in the second pistol. The RO won the match.

On the buzzer, the dueling started. The results were as expected. Sue finished first, and I had one round left over in my second pistol. I ended up with 4 reds and Sue ended up with 2 blacks. So I ended up with a 10 second penalty for that extra target and Sue had a 10 second bonus for that one target flipped to my side. Plus, I got a 15 second penalty for that live round left in my pistol. *I thought, she beat me again, but I was proud of her.*

<u>SIDE SHOOT #4.</u> Cowboy Clays–shotgun stage. The scenario, a pheasant hunt. The RO and assistant explained, "this is a game of doubles. The first set of doubles will be released straight ahead with the left bird going left and the right bird going right. The second set will be angled to the left and the third set will be angled to the right. The direction of the fourth and fifth sets will be randomly selected."

"As soon as you are ready, yell PULL. Since this is a timed stage, reload ASAP and yell pull again. You will get 5 set's of doubles. Every hit gives you a 5 second bonus off your time. There is no penalty for a miss." The RO gave a demonstration with the assistant operating the clay launcher. He got 5 birds and admitted that he never got the hang of shotgun shooting at moving targets.

I got 9 hits and Sue got 5. Even with her faster reloads, I finally beat her. I did admit that years ago I had shot trap, skeet, and sporting clays, which obviously gave me an advantage in leading birds for a hit.

SIDE SHOOT #5. Long Range active target–rifle stage. No scenario.

The RO explained, "Here we have two 8 inch targets at 25 yards. It sounds simple, but watch when I press this button." The two targets started moving in unison, right to left to right, back and forth as if attached to a metronome. "The size, distance, and motion of these targets, makes this a challenging stage."

"You have 10 shots and the clock stops on your last shot. Every hit is worth 5 seconds off your time and there are no penalties for misses." The RO demonstrated and got 6 hits with the exclamation, "this is my best score this season, and I hosted this stage last year with terrible results." I said to Sue, "them are not encouraging words!"

I went first and got 5 hits but Sue got a whopping 9 hits. When discussing our shooting technique, she said, "the key to this stage was to rack the lever and wait for the target to reach its apogee." She explained, "the apogee means the furthest point a target gets before it heads the other way." I then said, "I was chasing behind each target which got me nowhere. I will remember this 'apogee' thing!"

On our way to the next side shoot, I said to Sue, "you did so well on that last stage, that your score may be a contender for that stage's best score." She came back, "I am enjoying these side shoots. I try to shoot the best I can, and I try not to think of possible awards. If it happens that I win a stage, the more the sweetness of it all."

SIDE SHOOT #6. Long Range active target–pistol stage. No scenario, this is a pre match practice. The RO and assistant explained, "this is another powered exercise. There are two wheels with 8 inch red and black paddles, randomly spaced. The wheels, 10 yards downrange, are adjacent and both turning. The tricky part is that both wheels are behind this steel shroud, with a one 8 inch window, where you can shoot at the targets. You can shoot as fast as you wish, and keep in mind that this is a timed stage. For every hit on a red target you get a 5 second bonus, but every hit on a black target will give you a 10 second penalty. Any hit on the shroud is a non scoring miss. You can shoot your 10 shots at either wheels. My assistant will be the spotter and his scoring will be final."

The RO demonstrated the stage. He got 5 hits on red paddles, one hit on a black target, and 4 hits on the shroud. I commented, "this stage requires quick responses."

There were several shooters ahead of us, which gave us a chance to study their techniques. Our scoring reflected our worst stage performance. Sue got 4 red hits, and I got 5, but I also got one black hit. Our final scores were so close that we called this stage a draw. As we were leaving this stage, the RO said, "This exact stage will be part of the main match at stage 9 tomorrow. I hope that this exposure might give you an advantage, good luck tomorrow!"

Thursday evening day 19. By 4 PM we arrived on the main street. We went to investigate the pool and horse riding corral. The pool sign said, "Daytime is family time. Evenings, after dark, is adult time. Swimsuits required at all times, but evening suits can be a Speedo for men and a two piece mini bikini for women. Alcohol allowed during adult time." I said, "we are coming tonight and you can finally wear your mini bikini." Sue's gesture said it all, she punched her right fist high in the air and said, "Yes."

We then headed to the horse riding corral. We were eager to go on a ride. We reserved a two hour ride for 2 PM tomorrow. We then went to the registration office and paid for a two hour pass. We brought our gear to the camper, changed into more casual clothes, and headed out for dinner. At the cookie shack, Sue took the 8 oz. sirloin steak with mashed potatoes and I ordered the 10 oz. BBQ strip steak with a side of beans/green chile. We both took the peaches for dessert. Everything was well prepared and the steaks were incredibly tasty and tender. Sue commented, "you can never find steaks like these in a grocery store."

After a great meal, we retired to the camper for coffee. We sat outside in the shade and watched people moving about. Some of the shooters, we met at the side shoots, stopped by to visit and we wondered how many of these would be on our posse on Saturday.

With darkness well set in, we changed into our swimsuits. Fortunately I did not own a Speedo, I had the standard boxer trunks. Sue got into her mini and asked, "is this too much as she modeled her suit?" I answered, "well it certainly does not have too much material. However, every woman there will likely have the same suit. The difference will be the body in the suit, and you rank pretty high. Just wear your swim top, to get to the pool, and stop worrying. You will be a knockout." "That swim top you mentioned is called a Tankini, and it matches my mini–skimpy and bright orange. *I thought, oh great, another thing to turn heads, but I suppose, if you got it you might as well flaunt it!*

The pool and deck were perfectly designed. The pavers were light beige, the walls and pillars were a teal/ blue background with many designs of fish and ocean artifacts. There was a bathroom, changing room, as well as a bar serving alcoholic beverages. The lounging chairs were in differing bright pastel colors and of course the pool bottom was a bright blue. All these features created a pleasing and uplifting ambiance.

We swam and bobbed for a long time. The pool life guard announced that everyone was entitled to two free drinks. We each had a pina colada, which was heavy with white rum, and light with pineapple juice/coconut cream. We did not need a second one.

By 11 pm we were ready to head to our camper. On route, Sue asked, "why is it that women in a two piece look so good, and men in their Speedo look so obscene with their well delineated bulge?" "Well, I agree, the more a woman shows her body, the more voluptuous they appear. Whereas a man's body is simply a device to hold his functional tool!" She gave me that look, the one I don't fare well with, and said, "boy that was a deep revelation."

On arriving, we found a note on our door. It said, "please come to the foreman's home directly across the street, tonight, it is very important."

Without changing, we went over, and the owners were on the porch. We introduced ourselves, and the gentleman introduced themselves as Jim and Eleanor Beecher–foreman and registrar. Mr. Beecher explained, "call me Jim, today a man and lady friend requested campsite #26–the second row but adjacent to the porta-potties. No one ever requests a site so close to the porta-potties."

"Eleanor alerted me and I immediately did a search using the name he used at registration. As public knowledge, he was registered as a sex offender, and was still on probation three years after a prison sentence. That information did not exclude him from participation in the ranch shoot, but it certainly meant he was worth watching since I am in charge of security." I then asked, "how does this affect us?"

Jim paused and said, "Eleanor and I were at the pool this evening. Every time Sue got up without you at her side, his eyes tracked her every move." I held my hand up, "say no more, I spotted the man. Tall athletic build, blond hair but a striking black moustache and thick black eye brows." Jim added, "right on, and good for you for being aware of your surroundings. I would like to ask you, Sue, please do not go anywhere by yourself." Sue finished by saying, "thank you for your warning and let's hope that nothing comes of this."

As we were leaving, Jim added, "campsite #1 next to the porta-potties is housing one of our cowboys as a precaution. If there develops a problem go to him for assistance."

After we got home, Sue asks, "why didn't you mention your suspicions?" "Because, I do not want you to live your life in constant wonder! You deserve the right to live in freedom, like everyone else. Besides, when we get on the road this summer, I plan to be at your side at all times. I do not want you to experience another home invasion event–ever again." She gave me a warm loving kiss and said no more on the subject.

Friday day 20. We were up by 5 AM and planned to arrive at the cookie shack with all our gear by 6 AM, when the kitchen opened. I was standing by the main street waiting for Sue when I saw something shocking. I said, "Sue, look, campsite # 26 is vacant. At the same time, a 6 foot full size Cowboy wearing his pistol, came out of his camper at site # 1, and walked up to us. He said, "Jim asked me to tell you what happened after you retired."

"At 2 AM that dude was still sitting outside his camper and suddenly ran towards the porta-potties. He grabbed a woman exiting a porta-pottie and was trying to overpower her. I was on him in a matter of seconds, popped him a good one on the nose and laid him flat on the ground. I then called Jim who called in Sheriff Cummings. He was arrested and hauled off to jail. We then helped his friend to close up camp, and she drove their Class C camper out of the ranch, before anyone else was aware of the situation, end of story."

We thanked the Cowboy for his alertness and a job well done, and headed to the cookie shack. We both had pancakes, bacon, real Vermont maple syrup and plenty of coffee. By 7 AM we were at the side shoots and no lines had formed, yet.

<u>SIDE SHOOT #7.</u> Aerial Targets–pistol stage. No scenario. The RO and assistant explained, "this

is considered the most difficult stage because no one is accustomed to flying targets, and I have never seen a perfect score of 10 hits. A large coffee can is ejected straight up about 7 yards. The idea is to shoot it as the can gets to the top, its apogee, before it starts coming down. If you shoot at it while it is still climbing, shoot ahead or on top of the can. If you shoot at the can coming down, shoot below it. Either way, keep your pistol moving and leading the can."

"There is no safety issue, if you shoot at the can at its apogee, the angle of the shot will not exceed 60 degrees. This puts your shot in a safe downrange location. Each shooter gets 8 cans in the air. The first six cans get a single shot. The last two cans get two shots each for a total of ten shots. We tape each bullet hole so there is no doubt on your hit. Each hit gives you one point–there is no other scoring. When ready, just yell, UP for each can."

The RO demonstrated and got 4 hits exclaiming, "it's too early in the morning for me." Sue went next and got 5 hits, all single shots. I then called for my first can and something strange happened–I hit all ten cans. The RO was frozen like a statue and Sue exploded, "Wil, how did you do this, you even got the two doubles?" I said, "I don't know how this is possible, but the cans were climbing in slow motion, and at their apogee, they seemed fixed in mid air. At the 7 yard apogee, they appeared an easy target for me."

The RO finally spoke. "You have to be a natural talent, like the famous exhibition shooter, Ed McGivern. In the late 30's using a double action revolver, he hit an aerial tin can six times before the can hit the ground, and from a height of +-20 feet. He did a similar feat at another exhibition with 6 clay birds simultaneously thrown in the air."

While walking to the next side shoot, Sue said, "It is certainly a privilege to walk next to a natural wonder, and me only a significant other." Before I could react, she took off like a bullet for the next stage–where she could mingle amongst other shooters.! When I got to the next stage, she was still laughing.

SIDE SHOOT #8. Pop Ups–pistol stage. The scenario was about shooting outlaws, not town people. The RO explained, "This stage requires quick thinking and target acquisition. You walk with your pistol drawn on this boardwalk which is on the left of these continuous store fronts. Every time you step on a pressure plate, a face pops up in a window or door on the right, some are friendly and some are bad guys. This is a timed stage, for every outlaw hit you get a bonus of 5 seconds but for every friendly hit(such as a nun) you get a 15 second penalty on your time. If you miss a pressure plate because you took a giant step, that also is a 15 second penalty."

Before the RO gave his demonstration, he added, "this is the kind of stage where you can easily find yourself walking with a cocked pistol. For example, if you hear the pressure plate activating the target, you can easily cock your pistol before the target pops up. If the target is a friendly, what do you do with a cocked gun? If you walk forward with a cocked gun you get a stage DQ. The answer is to discharge your gun into the ground or on the friendly target and take your 15 second penalty. Next time, don't cock your gun before you see the target!"

The RO demonstrated this stage. He got all 10 hits on outlaws. He did admit that his demonstration was not realistic because he was walking too slow and he knew where the friendly targets were. It was clear to us that, the shooter needed to walk faster than the RO, in order to get a decent score.

I went first this time. I activated all pressure plates, hit all outlaws, did not shoot any friendly targets and my score was 60 seconds. Sue's time was quicker but she only hit 9 of the 10 outlaws–she hit a friendly kid with a toy gun on her 10th shot. Her time was 69 seconds. She came off the boardwalk and gave me a "new look", the kind that I better not say a word. I heard her softly say, "SHEEEE-ET!" *It was a real quiet walk to the next side shoot.*

SIDE SHOOT #9. Falling targets–pistol and rifle stage. No scenario. The RO explained, "standing on either the pistol or rifle firing line, you shoot the small green starter plate until you hit it, hopefully one shot will do it or you will waste your ammo. That will activate the two frontal targets to start falling. The two targets will suddenly and randomly turn 180 degrees, and become impossible to hit. They will also randomly return to frontal targets as they continue to fall. You have to alternate between the two systems to get hits. The stage finishes when you run out of ammo, or the two targets turn sideways at the base of the mechanism, and stop falling."

"Once I reset the targets, you repeat this stage using your rifle, but standing on the further firing line. This is a timed stage. Scoring is based on total hits. The maximum is 20 points for 20 hits, that includes the green starter plate–ten on pistols and 10 on the rifle. Don't be too slow, since the targets will stop before you empty your guns."

The RO demonstrated a nice shooting speed. He finished both guns as the targets came to a sideways standstill. He got a total of 15 hits, a low time, and was satisfied with his score.

I went first, I wasted several shots just to hit that darn green starter plate, with both pistol and rifle. Yet, I ended up with 14 hits. Sue did a heck of a job on this stage, she was so fast that she was out of ammo as the targets reached 3/4 of their total traveling distance. She ended up with 19 hits and a record short shooting time–a definite contender for the stage award. On our walk to the last stage, I said, "You just demonstrated one of your training mantras. Put a goof behind you and concentrate on the present. Clearly a good example of this stage, compared to the last one."

SIDE SHOOT #10. The Texas Star–pistol and rifle. No scenario.

The RO explained, "this last stage is a good practice since it will be one of the stages at the main match–after-all, this star must have originated in Texas!" He went through a quick review of "his" best method, to attack and control the star's spin. "Shoot the plates of a clock in this order: bottom 6 o'clock plate first, 10–2 and pause, and last 8–4 plates. Perform this stage with the two pistols and then repeat with the rifle. This is a timed stage and only left over plates are scored as a 10 second penalty added to your time. With leftover rounds placed on the dumping target, each cycle finishes with the shooter's last shot. Note, listen to the RO's instructions, since the starting plate may vary."

The RO demonstrated. He got all plates down with rounds to spare–with a good time. He said, "This is the type of stage that gets better with practice, and I have had a lot of practice in the past years."

Sue completed the runs with a time of 32 seconds with pistols, and 27 seconds with the rifle. My times were 42 seconds with pistols and 37 seconds with the rifle. Not contender scores but personally satisfying ones, and certainly adequate as a primer for the main match.

We finished the side shoots by 9 AM. Next to the Texas Star was a demonstration of the new sport, Cowboy Fast Draw. There was a sign that said the next demonstration was at 11 AM. So we took our main match brochures and started reviewing all 10 stages.

The fantasy scenarios were all about situations that could affect a ranch–cattle rustlers, horse thieves, Indians attacking a ranch, changing cattle brands, poisoning water supplies, cattlemen's Credit Union robbers and so on. There were many props to deal with, and long lines to say before the buzzer went off. All in all, great creativity at work.

The shooting sequences were generally complicated. Many had complicated sweeps, twisted sequences to challenge our memory banks, and some sequences difficult to understand. Fortunately, Sue was able to explain all these sequences. By the time we finished reviewing each stage, I was glad to have spent the time. This was an excellent primer for the main match.

At 11 AM we came back to the fast draw demonstration. The RO explained, "Cowboy Fast Draw was a new division in Cowboy Shooting but not part of the parent sport, CAS. The pistol used is a 45 caliber and the ammo is a wax bullet pushed into a 45 long colt casing. The fodder is a shotgun primer fitted into the drilled out primer pocket. Gunpowder is not necessary, but some add a minuscule amount of black powder or pyrodex for smoke effect. A special holster is used that allows cocking the hammer while the pistol is still partially in the holster. At the sound of the buzzer you draw and fire at a 2 foot steel plate set at +7 yards."

The RO adds, "I am told that Marshall Dillon performed this draw in 0.8 seconds. History books also mention that two actors, Sammy Davis Jr. and Jerry Lewis could perform this draw and shoot much faster. Today, champions can perform this feat in 0.3–0.4 seconds."

The RO demonstrated this "draw and shoot," with the timer attached to his shirt pocket. On the buzzer, his time was 0.7 seconds. He then added, "I have had a lot of practice to be in this range. If you plan to join this sport, you had better have a lot of time on your hands. It takes months, and many wax bullets, to even come close to Marshall Dillon. The nice thing about this sport is that you can practice in your garage or cellar–with the proper facial protection and backstops.

Note: wear jeans and leather shoes, better still, steel toes."

When asked how the timer works, he answered, "the buzzer starts the clock and the sound of the shot stops the clock–which is why I had the timer on my shirt pocket. Today serious shooters buy the latest electronic equipment that replaces a timer. The electronic plate has a white light that comes on to start the draw, and the bullet impact on the plate stops the clock. Clubs that host this sport, generally use the new electronic equipment."

After the demonstration, we brought our gear to the camper and headed for the cookie shack for lunch.

For lunch Sue had the cattle drive casserole and I had the beef stew. For a side we both had the sweet biscuits and coffee. Another great meal well prepared by the cook. We lingered after lunch since our scheduled horse ride was not till 2 PM. We had extra coffee and spent time talking to the shooters, we had met at the side shoots.

At the horse corral, Sue was given a Palomino mare and I was handed the reins to a gentle Sorrel gelding. We were a total of eight riders with two guides. We started in single file with a guide in the front and the other guide in the rear.

The ride was through the ranch's private and open range. Cattle were everywhere, and the number of calves confirmed the well-being of the animals. These first cattle were Black Angus and crossbreeds, but the crossbred cows were clearly larger than the Angus. The scenery started as flat prairies, with more than adequate vegetation for early spring. Half way through our trip we arrived at the base of mountains.

We stopped for a 15 minute break, at an old line shack, which was supplied with liquid refreshments. The horses drank out of a nearby creek. It gave us the chance to use the old fashion outhouse, to get rid of all the extra coffee we had at lunch. It felt good to stretch our legs and bring our sore hips back to a natural position. *I guess the guides realized that we were all tenderfoots when it came to riding a horse.*

After our short rest, we followed a loop through the pine trees, then headed back to the ranch via another trail. The cattle breeds changed to a mixture of Herefords, Shorthorns, and mostly crossbreeds. As we got closer to the ranch, we came upon a small herd of Texas Longhorns and again plenty of crossbreeds. Sue commented, "Will, look at the crossbred calves, they are much larger and livelier."

We arrived at the ranch by 4 PM. A bit saddle sore but appreciative of the opportunity to ride and see the ranch. Jim Beecher was leaning on the corral as we exited the horse area. We struck up a conversation, and I asked, "We saw extensive evidence of cross breeding. Some of the pure-breeds would herd together but had many crossbreeds with them. Are the crossbreeds the result of the open range and why do certain breeds herd together?"

Jim answered, "there is a natural selection where certain breeds tend to herd together, we "think" that is because of the type of vegetation available during different seasons. However, we could be wrong and some other factor may be the cause. Some believe that animals can recognize their own kind!"

"The other is the more important issue that you picked out. The crossbred animal is the current answer to beef farming. A 1 year old crossbred steer will weigh 25% more at market time than a pure breed. That is because of two reasons. The first is breed complementarity– an offspring advantage of desirable characteristics from two or more breeds. The other reason is hybrid vigor, an improved growth rate that results in a higher yield in weight. Crossbreeding produces a better quality of meat as far as tenderness and flavor. Actually, the crossbred stock is what is served as beef products at the cookie shack during this shooting event."

We thanked the guides, and with the end of the day at hand, we headed to our camper for R & R, and prepare for the evening's activities.

Friday evening day 20. We both had a cold vodka/7up cocktail and then took our showers. We dressed casually, while still in Western clothes with our Cowboy hats and boots.

The cookie shack was very busy, everyone wanted dinner before the variety show started. We were seated and the waitress took our order. Sue ordered a ribeye steak, medium with mashed potatoes. I asked the waitress, "I am told that the brisket is the least tender of all beef cuts, so I wondered what to expect from the cook?" The waitress quickly added, "The cook prepares this cut by braising or slow roasting. I personally prefer the slow roasted method. I guarantee, it will be tender enough to cut with a fork, and the flavor will never be matched."

I took the slow roasted brisket, medium, with a baked potato. Our meals arrived. Sue's steak was so tender it was falling apart in her plate, she never used her steak knife. My brisket was also tender but a steak knife was needed. The flavor was a wonderful taste I had never experienced. We then had the bread pudding for dessert with coffee.

The variety show started at 8 PM with the band leader giving us an introduction to Old West music. He said, "the 1800's Western Music was about people who settled in the Old West. and it celebrated the life of the Cowboy on the open range. The songs added serious and comical lyrics, as well as calls and hollers. Tonight's presentation will include old style music and songs, instrumental solos, jokes, comic skits, and a tribute to two singing cowboys of our era."

The introduction finished with the band leader sneaking behind the curtain, as the curtain opened with a lively classic western song, The Yellow Rose of Texas, that got everyone's attention and set the mood of the evening. The band's instruments included: a standard guitar, banjo, mandolin, fiddle and string bass.

They started their show with a series of songs made famous by the Sons of the Pioneers. Such tunes as: Ghost Riders in the Sky, Tumbling Tumbleweeds, Whoopie Ti YI Yo, and Cool Water.

Jokes were rattled off between songs, which kept the mood festive. The band leader started addressing his members individually. He got the fiddle player to play, Orange Blossom Special and Cotton Eye Joe. When the band leader pushed the fiddle player to play something less country, the fiddle player walked away and came back with a shiny expensive violin and proceeded to play Tchaikovsky's, The Swan Lake. This virtuoso violinist got the applause he well earned.

A short comedy skit followed, about a clumsy Cowboy on a trail drive, that brought the house down. Next, the band played what sounded like a regular two-step to Sue and I. However, a couple appeared doing the Texas Two-step. Sue commented, "I prefer our country two-step."

The band leader then addressed the banjo player. "It is your turn, Tom, please give us a good Western tune." The banjo player starts a beautiful rendition of You are my Sunshine. The band leader was waving his index finger, in the negative, and added, "I mean a typical banjo hoe-down." Tom came back with, Foggy Mountain Breakdown, by Earl Scruggs.

Another joke and a classic song followed. Then the band leader mentioned that it was time to jump ahead in years, with some more modern tunes and songs. He addressed the mandolin player, Harvey, and asked him to give us a modern tune. He answered, "I can't do that with a mandolin but I can with this guitar"–as he exchanges the mandolin for a beautiful electrified acoustic guitar. Harvey asked the band leader, "how about some Chet Atkins?" Harvey did a medley of Chet's top 5 popular tunes, and then went right into number one, Mr. Sandman, with a rousing applause from the audience. His musical talent was evident when he did a Chet Atkins' rendition of Yakety Axe(same as Boots Randolph's Yakety Sax).

After two hours of continuous entertainment, the band leader announced, "I would like to close this evening with a tribute to two singing Cowboys of the 40's to the 60's. Gene and Roy. On cue, they played: Rudolph the Red Nose Reindeer, STOP STOP STOP. My mistake, it is not Christmas and we are on a horse/cattle ranch. The band restarted, Back in the Saddle Again, by Gene Autry.

In closing, "Good luck to you Cowboy Shooters tomorrow, and I plan to take first place in the Silver Senior division!' As the band played their closing song, Happy Trails to You, by Roy Rogers.

FYI Sue, "Roy Rodgers was an original singer in the Sons of the Pioneers, under his real name, Leonard Slye." "Wow, what a pit!"

Saturday day 21. At 8 AM the cannon blast announced the mandatory Shooter's Meeting and everyone gathered at the clubhouse. The Match Director, Bull Slinger, started, "Welcome to the Bar W's annual shooting extravaganza. Let's begin with the Pledge of Allegiance to the Flag.........! I have several subjects to cover"

1. "We will have 7 posses of 15 shooters each. All posses were selected randomly, so get to know your posse members. The only two exceptions to the random pick are: the disabled who may use a shooting or non shooting assistant, and the newbies who can shoot with their coaches."
2. "It will be a hot and sunny day. Don't get dehydrated. Drink plenty of water or Gatorade."
3. "We will have a shooting order, randomly established by your RO."
4. "Loading and unloading tables must be manned at all times."
5. "This is not a SASS sanctioned shoot, but for safety reasons, we will follow SASS rules. We have several powered and unconventional targets that have become our signature. We can do this because we are a private ranch and organization."
6. "You all get along, this is a pleasant sport and do not confront a posse member. Take problems to the RO."
7. "Lunch will be served between 11 AM–1 PM. Your posse will be notified when it is your turn."
8. "Each posse will be identified by color code and each color has a starting stage. If you do not know your posse or starting stage, your name

by alphabetical order is posted on the clubhouse outside bulletin board."

9. "Have a safe and pleasant day. We hope to see you tonight at the dinner/dance gala, and at the awards ceremony tomorrow at 10 AM."
10. "If there are no questions……. Let's go shooting."

Sue checked the board and said, "we are the purple posse and we start on Stage 5. That means we will finish on Stage 4." The RO welcomed everyone, shuffled the score cards and did a roll call. Sue ended up the 7th shooter and I was the 9th. Sue added, "I will be the last shooter whose brass you will pick up. That will give you plenty of time to get ready for the loading table." I added, "After shooting, I plan to relax before we move to the next stage, take the time to read the next shooting sequence, and load up my shotgun slide and loading block."

STAGE #5. Pistol Knockdowns. The scenario was about horse thieves on the run. The RO explained, "the rifle and shotgun targets were standard displays but the 10 pistols were all knockdowns." I loaded my ammo block with all hot rifle loads as we had planned. I did well with a clean shoot but a bit slow since I was aiming to get a high shot on the pistol knockdowns. Sue was much faster than me, but ended up with a knockdown that stayed up. We decided after this stage that we would not check our stage times, like gamers do. We would wait to see the master list tomorrow, and try to shoot as best we can while enjoying the day.

Early in the shooter's sequence, we got our first blooper. The shooter, by the name of Manor Queen, took off on the buzzer but tripped in her long dress. The RO caught her in time and said, "maybe you could pull up your skirt." She thought, "I have a better idea" as she tore off the bottom frill and added, "I hate dresses, I knew I should have worn pants!" The RO restarted her and she had a respectable shoot.

STAGE #6. The Lawrence Welk sweep. The scenario was about Indians attacking a wagon train. The RO explained, "there are 4 pistol and 4 rifle targets. You place one shot on target 1, then two on 2, then three on 3 and four on target 4. Just like Mr. Welk would say, 1 and ah 2 and ah 3 and ah 4. That makes ten shots in my book."

We both did well and we realized that this was a smooth and pleasant stage. The talk among the posse was that these two stages were the only uncomplicated ones in the match. The fun was about to begin.

As we watched the last of this stage's shooters, Sue mentioned that the last shooter had shot field grade hot shotgun loads on Stage 5 and would likely develop a flinch if he stayed with this ammo.

The last shooter, Trak-Man, was extremely fast with the pistol and rifle. When he got to the shotgun, he closed the double barrel without loading it. Before the RO could stop him, the gun went click. The flinch was so bad, that the barrel almost hit him in the knees. Laughter broke out, but Trak-Man simply loaded the shotgun and finished the stage.

STAGE #7. The Texas Star. The scenario was about an arcade shoot at the local fair. The RO explained, "The rifle and shotgun have standard targets but the pistols will be shot on the star. If you get the 5 plates off with rounds left over, then dump them on that small red target. This is a timed event, left over plates are 10 seconds added to your time, and a miss on the mini dump is a standard miss."

The gamers had already made their identities known on the first two stages. They were not happy with this star. It would slow them down, and they would likely have a tough time as they usually did with moving targets. To make it worse, dumping extra rounds on a mini target was another problem for speed shooters–who like large, fixed, and up close targets.

After all the practice we had gained at Dusty's range, we did well on this stage. I got into a good cadence with little rotation of the star. Sue was amazing. She shot the plates so fast that the star barely moved.

Right after my shoot, we had another blooper. The next shooter to head to the firing line was not responding to the RO's order of "next shooter." Finally the RO went up to Jo-Bag who was holding his rifle/shotgun, and asked him what the problem was. That old coot said to the RO, "Take my rifle and shotgun so I can bend down and unlock my intertwined spurs."

Sue added, "this is a jovial bunch of shooters and I suspect why we are getting so many bloopers." Someone added, "this is historically classic of this shoot, but as long as things stay safe, who cares."

STAGE #8. The four corners. The scenario was about an ambush by outlaws hiding behind rocks. The RO explained, "there are four targets set up to make a square. This is a test of memory for all three guns. The shooting sequence for the first pistol is top left, bottom right, bottom left, bottom right and top right. Or remember, TL/BR/BL/BR/ TR. Repeat the sequence on the next pistol. For the rifle, reverse the sequence, TR/BR/BL/BR/TL and repeat for a total of 10 shots. Then go back to the pistol sequence for 5 shotgun rounds."

"Scoring is based on misses and the wrong shooting order. For every missed target, you get a 5 second miss. If you mess up the order you will get a 10 second procedural. However, you can only get one procedural for the entire stage. So if you mess up the order, work on not getting any misses and try to maintain some similarity in the expected shooting sequence."

The stage started, both Sue and I were running the sequence repeatedly in our heads. Finally, I got it. Both of us did well with a few misses but we got the sequence right–for all three guns.

The early shooters did not fare well. The second shooter by the name of Jay-Dee who thinks he will always be 49, stepped up to the firing line with a swagger of confidence. At the buzzer, we all saw a typical "fruit salad." He attempted to salvage the stage, but to no avail. He was all over the place, even from one gun to the other. Old Jay-Dee walked to the unloading table grumbling over and over, "what a mess."

STAGE #9. The Windmills and Falling Plates. The scenario was about shooting prairie dogs that were a hazard to animals on the range. The RO explained, "the pistol target is the windmill, and the rifle target is the falling plates." He went over the instructions which we already knew. "The shooting sequence finishes with two standard shotgun targets."

A posse member asked, "why is it that the shotgun targets are always last in the shooting sequences?" The RO answered, "the timer will detect the shotgun blast much better than the rifle or pistol. This guarantees a uniform pickup of the shooter's last shot, which transfers to correct shooting times."

The RO walked the posse to check out the 10 falling plates. Each plate was larger than the next plate, making it impossible to hit the second plate, till the first one fell. The real shock was that the next to last plate was the size of a tea cup, and the last plate was in the shape and size of a chicken egg–even painted eggshell color. This egg size target could be a game changer, for those trying to get a Clean Shoot.

As we were getting ready, I said to Sue, "I have been thinking of a better way to attack these windmills. Hold your gun at the space between each windmill. Keep an eye on both windows. When the red paddles appear, move to that window and shoot. Come back to the space and wait for the next red paddle, which can come from either side. By the time your eyes pick up some red, you can get there from the space, as the red paddle comes into the window's full view."

"A timed event with a bonus of 5 seconds on pistol hits, and 10 seconds penalty on rifle plates left standing after 10 shots.

Our results became routine for Sue and I. She was a quicker shooter with more misses, and I was a slower shooter but with more accuracy. The final scoring will determine who was ahead. I kept thinking of the old adage to CAS, "the average shooter can't shoot fast enough to make up time from a miss." The gamers were certainly fast enough to overtake a miss, I was wondering if Sue was approaching this group?

One shooter, Lady Stitcher, got quite rattled from the windmills and that egg shot. Coming off the firing line, adding a few expletives to that egg, she went directly to her cart instead of the unloading table, and lit a cigar!

Fortunately, the unloading table officer came over and escorted her back to his table.

Another shooter, an irritated super gamer, could not thank me for picking up his brass as most shooters do. Instead, he harrumphed and shooed me away with a waving hand. *I thought, people like that should take up underwater basket weaving–meaningless and without human contact.* When Sue spotted his behavior and saw me walk away with a smile, she added, "this is the kind of day I live for, thank you match organizers for making my day with a level playing field."

STAGE #10. Plates on a fence. The scenario was about a young ranch hand, drawing and shooting at beer bottles. The RO explained, "there are two racks of 5 falling plates for the pistol and rifle–at differing distances. There are four knockdown shotgun targets. Each plate and knockdown can be shot at, only once. Each standing target is a miss. The plates are all of varying sizes, and some are real small. If a plate falls on its own, you get a freebie, but you must shoot that round in the vicinity of that free plate. PS, those small plates need careful aiming." The last RO's warning was that the shotgun knockdowns would not go down easily. He added, "so hit them hard in the center with as many pellets as possible."

Fortunately, the smallest of targets were the ones that fell prematurely, generating the most pleasure for the lucky ones. We were ready for the hard shotgun knockdowns. We had a box of hot field grade 12 gauge shells, as proper fodder for these stubborn knockdowns. We knew that these hot shells were legal, since most shooters did not bother to load lighter shotgun loads, and only used these box-store shells.

The results were the usual. I was slow and accurate, Sue was much faster but with two misses on the very small targets. All the shotgun targets went down with a vengeance, but our shoulders took a heck of a beating, with those shells–we would continue loading our own shells.

Our posse was then called to lunch. We agreed on a half hour break, meaning we could finish the match early. We both took the burgers with steak fries and coffee. We got back to Stage 1 for our last four stages, and Miss Productive was the last to arrive. I happen to notice that she had an empty holster. I pointed it out to her and she said, "well I went to lunch with two pistols." So I added, "well it must have fallen in the cookie shack." With a look of panic she added, "or the porta-potty #3 I used after lunch." As she took off on a run, Sue added. "I hope it is on the floor of the porta-potty and not in the!@#$%^&*"

<u>STAGE #1.</u> Shooting through Bars. The scenario was about the Sheriff shooting through window bars, and outlaws trying to break out their friend. The RO explained, "there are two targets on a center spindle. One

set is for pistols and the other is for the rifle. No shotgun targets. Each white target has black jail bars painted on. If you hit dead center between the bars, the target will not move. If you hit to the right or left of center, the target will swing in the direction you hit, and take time to come back to its frontal view. This is a stage where speed related poor accuracy, can ruin your score because of a target that is slow to return. This is a timed stage where misses are scored at 5 seconds. The stage starts with pistols and finishes on the rifle's 10th shot.

This is a stage that Sue quickly mastered. She slowed down and was so accurate that the target barely moved. My score was not much to talk about, I did a lot of waiting for the target to come back to frontal view. There were no bloopers on this stage.

STAGE #2. Paste Boards(an Old West name for playing cards). The scenario was about a gunfight between ranch hands and card cheaters. The RO explained, "You are sitting at a card table and flip up a card, say 3 of clubs, and you look up and shoot at the target labeled 3 of clubs. But you must yell out the 3 of clubs so the spotters know what you are shooting at. There are ten targets with varying numbers for clubs and hearts, meaning red or black, and the cards match the targets. This is a timed stage with misses at 5 seconds. The side four shotgun targets are not numbered and they are either a red or black target for the corresponding card color.

The first two shooters did well. The third shooter was Karut-Hed. She started off seemingly well but after 4 shots, suddenly the RO yells, STOP. He leans over and says to Karut-Hed, "you can see the clubs and hearts ok, but you are shooting at the wrong number every time. Let's put on your half reading glasses so you can read the numbers, and you will be able to shoot over the lenses, to hit the targets downrange." The RO turns around and orders a reshoot.

Our scores were wildly different, since everyone spent too much time finding a 7 of hearts on a large board, where all the targets were randomly situated. Quick target acquisition made all the difference. Since we were not shooting against 30 year old shooters, the stage was well matched to age related groups. Our comparative scores would appear tomorrow.

<u>STAGE #3.</u> Riding Shotgun. This scenario was about a woman riding shotgun on a stagecoach. The RO explained, "This is a shotgun stage. The shooter gets on the stagecoach and shoots as many rounds he or she can carry on the body. You are shooting at six randomly placed knockdown targets–all knockdowns must go down. This is a timed stage where all targets left standing are a miss." Someone says, "seems too easy, what's the catch?" The RO pushes a button and the stagecoach starts to bob up and down and sway left to right.

I said to Sue, "we were told that the stages would not stay simple. Sue adds, "boy, this stage looks like fun." Everything was going well till we got to Ran-Dee. This was an older lady in the 65 plus category. She only had a shotgun slide that held 4 shells and her dress had no pockets. Sue and I saw her fill her bra with handfuls of shotgun shells, as she winked at us on route to the loading table.

When Ran-Dee got up on the stagecoach, the RO said she did not have enough shells for this stage. "Not to worry" she said, "Start the buzzer and press the power button." The RO did not argue. Shells suddenly went flying all over the place because of the stagecoach gyrations. The RO was ducking and Ran-Dee was digging deeper and deeper, pulling out more than shotgun shells. The RO covered his eyes and everyone was whistling, screaming and clapping. Finally all targets were down. The RO said, "If you are done shooting, you might consider putting things back in their proper place." Ran-Dee looked down and said, "OH MY." The RO added, "thank goodness this is over with, next time, sew some pockets on your dress." The RO finally broke down while trying to give her score to the scorekeeper.

On route to Stage 4, the last stage of the day, a ruckus was brewing at Stage 5 next to us. Suddenly a woman screamed and yelled, HELP. I ran over and pulled the lady aside. The man on the ground had an extremely fast pulse that stopped suddenly as I was trying to count the heart rate. I immediately started cardiac massage and yelled for someone to get a defibrillator, emergency medical bag and the EMT's. A lady nurse quickly arrived with the bag, oxygen, defibrillator and said "the EMT's are 5 minutes away–delayed because of a fire."

That is when I said, 5 minutes will be too late. I told the RN, "apply the defibrillator, Sue take over cardiac massage." I opened the emergency bag and grabbed a syringe with 150 mg of Lidocaine and injected it into his elbow vein. Suddenly the defibrillator said, "Ventricular Fibrillation, stand back for a shock," the man's body had an immediate contracting muscular response. The defibrillator said, "ventricular tachycardia." I immediately gave the patient a strong punch to the sternum(a precordial thump), the machine responded with a regular rhythm, but it quickly deteriorated to fibrillation and a 2nd shock followed.

The machine then said, "Asystole start epinephrine drip." I then took over, "Restart cardiac massage," and I saw Sue and Ranger Rooster alternating, and relieving each other. I took the cardiac syringe with a 6 inch needle, and plunged it into his chest, aspirated bright red blood from the heart, and injected the entire syringe content of epinephrine. I restarted cardiac massage and after a while, suddenly a man caught my wrist and said, "that hurts, please stop."

I immediately propped the man up, put portable oxygen on him, sprayed nitro under his tongue, and gave him an aspirin to chew and swallow with water–followed by a whole aspirin, and he laid back down.

The EMT's arrived and I gave them my name and a quick synopsis. The head EMT said, "what do you need Doc?"" I said, "start a lidocaine infusion and put the leads on to run a full EKG. The tracing quickly came out, and there it was, a massive anterior myocardial infarction. Meanwhile, one EMT had started an infusion of more lidocaine to prevent another run of fibrillation. I said out loud, "start the CLOT BUSTERS, NOW. Without hesitation, the head EMT was hanging up the magic medicine of the century. The EMT said, "that was an order, right, Doc." The EMT said, "I am not calling the medical center for permission–and waste precious time. I am taking your order."

The EMT's were making preparation for a 1+ hour transfer to the nearest medical center. Suddenly, I yelled, LOOK. "The EKG is changing, he is reperfusing his left anterior coronary artery." The EMT said, "Nice job, Doc." I asked the patient how he felt and he answered, "other than sore ribs, that squeezing chest pain is gone."

Shortly thereafter, after more IV infusions of standard meds, the patient was loaded onto the ambulance. Before the EMT's departed, the head EMT came over and said, "well Doc, you saved that man's life, nice work"– unfortunately in ear shot of all present. Finally, with a black car following, the vehicles headed out of the ranch.

That is when the RO came over and asked if I knew who the patient was. I said no. "Well that was Amos Whitehouse, the lady you pulled off the man was his wife, owners of this ranch."

With the commotion over with, the Match Director, Bull Slinger, called a 15 minute break. Apparently, there were several shooters who turned green seeing a precordial thump, and many more ended up on hands and knees when that cardiac needle was whipped out and plunged.

The RO offered me the last position to shoot and I accepted since I was still full of adrenaline and a bit shaky.

STAGE #4. In the Saddle. The scenario was about a Cowboy on horse-back shooting at would be cattle thieves. The RO explained, "this stage has all standard SASS targets, 10 pistols, 10 rifles but no shotguns. The catch is this:" he presses a button and the horse starts rocking back and forth. "Standard scoring, misses are 5 seconds. The pistols are staged in the saddle pommel holsters and the rifle is in the saddle scabbard."

Sue and I watched several shooters when Sue pointed out, "when the horse rocks backwards, it is quick and snappy. When the horse rocks forward, it does so a bit slower and there is a momentary hesitation as the horse is in full forward position, before it snaps backwards. We need to fire during that momentary hesitation."

That was a difficult stage to shoot. The mechanical horse caused many misses for everyone, including us. Yet, it was the last stage and we were glad to head back to camp.

At camp we had a glass of wine and sat in long silence. Sue finally asked, "are you OK, Wil?" I looked at her and said, "you know that a physician maintaining an office practice does not get much exposure to catastrophic cardiac arrests. Fortunately, every year I took the refresher course in Advanced Cardiac Resuscitation for physicians. For the first time in my life, it certainly paid off. Now in retirement, I hope that never happens again. But yes, I am OK."

Saturday evening day 21. This evening was an upscale gala event with fancy western outfits. I was told that this evening was like a black tie tuxedo event, of the rich, at a charity ball. So I wore my best outfit. Charcoal grey gabardine pants with a wool black stripe on the pant legs. Pockets and cuffs of Western design. White silk shirt with knitted edges and cuffs, a comfortable non banded collar, and an 1800's style black bow-tie. For my dinner jacket, I had a choice of two–both made of a fine twill mixture of polyester and cotton. One was a black Western tuxedo coat, and the other was a dark blue Western floral embroidered jacket. Both jackets had the classic cuts on the lapel, pockets, coat tail and other areas.

I displayed both jackets to Sue and she said, "tonight wear the black tuxedo coat and keep the embroidered one for a less formal event." The outfit was enhanced with well polished dress Cowboy boots and a black bowler Cowboy hat–with a round dome and a well shaped crown.

Sue had all her evening gowns displayed on the bed. She asked, "which one should I wear tonight?" I answered, "need to see them on you to be certain." So she started modeling. The first four had their own niche, but not for this evening. The fifth one was a black strapless long dress, form fitting with attached braw. The bottom of the dress had an embroidered flare. Matched with her diamond earrings, a well place hairdo, some moderate cleavage, she did look like a super model. I said, "the choice is clear, Princess Lady Slipper."

While she was putting the finishing touches to her makeup, I said, "I find it hard to believe that your ex gave you those expensive earrings." She looked surprised and said, "I think I misled you when I said these earrings came from my ex. After the divorce, I took all the jewelry that I had received from him, to an estate jeweler, sold them, and placed the money in a special savings account. Years later after my depression, my physician said that it was time for me to develop my own identity, even if it still had traces of my married life. So I went shopping and used all the funds from my jewelry account, and bought the most expensive and brightest diamond earrings that the special savings account could buy. And here they are."

I added, "that is the most wonderful story, now when I see those diamonds, I will know that it represents a new person–my companion and lover. She did not miss a step, "so now we have gone from companion, to significant other and now to lovers, heh?" This time, instead of yanking on her new dress and wrinkling it, I thought, *I wonder if she is anticipating the next step of our relationship?*

On arrival at the meeting hall, we were greeted by Jim and Eleanor Beecher and Bull Slinger. Normally, such honor was reserved for the Whitehouses. I could not wait any longer and I asked Jim if he had heard any news about Mr. Whitehouse. "Yes, and it is all good news, I will announce it tonight. Please do not mention this to anyone."

I knew that Eleanor was having a chat with Sue. *Little did I know, she was telling Sue that we had a record setter in the side shoots, as she rolled her eyes toward me.*

As we walked in we saw 30 round tables seating 10 people each–for a total occupancy of 300 guests. The usher asked us our posse color, as we noticed that there were 7 different table colors, plus several white ones. We had 3 tables to cover our purple posse and a total of 21 tables covered all the posses. The usher explained, "the nine white tables are for shooters from the side shoots, most came with guests for dinner and some also came with guests for the dance."

The menu included one of two choices, tenderloin beef steak or prime rib, both with all the fixings. There was an interesting comment on the menu. There is no well done beef served at this ranch. Your choice is medium rare or medium. I looked at Sue and said, "the prime rib is more uniform since it is oven roasted to a certain meat temperature monitored by a thermometer. The steaks can be rushed, especially when the early cooked supply runs out, so a rare steak would ruin our dinner." Sue said, "not a problem since I prefer prime rib."

With everyone seated, the master of ceremonies announced that each table was numbered and would be randomly called to the banquet table. We were table #7 and we were the fourth table called up. The first round was for assorted cheeses with either beef soup or salad. The second round, using the same numbered sequence, was for the main meal. It was hard to fathom how they could come out with different meats all properly cooked. Sue and I had the medium prime rib with a baked potato and several hot vegetables.

The last round called was for desserts. They had an array of all the desserts the cookie shack had offered in the past three days. Coffee and assorted teas were self serve.

The dinner came to a closing, and guests were asked to move to the outside boardwalk, so tables could be rearranged. Apparently not all dinner guests stayed for the dance. This allowed for some tables to be removed, thereby creating a dance floor.

Upon returning to the hall, we sat with the same guests we had dinner with. Talk around the table continued, and too many questions were regarding the kind of practice I had and why I retired early. Sue was very good at changing and redirecting the subject matter. Finally we were saved by the microphone coming alive.

Jim Beecher's voice came to the microphone and he said, "before the dancing begins, I have good news. Mrs. Whitehouse called before dinner and said that Mr. Whitehouse, on arrival at the medical center, had received an emergency coronary angiogram, followed by a coronary angioplasty and stent. The procedure was without complications and he was stable in the ICU." The applause started but Jim Beecher raised his hands and added, "many thanks to all who assisted in his emergency care, and we all know who I am talking about."

The applause restarted and seemed to have no end. Sue leaned over and said, "the applause will not stop until you get up and acknowledge them–in Texas any job well done deserves respect." I got up, counted to 10 quickly and sat down. Thankfully, with the applause waning out.

The band, The Texas Wanderers, started with a classic song, Texas when I Die, by Tanya Tucker. No one got up to dance since the local people knew that they always started with that tune. Then the band leader said that they would play, two-steps, country waltzes, line dances and slow dances. They would play as many songs as possible about Texas. I said, "that might be interesting."

They then started and called up line dancers, the leader started the group with the count, 5-6-7-8. The first two songs were: God Blessed Texas by Little Texas, and, If you're going to play in Texas, you've got to have a Fiddle in the Band by Alabama. The dance floor was packed with all women dancers–par for the course.

Sue sat down after the line dances, and said, "as soon as they play a two-step or waltz, the men will get up. Just like at the Country Roadhouse. The first two-step was a medium tempo, what Sue called a starter for men. The band played, All my X's Live in Texas, by George Strait. No one was getting up to dance. Suddenly, Sue grabs my hand and drags me to the dance floor. We started two-stepping and Sue said, "men are like cows, once the lead cows goes through the gate, the herd follows." Before we got half way down the hall, couples were getting up and by the time we got to the end of the hall, the dance floor was full. After two more two-steps, Love's got a Hold on You, by Alan Jackson, and Mama Knows the Highway, by Hal Ketchum, the men were glad to sit down. Several line dances followed, of which Sue did half of them. Finally they announced the first country waltz, West Texas Waltz, by Joni Harms. We got up and I said, "I suppose we are going to be the lead cow again!" We started waltzing and quickly got into the elegant moves of skating, reversing, simple turns and feeling like we were floating over the floor. Suddenly, I said, "the herd is balking and is not following the leader, what do we do? She calmly added, "They will get up" and she was right. They got up and stood at the dance floor sidelines, gawking at us grandstanding. I gave up my resistance, continued to dance, and added all our turns. We eventually came to a stop in front of the band who followed our lead and phased out of the song. People applauded till we got back to our table. I looked at Sue and said, "so much for your follow the leader philosophy." Sue just started laughing, touched my hand and said, "despite all the showing off, you certainly guided that waltz like a pro."

The highlight of the evening was when the band played, Baby Likes to Rock It, by The Tractors. I said, "unless I am wrong, the men have had enough alcohol to really loosen up. This is a lively tune and we should see some wild dancing." We started dancing, and finally we were the ones on the sidelines, watching these basic two-step dancers provide some spontaneous twists and turns. We did not miss a chance to give some payback to several dancers–who definitely needed it.

During the course of the evening, we got to know the people at our table to include their partners. They were all pleasant people to talk to and be with. We both hoped we would get to see them again in the year to come in our travels, but would certainly be back here next year.

True to their word, the band played more Texas songs to include: Waltz across Texas, by E. Tubb and Stars over Texas, by T. Lawrence.

At nearly 1 AM they announced the last dance. A closing medley starting with Crazy by Patsy Cline, followed with Neon Blue by the Mavericks and finally, Goodnight Sweetheart by David Kersh. Sue seemed to be asleep in my arms but still following my steps. At the end of the dance we kissed–and it did not matter who was watching. We got to the camper and went straight to bed. I heard Sue say, "thank goodness that the award's ceremony doesn't start till 10 AM. We were both exhausted from a busy day shooting, dining, dancing and of course the nerve racking cardiac resuscitation.

Sunday day 22. We were up by 8 AM and were at the meeting hall at 9 AM for the buffet breakfast. I was just finishing my meal when I felt a hand on my shoulder. I recognized her immediately, I stood up and she gives me a hug and says, "I am Emma Whitehouse and thank you for bringing my husband back to me. Could you join me, and my son Charles for a few minutes?" "Certainly." She touched Sue's shoulder and asked her to join us.

We stepped to the side and Mrs. Whitehouse asked what my fee was for services rendered. I could see her son had his checkbook in hand. I said, "a retired doctor does not charge for services, besides there is no physician that could ethically charge for a Good Samaritan act. Let it be that your hug was payment in full."

She then stated that although she watched the entire resuscitation, she was not certain who had assisted me. I said Sue, Ranger Rooster and the RN who arrived with the defibrillator, med pack and oxygen. She then said that the RN was of no concern. Charles spoke up and said that the RN was his wife, Tess. "My wonderful daughter-in-law will be thanked appropriately."

She then said, "out of the 100 shooters present, 4 people did all the work. I came back, "well after my precordial thump, I had lost at least a dozen potential helpers. Then after whipping out the cardiac needle and plunging it, it appears that I had lost everyone within eye sight, to their hands and knees. Charles added, "and I was one of them losing my lunch in the bushes. She added, "I must admit that the needle is firmly implanted on my retina, and every time that I think about it, I get goose bumps. The doctors reviewed Tess's flow sheet of the resuscitation and they all agreed that you did a magnificent job, and they all claimed that the definitive procedure of the cardiac injection was the saving act."

The lady kept going back to paying for my services. She asked which club I belonged to. I answered, "the Desperados" and the match director/president was Ranger Rooster." As I pointed to him, "you mean the man who did cardiac massage?" "Yes."

After more haggling, Sue had a solution, "When we register at the next year's shoot, give us a 25% discount as full payment." The lady smiled, hugged us both and said, "Thank You," and walked away.

As the award's ceremony started, the master statistics sheet was handed out. We did not have time to review it in detail but quickly ascertained that Sue had placed 23rd and I had placed 35th out of 104 shooters. The 105th shooter, Amos Whitehouse, was not in the count.

The first award was the "Clean Shoot" certificate. Bull Slinger said, "I cannot believe that anyone could get through all of those mechanized stages, and the egg at Stage 9, without a miss, but two did. Two shooters got up to get their "Iron Man Award" and were then herded to the photo stage with the Bar W logo behind them.

The next awards were the stage winners. They awarded 1st and 2nd place certificates for all 10 stages. They started with Stage 1 and worked their way up. At Stage 5, Sue had hit 9 out of 10 targets but with a low time. She won first place and smiled all the way to the podium.

The next stage in contention for us was Stage 7 where I had hit all 10 aerial shots. Bull Slinger said, "this was the most popular stage with the lowest number of hits. However, we do have one shooter who hit all 10 cans.

This is a newbie and I suspect he is a natural talent, Doc Derby. I got up to get my certificate and the applause was loud and clear. After the photo shoot, I sat down, and Sue just squeezed my hand with pride.

Moving on to Stage 9, the falling targets. Sue had shot 18 falling targets and both starter plates. Along with a slow time, Sue got 2nd place. This was a windfall for Sue, and was proud to get her award.

The scores for the main match were then reviewed, and the number of awards per each category was determined by the number of shooters in each category. For the next hour, every category was visited. The next to last category was the silver senior category. The band leader from Friday did win first place.

The last category was the Senior division. Bill Slinger said, "this category encompassed 25% of the match shooters and many of the best shooters at the match. There were 16 men and 6 ladies in Senior. To our surprise, Sue got 2nd place in ladies, and I got 5th place in mens. We both got a certificate. I had my second photo shoot and Sue had her third trip to the camera. *I thought, what a day to remember.*

With the event coming to a close, we said our goodbyes. Walking out of the hall, Ranger Rooster came up to us and said, "may I walk with you? Mrs. Whitehouse looked me up and thanked me for doing CPR on her husband. She inquired about our club and one thing led to another.

She asked what our expected cost for our last 7 permanent facades and I told her $2 K."

"She looked at her son and they agreed on something. She then hands me a check for $7 K and says, "Build your facades, include a connecting boardwalk and get carpenters to do the job. Let you club members enjoy themselves without working on their time off. I only ask that one of your new facades be about a medical clinic with the doctor's name, Doc Derby. The other thing, she hands me this envelope and asks me to tell you," "since you won't charge me for services rendered, well, I refuse to charge you your registration fee!" Ranger Rooster adds, "What do I do with this check?" I answered, "take the money and build the facades. There is no way you can refuse her generosity."

On the way to the camper, Sue opens the envelope and says. "I thought our registration fees came up to $295. What are you going to do with this refund?" She hands me the check and I see the amount of $5K. Sue adds, "I guess you cannot refuse her generosity, heh!"

With the end of the festivities, everyone was hooking up their campers. We did the same. Before leaving, we went to say goodbye and express our thanks to the Beechers. We exchanged phone numbers and e-mails. We told them of our traveling plans, and the fact that we would be going by their local town in the near future, on route to New Mexico. Jim added, "it's likely that Amos

Whitehouse would be home by then and may want to meet you. We will be in touch."

With the end of a great holiday, we headed home to prepare for our next adventure–on the road.

CHAPTER 10

On The Road–Preparations

Sunday evening day 22. On our way home, we talked about all the different events, the location, the ambience and the many shooters we met. We finally stopped rejoicing about our holiday, and had a period of silent reflection. I then said, "Sue, this is a kind of life that is uplifting and worth pursuing." I gave her time to think and then said, "Let's go home and get ready to go on the road for the summer."

I could tell Sue was boiling over with delight. She added, "I am in complete agreement. It is time for us to do this. Before we take off for the summer, we have two commitments: The condo association annual meeting, and the family meeting we promised."

"Done," I said. "Since you are driving, and with your input, let's make a list of what needs to be done before we get on the road, in order of priority"

1. Set up an MRI and physician visit.

2. Change Sue's mailing address to #24.
3. Arrange for home security at #24 and #97.
4. Attend condo meeting.
5. Set up a family meeting.
6. Set up two durable powers of attorney.
7. Prepay all bills with an estimated credit for 4 months.
8. Prepare a financial and communication file.
9. Arrange for a 4 month supply of meds.
10. Schedule a vacation date for TV and Internet.
11. Add Sue's digital camera with extra lenses. Numbers 12–16 are to be done within 24 hours of departure
12. Close refrigerator and water.
13. Set humidistat and security system.
14. Notify credit card of traveling schedule.
15. Disconnect Sue's car battery.
16. Pick up groceries and miscellaneous items.

I then added two items to the list, which I would explain to Sue at a later time. A joint checking account and a codicil to my will.

We did the +-425 mile trip in 9 hours, allowing time for fueling, rest areas, and meals. At home we parked the camper in the driveway, connected it to power and brought perishable food items into the house. After a shower, we went to bed, tired from the road trip.

Monday day 23. We had the first 4 days set. Today we started eliminating the preference items on the list. Tuesday morning gave us more time to work on the list and supervise the security system installations. In the late afternoon and evening, was the association meeting and dance. Wednesday was my doctor's meeting in the AM, and the family meeting in the afternoon and evening. Thursday was the last day to work off the preparation list. Friday would be our first day on the road, if everything went according to schedule, or it would end up a catch up day.

On this first day, we took different jobs and actually went different ways. I immediately went to the bank and set up a joint checking account with Sue. I started the account with 50K, and set up an auto refill, every time the account dropped 5K. The new checks would be ready tomorrow. Sue would pick up the checks. She would need a photo driver's licence, social security card and the application signed by me. She would have a photo taken and her signature registered.

Then I went to see my paralegal and wrote a codicil to my will. Upon my death, Sue would inherit my truck, camper and the balance of the joint checking account. All identified by proper numbers, I signed the document and my paralegal notarized it. I then went to the Probate Court and registered it. I left with a copy for Sue.

We met for lunch and then took on new tasks. Some of these tasks were not easy to get scheduled within the next 48 hours. However, when we added that we would be out of the state for the next 4 months, things got done. Tuesday morning both security systems, approved by the association, were installed. Then came the association meeting.

Tuesday day 24. The "Easy Living Condo Association" has an annual gala event to include a business meeting, dinner and dance. I wore my light grey pants with the blue embroidered Western sport coat. Sue came out of the bedroom wearing a full length green Western gown, her diamond earrings, and a necklace with a diamond pendant. I asked, "where does this beautiful diamond pendant come from?" She said, "this belonged to my mother, how do I look?' "Gorgeous, simply ravishing!"

We met Jack at the clubhouse and I saw Jack staring at Sue. He whispered to me, "lucky fella, she certainly cleaned up nicely didn't she." Sue asked what he said and I told her. She reacted by smiling. With no one in ear shot, I said, "how come you never dated Jack?" She answered, "we became good friends as he helped me out of my depression and got me started in CAS. Yet things never progressed beyond friendship. That is the way relationships can develop or fail to develop. I asked, "what about us?" She squeezed my hand and said, "isn't it obvious."

I introduced Sue to my two neighbors, and she did the same with her's. After small talk, the president of the association invited everyone to take a seat. He explained how the tables would be called to the banquet table in three stages–salad, main meal and dessert.

After dinner, the annual meeting was held. The association president quickly went over formalities, and said we had six major issues to discuss:

1. "Our roofs are now 15 years old. A roofing company will check your roof, make repairs, and spray it with a roof coating to extend the life of your roof. Starting this summer, we will start a three year program of replacing the oldest and more damaged roofs."
2. "We will start recycling next month. You will all get a separate dumpster for recycling. You can mix all recyclables in this dumpster. No glass or styrofoam. The recyclables will defray an association fee increase for the next 2 years."
3. "This year we will paint 50 of our 200 condos. Each 10 unit section will have the same color, and will match the existing colors."
4. "A reminder, this is an over 55 association. If you plan to rent your condo, the association has to

approve the proposed renters before you sign a lease or agreement."

5. "The next election of association officers is 1 year away. We have a vacancy for this next year. A volunteer is needed. This is an excellent way to serve, and find out if you wish to run for the 5 year position, come election time."
6. "The most important issue, saved for last, is security. We have had three home invasions in the past year. Times have changed, and it's time for homeowners to add a home security system, that is tied in with the police department."

He explained how the system works, and which company they have an agreement with. "After a $150 installation fee, the monthly maintenance fee would be $39 per month–guaranteed for the next 2 years. If interested, pick up a brochure for more info and contact numbers."

As the meeting came to an end, the Wilson's at unit #96, adjacent to Sue's condo, approached us. Mrs. Wilson said, "I don't mean to be out of line, Sue, but you haven't been in your condo for several weeks. Would you consider renting it to my parents? Sue came back with, "I have met your parents and they seem quite capable of maintaining the family homestead." "Yes, but they are now in their early 80's, and they wish to be closer to me and live in a smaller apartment. Their large 4 bedroom house on 3 acres has gotten to be a burden."

Sue looked at me and I nodded, "Yes." Sue then addressed Mr. Wilson. "I know you own two rental units in our condo complex, what is your monthly fee and what do you include for services?" He answered, "I rent to elderly couples who do not like to pay bills. So I charge $1700 per month and include: water, sewage, electricity, heat and association dues. With the new security system, you could easily ask for $1750. That would only leave, TV, internet and phone bills, for your tenants to pay. At this rate, my end of year totals show a profit of $1K per month, plus the tax advantage of having rental property."

Sue again looked at me and I again nodded, "Yes." "OK, why don't you come over to #24 in the morning. Bring me a copy of the lease agreement you presently use, and a copy of the association's application for renting."

Shortly thereafter, the tables were cleared and the band came alive. We danced the usual two-steps and waltzes, but the crowd was a bit older and so more slow dances were performed. We were so preoccupied with our traveling preparations, that we danced less than usual.

We had long visits with our neighbors, and explained that we would be gone this summer, visiting the American West. I asked them to report any problems to Jack, who they all knew, and we exchanged phone numbers and e-mails.

After getting home, I brought up the issue of renting Sue's condo. "What happens if our relationship breaks up–you are going to be without a home". She answered, "I am sure of myself, I know what I want, I know how I feel and I have no doubts."

I put my hand up and said, "I am more sure about our relationship, than anything else that has happened to me in the past 10 years. I am falling in love with you, and I don't want to live without you." Sue came into my arms, started crying, and I heard her mumble, "every minute of every day is a joy being with you and I have already fallen in love with you."

After our emotions cleared, I said, "Sue, we need to agree on these issues:

1. "If our relationship falls apart, I will buy you a replacement condo."
2. "Your rent profit of 1K/month is to be placed in your bank."
3. "I will start a joint checking account of 50K to cover all our expenses. When the balance drops 5K, it will auto replenish from my account."
4. "I will add a codicil to my will. If I pass away and we are still living together, you will inherit the truck, camper and the balance of the checking account. This will cover #1 of this agreement."

Sue was somewhat surprised and was about to object. I stopped her and added, "our relationship is not based on money. It is based on care, respect and love. I want you to enjoy life with me, and not have to worry about money. This financial commitment is for your security and piece of mind. Some people call this a companionship agreement, I prefer to see it as an expression of my feelings towards you."

Wednesday day 25. Morning came and the Wilsons arrived with her parents. We signed a one year lease, filled out the association application and told the new tenants they could move in as soon as their application was approved. We would empty the condo, of any left over personal items, tomorrow AM. After they left, Sue was heading to her bank to set up an auto payment for all the utilities, the association dues and the new security system.

I went to my doctor's appointment. The MRI was negative and my physician wished me a pleasant trip. When I got back with the good news, Sue was obviously relieved. We then started preparing for the family meeting.

Setting a time and day for the meeting was easy, since everyone was eager and waiting. We agreed to meet at 3 PM at #24 and all the ones who were working took personal time off. It took Sue a long time to find the right outfit to wear–probably caused by some anxiety.

Sue's daughters and husbands were the first to arrive. They hugged for a long time. One daughter said, "mom you look so radiant." The other said, "there is a glow in your eyes." Sue added, "that is probably because I am so happy." The oldest daughter, with tears flowing, said, "that is so nice to hear after these difficult years." The youngest daughter came up to me and said, "it appears we have you to thank for mom's state of mind." After Sue finally introduced me, one of the husbands shook my hand and said, "I haven't seen my mother-in-law with such a smile in the past 8 years." The other said, "thank you and welcome to our family."

My daughter and husband were next to arrived. My daughter gave me a hug, saying, "dad, you look 20 years younger than when you were practicing medicine." She then went to Sue and said, "so you are the cause of his healthy and zestful rebirth, thank you."

My youngest son and wife were next to arrive. He came up to me and said, "OK dad, where is this blonde bombshell you are shacking up with?" As he turned around, I heard him say, "WHOA" as he was introduced to Sue. My oldest son and wife were last to arrive. My son immediately spotted Sue in the crowd, came up to me and said, "dad, that is robbing the cradle." I then explained to him that we were almost the same age, but obviously not the same genetic inheritance.

After cocktails were served, introductions were finished, it became clear that everyone was getting comfortable. I invited all to sit, so we could talk and have a Q and A session, where everyone could have their say.

I started by saying that Sue and I had made a list of ground rules but that only one will be followed. "We are not here to hide anything, all and any question will be truthfully answered. So let's begin."

1. "Tell us about this trip you are planning." The details were given about visiting tourist attractions and shooting.
2. "How did you get into CAS." "After retirement, I was desperate to find a hobby–something I could do every day. Saved by Jack and Sue.

   Now, I have 4 hobbies, Reloading, shooting, traveling and Sue." "TMI-TMI-TMI." Sue turned red as a tomato and gave me that look, the one I don't fare well with. Overall laughter save the day.
3. "Who is paying the expenses?" "I am, and Sue is renting her condo. The profits will be deposited in her bank account."
4. "If mom is renting her condo, what happens if your relationship breaks up, she would be left without a home?" Sue gave me the nod of approval. "Your mom is well protected. If we do break up, I will buy her a replacement unit in this complex–and you are all a witness to my promise. In addition,

I have started a joint checking account of 50K to cover our expenses. If I suddenly pass away, as long as we are still together, she will inherit the truck, camper and the balance of the joint checking account–to cover my promise." There was silence until her oldest daughter said, "that is very generous of you".

5. "Does your doctor approve of this trip?" "I just had a negative MRI and my doctor is all in favor of this venture."
6. "How are you going to pay your bills?" "I have prepaid all 'our' known bills, with a large credit amount to cover the next four months." The only expense Sue has is her car payment which has also been prepaid for 4 months."
7. "In view of the home invasion, how secure is mom while traveling?" "Your mom will never be alone, she is not going any where without me at her side. In addition, we both have a concealed weapons permit, and both carry a self defense revolver."

When there were no further question, my youngest son said, "well that really covers all our concerns. I really like everything I heard, what about you all?" There was a general wave and buzz of approval as my daughter said, "what do you say we visit your camper?" "Great, let's do that, and then we will all gather at Joe's place for dinner and hopefully answer more questions."

We showed the camper in groups of five. The men had more questions about the truck. The camper was liked by all. The one thing that impressed everyone was the conversion of a bunk room to a gun room. One son noted that there was only one bedroom. Sue was giving me that look again, so I just got off the subject before I got myself in trouble. The women really liked the large pantry. The men liked the power awning and push out.

The dinner was held in a private dining room. We were sitting at a large circular table that held all twelve of us. Everyone ordered wine or beer. We all chose an entre from an American or Italian menu.

The conversation during dinner was congenial. It was clear to me that everyone was comfortable with their new family. There was only one question that surprised my sons and daughter. "Mom, is this financial and living situation going to affect your alimony checks?" "No, my alimony and health insurance are protected by court order till I reach the age of 65. The only thing that would cancel this, is if I get married or die." *I clearly heard, and would take that into future consideration–or possibly ignore it.*

After dinner, coffee, drinks and dessert extended the evening. We were approaching 10 PM and no one was giving any signs of running out of steam. Finally my oldest son got up and said, "I have to leave, but this family get together has been enlightening. I came today dreading the thought of meeting a gold-digger and an old fool. Instead I found a distinguished father and an elegant lady–two late middle age people who were lucky to have found each other. Sue, welcome to our family, you may be a bombshell but you're no gold-digger."

Across the table I heard, "HEAR-HEAR, HEAR-HEAR."

As everyone was leaving, Sue's oldest daughter came up and said, "A parent feels accomplished when a child finishes their education and become financially independent. That feeling is very similar today. I know you are safe, financially secure and happy. I love you." And so we went home feeling quite proud of our children and spouses.

Thursday day 26. We got up early with many things to do. We went together at #97 and cleaned the condo of the remaining items. Left Sue's keys with the Wilsons. Then, I gave Sue her copy of the will codicil and informed her she had to pick up our checks, with all the identity proof that was required. Then she would pick up groceries and additional items for the camper. I had the remainder of the list to attack. Fortunately, my tasks were all phone calls. We both finished around 4 PM. After a relaxing evening at home, we retired early anticipating an early rising to get "On the Road" by **Friday day 27**–making it about a month since we met!

CHAPTER 11

On the Road–Deming, NM

On our departure, from the southern suburbs of Springfield, we headed north to the highway of Route 44. We decided to stay on the highway until we arrived in the Texas Panhandle. This required that we change to Route 40 in Oklahoma City. Our total mileage would be +-400 miles to the Texas-Oklahoma border and another +-100 miles to circumvent Amarillo. Thereafter, we would take secondary roads to Deming NM.

We had traveled 100 miles when my phone rang. It was Jim Beecher who said, "Amos Whitefield got home yesterday, one thing led to another, and he found out you were headed for the Texas Panhandle. He hopes you would stop over for a visit, dinner and camp overnight." We thought about it, and Sue gave me a positive nod. "Certainly, at 400 miles, we would be stopping for the night anyways. Our ETA is 2 PM."

We arrived at 2:30 PM and a Cowboy directed us to the camping area. We set up the camper and headed to the main house. Amos was sitting on the porch with his wife. Introductions were made and Amos said, "so I hear Mam, that you were the one who provided those deep and effective cardiac compressions–still painful today. Every time I breathe, I remember awakening and finding you Doc, crushing away on my chest. But all in all, it is nice to be alive, thanks to you. Incidentally, I hear that my son lost his lunch. It must have been something dramatic, since he is one tough fella." Emma interjected, "oh it was, believe me." As she was seen rubbing her goose bumps.

Changing the subject to ranching, Amos said, "cattle ranching today requires raising organic beef with high yielding crossbreeds. We have an estimated 2000 cattle, producing +-1000 calves per year. We have 1800 fenced in acres, utilize the open range, and raise 300 acres of hay for winter use. To protect our herd, from winter blizzards in the Panhandle, we have several clear span huts where they have shelter, and we have a location to feed them. We still use horses, but with the extensive acreage, we have to use ATV's and satellite radios. We have a major coyote problem and so all Cowboys on the range carry a rifle."

"We do well on this ranch because we have tamed most of our fenced in 1800 acres. The tamed pastures are seeded with grass, and some of the recent ones have been cultivated and fertilized with organic soil supplements. Our tamed pastures will support 1 cattle unit(a cow and calf) over 2 acres. The open range requires anywhere from 8–15 acres per cattle unit."

"Sue asked, "on our horse ride, we noticed that every animal has an ear tag. Has this replaced branding? "Unfortunately no. Our pasture stock is usually herded into branding stations, where animals are herded into restraining stanchions, for cold branding with dry ice or liquid nitrogen. On the open range, hot branding is still practiced. We brand for ownership proof and we ear tag for farm identification purposes. Of note, a hot branded animal has no hair regrowth, whereas a cold branded animal has white hair as regrowth. This allows us to detect cattle that got out of the pastures and escaped to the open range."

"We have 12 full time range Cowboys and several part time utility workers. Round up time and calving season is when we hire on the road Cowboys, who arrive a with camper–which is the major reason we have a camping area."

The house cook came to inform us dinner was ready. Amos said, "I now have to start eating cardboard, nuts and twigs. But that will not start till tomorrow. Tonight we are having the best filet mignons this ranch can produce. During dinner, Sue kept directing the topics away from medicine. Eventually we said our goodbyes. We wished Amos a good extension of life and I managed to say to Emma, "thank you for your generosity, to me and my club–that was way more than just a nice touch." In the morning, we were off very early, on the road to Deming.

Once on the road, we computed that we had +-550 miles to Deming. We had planned to stop at the Palo Duro Canyon, and so we decided that our goal for the day was Roswell. That would put us 250 miles to Deming for tomorrow.

Circumventing Amarillo, I asked Sue what this city was known for. She said, "It is a metropolitan area of 200,000 people. It has been a large cattle market since 1850. Today, it is a huge meat packing center that processes one quarter of the US beef supply."

As I was driving, Sue was on the internet, and gave a summary of the Palo Duro Canyon. "This canyon is located in the community of Canyon Texas–population 15,000. The canyon is the 2nd largest in the US. It is approximately 100 miles long, 20 miles wide and 800 feet deep."

"This canyon was inhabited for 12,000 years by natives until 1874, when the Comanches and Kiowas were removed. In 1876, Charles Goodnight entered the canyon and started the J A Ranch. At its peak, there were 100,000 cattle on the ranch."

We stopped and walked up to the canyon. This first sight of a canyon will likely stay imbedded in our minds forever. I said to Sue, "this is one heck of a crevice on the earth's surface." We took photographs, went into a visitor center and read display explanations. Within a short time, we were back on the road–rather pleased with our first encounter with the American West.

Sue was driving, and so I manned the internet. The next town was Hereford Texas. "Population 15,000, This is the only incorporated city named Hereford in the US. This is another large beef feeding and processing center. It also has a large dairy industry." As we arrived at the city limits, a sign said, "city without a toothache." I said, "that's because they have a natural water supply high in fluoride!"

The next town was Farwell Texas. I continued, "a small town of 2,000 that borders NM. This town is the site of the famous Red River War when the Comanches were finally defeated. Shortly thereafter, the XIT Ranch was formed–the ranch that boasted having 800 employed Cowboys and having strung 6000 miles of barbed wire."

Finally, we crossed into New Mexico. The first community was Clovis, "population 37,000. The area was developed in the early 1900's by the railroad industry. Even today, it is still a major hub of operations for several railroad companies. Of interest, this city hosts the largest cheddar cheese producers in North America."

At the end of today's journey was Roswell. I checked the internet and found, "Roswell, population 48,000, is known for area 51, the alleged crash site of a UFO in 1947. Despite the many witnesses, the government kept explaining the event as a crashed weather balloon. 50 years later, their explanation changed to a top secret atomic espionage project. There are many disbelievers to the government's explanations. Today, Roswell has become a tourist center because of the alien decor and the International UFO Museum."

We found a camping area just outside city limits. Set up for the night and headed for the UFO Museum. Whether, the drawings of aliens and crash site revelations, were real or fiction did not matter. They were part of the American West and we wanted to experience them. We still do believe that one day a UFO will land and communicate with us. Visiting this area certainly kept my mind's imagination active, and kept fueling my dreams.

The next day on the road brought us to two small communities. Sue started with more internet information. "Ruidoso, population 8,000. A mountain resort community with ski slopes and Apache Indian casinos. Tularosa, population 5,000. A town known for its abundance of cottonwood shade trees, and a long standing irrigation system. Also well known for their preservation of the adobe architecture."

"The next big city was Alamogordo, population 30,000. A city in the Tularosa Basin of the Chihuahuan Dessert. The area is known for the Trinity Test, the first explosion of an atomic bomb. Today it is a tourist center, and hosts a large military base, Holloman Air

Force Base. It has now become a retirement center for military personnel–especially the snow-birds. We will be returning to this location in a few days on our trip to the White Sands National Monument."

The last location before Deming was Las Cruces. "Population 100,000 and the 2nd largest city in New Mexico. It serves as the metropolitan center for Deming. It's major employer is the White Sands test facility and the Missile Range. It is the headquarters for Virgin Galactic, with their sub-orbital space flights. And last, it has historically been a site for movie making, for both city and nearby desert.

Deming is in the south of New Mexico. Warm weather the end of May and only 30 miles north of Mexico. As we parked our camper on the outskirts of town, I said, "it is 78 degrees today and that is why we started our circuitous route here." Sue even added, "and let's not head north till the temperature goes up." "Guess we will follow the weather report to move on!"

I said to Sue, "tell me about Deming." On the internet she added, "population 15,000. City named after Mary Ann Deming, wife of Charles Crocker who was one of the original big four railroad builders. It was the site of the 2nd transcontinental railroad union, connecting the east/west southern route. It still sits astride the major railroads, that link the east/west southern route. Homeland security and the Border Patrol have a large presence in the community. The great temperatures from November to April bring the snow-birds, and so it's become a popular winter retirement community. It has become a hub for access to four surrounding communities, one of which is a metropolitan area."

After two long days traveling, we decided to take it easy today. After planning our daily trips, we decided that the first day at a new base should be spent checking out the area, the streets and the secondary roads to tourist sites. So today we drove around Deming, and found the secondary roads out of town. There were only four roads out of town to the tourist sites we had on our list–east, west, northwest and northeast.

With ample time left over, we decided to visit some of the local Cowboy Shooting clubs since this was a shooting day. There were several within reasonable distances. We did not want to shoot since we had just been at a big shoot, we wanted to see how CAS was done in this area.

One we visited was in the desert. This was a club that sets up the day before the shoot. Sue explained, "they arrive with an enclosed trailer and pull out the facades, props, targets and set up for the day.

At the end of the shoot, they pick up everything and place it in the trailer. The trailer is usually left in a secure lot or taken away to someone's home. This kind of club requires many volunteers to do the work. If all club members help out, it goes well. If it's always the same workers, they burn out and the club falls apart." This club certainly looked like a successful endeavor.

The other club had permanent facades and stage designs. We took photographs to send to Ranger Rooster who was designing our club's facades. This was a nice location on the edge of the mountains. The shooters were a lively and happy appearing bunch. Sue added, "it's no surprise to see that the scenarios and shooting sequences are the same as ours–that is the universal advantage of following SASS rules and methods."

The next day, we decided to head northwest some 55 miles to an area with three tourist sites. The first was the "Chico Mine" or the "Santa Rita Mine." This was an open pit copper mine, with several minerals as byproduct–the major one being silver. Arriving at the scenic viewing site, the view was an eyeful. The pit measured 1.75 miles across and was 1350 feet deep. Excavators were perched on a rock platform and were loading trucks. These rock trucks were transporting the ore, through a series of switchback roads, all over this massive mountain of rock. This was a site that would be difficult to forget. The visiting center gave us all the facts we were looking for.

The second location was Penos Altos. This was a gold mining town formed in the 1860's. Population today was

200 from a high of 9,000 in 1880. Today it has become a tourist center, because many of these old buildings were still standing. Driving through town, in it's narrow streets, gives you an idea of the construction styles from long ago.

One historical location was the Opera House and Buckhorn Saloon. The Opera House has now become a restaurant and, during our visit, they were serving a tourist bus. The saloon had the ambience of yesteryear in the Old West. We had drinks and dinner in the saloon. While I went to the men's room, Sue told the tour guide that I would be glad to sing to the full house in the Opera House. Needless to say I had to do some fast talking and had to get the heck out of Dodge, real quick. *I knew this was payback for that swimsuit mayhem I had caused, but I kept a stiff upper lip.* Sue laughed all the way to Fort Bayard.

Fort Bayard was founded in 1866 as a military installation of Buffalo Soldiers. Sue added, "their function was to provide settlers protection against American Indians, especially Apaches. In later years, it was converted into a TB sanitarium, then into a VA Hospital, and today it serves as a nursing home for Veterans. It was a large institution that had undergone many renovations, and today had some buildings appear modern and some more consistent with the late 1800's." It took quite some time to go through the history of this fort's many faces.

That was the end to a pleasant day acting as tourists–gaining experience, knowledge and history from direct exposure.

The next day provided a long ride of 100 miles to the White Sands National Monument, just outside of Alamogordo. On route, I searched the internet on this natural wonder. With Sue driving, I said, "this is the world's largest dune field of gypsum and it encompasses 275 square miles. Gypsum, calcium sulfate dihydrate, is a water soluble mineral that flows from nearby mountains via the waterways. However, when the rivers hit the Tularosa Basin, there is no escape to the ocean. So the water either evaporates or seeps into the ground, this leaves crystals of gypsum called selenite that are broken down to sand by wind and rain."

"The sand size crystals are swept away by wind causing dunes to change shape from day to day. Also, the crystals are cool because the crystals do not convert the suns energy into heat." Sue interjected, "very interesting info, but what is gypsum used for?" "Gypsum is mainly used in the manufacturing of dry wall(sheet rock), cement, plaster of Paris, fertilizer and blackboard chalk."

When we got to the White Sands entrance gate, guards were just removing road barricades. We were told that the monument had been temporarily closed because of a missile launch at the Missile Range. We then drove in and eventually were surrounded by mounds of white appearing salt or snow. Eventually the mounds changed to large dunes.

Driving around, we saw kids sledding down the dunes and so we decided to stop and check this out. I said, "Sue, feel this material, it is cool to touch. Let's climb to the top of this dune." Every two foot step we took only yielded 6 inches of elevation. So we started running uphill, since this did not allow time for our feet to sink in so much. Eventually, we got to the top.

We walked around for a while, but quickly noticed that the wind was erasing our shallow footsteps in the gypsum. I said, "I have heard that people have gotten lost on long hikes because the wind was erasing their steps. Let's not go further than within visibility of the truck." Sue added, "then we better turn around now since all we can see are the black tires of our white truck!"

Walking back down to the road was another surprise. Every step yielded a three foot slide, since the gypsum was cascading ahead of our feet. Before we got into the truck, we cleaned our hands and feet by simply rubbing the skin, since the crystals did not stick to the skin. Fortunately, we had worn sandals and not sneakers. Cleaning sneakers might have been a different matter.

On our way back to our camping base, we decided to stop for lunch at the Old Mesilla Village in Las Cruces.

"This is a community that has preserved it's cultural identity and it's architectural history of adobe structures. Today, it hosts a mix of cultures: Indian, Spanish, Mexican and Anglo-American. The area also boasted of booming times of the 1880's–a hub for the Butterfield Stagecoach, the trial of Billy the Kid and other historical events."

We walked through the shops of boutiques, unique stores, galleries and many specialty restaurants serving traditional New Mexican food. It quickly became clear that chile(with an e) was the main ingredient in most dishes. We decided to ask our waitress about this "chile." She willingly said, "chile is the state vegetable and the major staple of south NM. It comes in either green or red. It is not the same as chili, which is a stew of meat, red chile sauce and beans. If you want to know more, take a trip to Hatch NM, the chile capital of the world."

"For today, you should order one dish with green chile and the other with red chile." We agreed and I ordered the Green Chile Stew, and Sue ordered the Stacked Red Chile Enchiladas. The waitress said, "good choices, and the hotter chile today is the green chile, which has been preserved since the last harvest! The degree of 'hot' depends on the year, source and variety–that's why you check with a store owner or a waitress."

Enjoying our meals, we could not believe that the green chile was so hot. I eventually suggested, "I agree with the waitress, let's interrupt our tourist schedule tomorrow and go to Hatch to get informed. On the way back, I am certain we can find some location to visit and complete the day."

Heading back to Deming from Las Cruces was a 50 mile stretch of desert. Checking the internet, Sue said, "the deserts in southern NM are not like barren sand dunes as one expects or can visualize. These deserts have some vegetative growth to include bushes, grasses and browse."

Driving along we spotted a mix of plants to include: scrub junipers, cactus, creosote bushes, prickly pear, cholla, rabbit bush, green wood and pinion trees. Grassy patches appeared randomly and were usually hosting feeding cattle. Ranches and water wells were widely scattered. The cattle were usually Black Angus. We were later told that this breed could go longer before returning to a water hole.

We got home in the late afternoon. Enjoyed sitting in the shade, with liquid refreshments, and planning our trip tomorrow–to Hatch(for chile) and Lake Valley(to visit a silver mine/ghost town).

The next day we had a late departure for Hatch NM–some 50 miles north east. Sue started her presentation, "the internet says that this small town has a population less than 2,000 people, yet is called the chile capital of the world. The town is nationally known for it's Labor Day festival celebrating their world famous crop."

"Both chiles are high in Vitamin C and antioxidants. The green chile is harvested early and served peeled, roasted, de-seeded, and chopped. It can be used in soups and chowders and many dishes, especially stews. Red chile is harvested late when it ripens and turns red. To be eaten, it must be dried and powdered to make a red sauce. The red sauce is used to make many dishes but it can also be ladled over enchiladas or tamales."

Sue suddenly stopped reading and said, "I really think that, if we want to learn more about chile, especially about Relenos and Ristras, we should talk to a market owner for both verbal and visual learning." I gladly added, "we are now arriving and will proceed to a market."

The town was full of markets. Some small and some well known such as the Hatch Chile Store. We found a very talkative market owner who also had a deli of hot chile dishes. He proudly explained, "rellenos are de-seeded green chiles, stuffed with cheese or chicken. They are then dipped in an egg batter and fried." He then had us taste both kinds.

"The Ristra is a strung pod of red chile that is hung in the sun for drying. As a decoration, it is hung in doorways or arches, as a welcome and good luck symbol. This method of drying was designed years ago in an attempt to stop contamination with bird and rodent droppings–as was common when red chiles were dried on sun exposed tables. Once the red chiles are dry, they are then converted into the red sauce."

As we were about to leave, Sue picked up some rellenos, several green and red chile dishes, and picked up a dry Ristra for a camper decoration. When the market owner heard that we were traveling north, he added, "These dry Ristras must be displayed in a dry climate. It you are heading north into a high humidity area, the humidity will ruin a Ristra. In your case, take a Ristra that has been treated with a lacquer to preserve them in other climates."

On our way back to Deming, we made a detour to Lake Valley, a ghost town. Reading on the net, "in the early 1880's, silver was discovered and a town, Lake Valley, grew up around the silver mine. The mine was called The Bridal Chamber Mine. It had silver so pure that large amounts of nearly pure silver were shipped unsmelted directly to the mint. There was so much pure silver that a railroad spur was built into the mine to load ore directly onto cars. A total of 2.5 million ounces of silver was removed between 1881–1893, when the silver crash closed the mine."

"The town grew to 4,000 people, and served to supply goods and equipment to the mine and it's workers. The town provided retail stores, stamping mills and smelters. Mining operations had a resurgence in mid 1950's when manganese was found and mined for a few years. The town eventually lost all its habitants, since employment moved out to Hillsboro, after the mine closed. The last residents left in 1994."

With this information already in mind, visiting the town was much more meaningful. On arrival, we found that there was a caretaker 24/7. The caretaker lived in a house located behind the school. When we pressed a buzzer, per directions, the caretaker came down and opened the doors. He was very helpful with more history and we eventually went on our self guided tour.

We saw old buildings, from the early years, that were falling down. Some of the buildings were more modern but obviously showing years of weathering. We saw much evidence of old mining equipment and a railroad terminal. There was no entering of buildings and the entrance to the mine was blocked off. Later we were told that if a renovation program was ever approved, buildings would be open to the public–and possibly a short distance in the mine.

During our walk, one feature was noted–rusted tin cans everywhere. There were mounds of rusted tin cans behind most homes, and mounds of cans collected from the walkways and placed into dumping areas. We were so impressed with this finding, that when we were leaving, we stopped and asked the caretaker what this meant.

The caretaker explained, "in early days without refrigeration, groceries had to be purchased as fresh perishable goods, or bought as canned non perishable goods. Canned goods were a quick meal for busy miners that did not have a home domestic. Without a recycling program or a dump, the cans were just thrown out the window. As long as they had been rinsed clean, they did not attract flies or rodents. Today, the rusted tin cans are part of this town's history."

After we got to the camper, Sue was writing the days events in her diary and reviewing the photos taken. Deleting some poor shots and making a file of the good ones for each location visited. She even referred each photo file to a specific page of her diary. When Sue asked me what I thought of her documenting their trip, I said, "memories are for those who have lived them." Sue pondered my answer, but quickly continued working her diary and photo shop.

The next day, we decided to visit a real and much older ghost town–Shakespeare. Sue read, "this area in the 1880's, served as a stop for the Butterfield Stage Line and a watering hole for travelers to the gold mines–it was named The Mexican Spring. When silver mines opened up, a town grew up and eventually was named Shakespeare. It was totally abandoned in 1929, when the mines closed down, and the railroad bypassed the town and went to Lordsburg.

During its hay-days, as in Lake Valley, the town served the mines. It was also well known as an area visited by historical characters such as Billy the Kid, Johnny Ringo, the Clantons and many others.

Today it is a tourist attraction. As we walked the main street, we saw: private homes, sheriff's office, a mercantile, blacksmith shop, harness shop and many other utilities used in the 1880's. The main street was full of wagons, stagecoaches, agricultural implements and miscellaneous hardware of the times.

This attraction revealed the way things were over one hundred years ago. It was amazing to see how some basic structural renovations had preserved the buildings, as they were so long ago. I commented, "if we don't see another ghost town, this place will always stay in my mind, as one of the memories I was referring to." Of course, Sue took a photo of every wagon, building and its contents.

On our way back to Deming we took a detour north to the City of Rocks State Park. I read along, "this one square mile park was formed 35 million years ago as a result of a massive volcanic eruption. The erupted rocks were then sculptured over millions of years by wind and rain. Today we have the incredible monolithic rock formations of pinnacles and columns."

As we walked amidst the formations, some reached a height of 40 feet high and some seemed to aggregate into groups of pinnacles. At the visitor center, we learned that this eruption was estimated to be 1000 times greater than the eruption at Mt. Saint Helens. I said to Sue, "now how can they estimate something that happened 35 million years ago?"

On our way home, Sue said, "this park is the best example of a natural wonder that cannot be properly described in books or pictures. I agree with you, some places have to be seen to appreciate them."

The next two days were spent relaxing in the sun. Their heated pool was a pleasure to use, and we went to Las Cruces one evening for a country dance–where their specialty dance was, two-step, two-step and more two-step. We also started reading Gary McCarthy's historical fiction, Grand Canyon Thunder. This book was about the natives who lived in the canyon, and about the Powell expedition down the Colorado River.

One afternoon, our neighboring campers hoodwinked us into playing cards. They taught us how to play Dirty Board–also known as Pegs and Jokers, or Jokers and Marbles. The game was a riot, especially for us non card players. It was certainly well named, dirty plays were the norm against our opponents–men against women! It was such a pleasurable game that we talked of buying the board game. How to accomplish this while on the road was solved by our neighbors. 'They sold us their game, and since they were heading home, they would order a replacement for themselves from Amazon. It would arrive even before they got home.

So after a great visit of tourist sites, wonderful weather, and pleasurable days at the campsite, it was time to move along to our next base of operations, Albuquerque NM, some 250 miles north.

CHAPTER 12

On the Road–Albuquerque, NM

Heading north, Sue asks, "why are we heading to our second base but staying in NM? I expected we would be going to Colorado." "As I was planning our trip, I could not bypass some crucial locations before moving on to Colorado. Such sites as the Grand Canyon, Los Alamos, Bandolier, Acoma Sky City and others. Let's not forget the two big ones, Founders Ranch-End of Trail and a hot air balloon ride." Sue's comment was, "well I guess Durango can wait."

On route, Sue read, "Albuquerque's population is 500,000. A large metropolitan area with a concentration of high-tech private and government institutions. Companies such as Intel have a large semi conductor manufacturing plant. Other major employers are Sandia Medical Laboratories, and Kirkland Air Forse Base. Despite being a large city, it always ranks high as best cities to live in."

As I was driving, I asked Sue, "find us a camping site northwest of the city. That will give us easier access to our many western and northern tourist locations. After finding a suitable site and setting up, I got on the phone to make reservations for our first hot air balloon ride.

After registration, signing a waiver of liability, and agreeing to help our pilot filling our balloon, we headed to the field. There were three balloons laid out on the ground. We went to our designated spot. There was only one other couple as passengers in our balloon. With Sue and I on one side and the other couple on the other side, we lifted the balloon intake. This allowed the pilot to release propane, to cause a flame that heated the air, and filled the balloon with hot air.

At a certain point, the pilot instructed us to jump in the basket. After that, the pilot released more propane, and the raging flame immediately generated enough hot air to lift the balloon off the ground. Then with more heat, the balloon lifted higher and higher.

The higher we got, Sue kept getting closer to me. It didn't take long for her to stop looking at the ground. By the time we got to 1000 feet, Sue was trying to get in my back pocket. Finally I said, "I did not know you were scared of heights, had I known we could have skipped this experience." "I was always leery, whenever I climbed on a house roof, but this is no house roof. The pilot just said we were 1000 feet high, with no maneuvering capability, kept up by a plastic balloon, and flying around at the whim of the wind–really reassuring, heh!"

I smiled at her and said, "wonderful, isn't it?" Needless to say, the camera never came out of Sue's backpack, and I got that look again–the one I don't fare well with.

After flying around for 45 minutes, the pilot said that we would start our slow descent. He would open a flap to release some hot air and we would descend slowly. The pilot pointed out a red van on the ground. He then explained, "that is my team following us. As soon as we are in a clearing, the team will be on the ground to secure this basket and balloon. First manually, and then with ropes anchored to the ground. You will then disembark and my team will help me lay the balloon down on its side.

As we were clearing the houses, the last one before the leaving was a three story structure. Sue suddenly said, "Jeeeez, we are only 20 feet above the roof, I hope this house doesn't have a chimney!"

Reaching the clearing, the pilot picked up a gust of wind. He reacted, by pulling the rope for a quick flame, and he aborted the landing. Shortly thereafter, he made his second attempt and was successful. The problem is that the basket was almost on the ground, but the team was just arriving from the aborted first landing site. A few minutes waiting felt like an hour, but all went well and we jumped out.

On way to our other tourist site, Sue said, "I am glad that this venture is off my bucket list, although it was a once in a lifetime experience. Where are we going this afternoon?" I answered, "we are on our way to visit a pueblo village, but we are presently driving on our current tourist site–driving on the historical Route 66."

Sue read, "this is a historical route of the 30's through the 80's, when it was decommissioned. Today, it still has many of the buildings of the times, intermingled with modern counterparts." As we drove west, we saw whimsical neon signs, classical metal diners, retro motels called motorcourts, old style gas stations and trading posts–displaying native rugs, pottery and jewelry.

At lunch time we stopped at an old fashioned metal diner. Walking in was stepping back in time. The booths had pastel bright colored leather seats, retro wallpaper, disco music, and waitresses wearing uniforms not seen in the past 30 years. This was another one of those places that required one's physical presence to enjoy and appreciate. As old as it was, a burger/fries/milkshake was still the same.

Arriving at the pueblo called, Acoma Sky Village, I read on the net, "NM has 19 distinct pueblos. This Acoma Pueblo is made up of three villages. These Puebloans are a federally recognized tribal entity, and are ancestral descendants of cultures from Chaco Canyon, Mesa Verde and Bandolier. These Puebloans offer a window in time, where native people still carry customary traditions, in their pottery and tribal celebrations."

"The Acoma Sky City sits on a 370 foot long sandstone cliff, and it's the oldest continually inhabited Puebloan city in North America. We drove through the narrow city streets, we saw natives sitting outside, cooking by the sidewalks, and selling pottery by the roadside. The adobe buildings seemed to be two or three story structures. There were exterior ladders to upper levels.

At the visitor center, we were told that the lower levels were for storage, and the upper levels were for living and sleeping. The volunteer also said, "there is no running water, electricity or sewage disposal. These people live the way they did hundreds of years ago. Also, there is only +- 50 Puebloans that live permanently in this pueblo. However, the population explodes on weekends when families come to visit. The other 3,000 Puebloans live in surrounding more modern villages. You are welcome to walk through the village and inspect their pottery, wares and their specialty breads–but cameras are not allowed!"

The next day, we headed north to Los Alamos and Bandolier, two adjacent tourist attractions some 100 miles north of our camp site.

Our destination in Los Alamos was the Bradbury Science Museum, home of the WW II Manhattan Project. On arrival, we attended an introductory movie which prepared us for the enormity of the museum's contents. As we walked throughout the artifacts, documents, and the 40 exhibits of the project, we got an eyeful in one room. We were face to face with a full size model of Little Boy and Fat Man Atomic Bombs. I said to Sue, "Whoa, this sight will never leave me."

We spent at least one hour reading the information on many displays. There were many hands-on models. One item caught our attention. It was a copy of the leaflets dropped on Hiroshima, warning of further atomic attacks, if the government did not surrender.

Then we moved to the newer artifact section to include: a missile warhead, a communication satellite, an air launched cruise missile and many others. One tourist asked a poignant question. "How does a missile, carrying a nuclear warhead, bring down a squadron of enemy planes?" The attendant quickly answered, "a nuclear device detonated several thousand feet above the planes would liquify every plane while in flight."

After an amazing and enlightening visit, we moved along to the Bandolier National Monument. Sue read, "this area has preserved the homes and territories of Ancestral Puebloans–dating back between 1150–1600 AD. Frijoles Canyon has a number of ancestral homes, rock paintings, kivas(ceremonial structures), and petroglyphs."

As we entered the park, we walked the one mile, Main Loop Trail. There was evidence of dwellings of rock structures on the canyon floor. The majority of dwellings were in the rock wall, homes were carved in the rock. Some were multistory structures and many showed evidence of wood holes in the rock–some with poles sticking out of them. Other dwellings were "cavates," voids in the canyon walls, and carved out further by humans into single or multistory dwellings.

Sue asked, "how did the people access their homes?" "Like we saw at the Acoma Sky City, exterior ladders. This offered some degree of security, since the ladders would be pulled up at nighttime, to ward off enemy attacks."

As we walked back to the truck, I said, "this first exposure to Ancestral Puebloan civilizations was a great primer, prior to our visit to Mesa Verde and the Cliff Palace in Colorado."

Our next tourist attraction was the Grand Canyon. It was a 400 mile trip and we decided to stop in Flagstaff AZ, some 325 miles from Albuquerque. This would make it a short jaunt to the canyon the next day. Before our Arizona trip, we took one day's rest at the camper, visiting surrounding sites around Albuquerque and reading Gary Mc Carthy's historical fiction, Grand Canyon Thunder.

This story describes Powell's 1869 expedition down the Colorado River with all the historic canyon sites still present today. A mountain man is intertwined in the lives of Navaho, Hopi, and Havasupai Indians, who lived in the canyon in the 1800's. This story is a primer to our visit since it is a mixture of real figures/locations, and fictional characters.

We shared driving to Flagstaff. Sue asked, "why did you choose this location for our overnight stop?" I answered, "I figured that it would be impossible to find a campsite at the Grand Canyon and I wanted to go to Black Bart's Steakhouse.

Searching the net, I said, "this is a unique restaurant and I would rather not tell you why it is so unique. Let this be a surprise." Sue agreed but asked, "who was this character named Black Bart and why do we immortalize him?"

I read, "Black Bart's real name was Charles E Bowles. He was known for robbing only Wells Fargo stagecoaches in northern California and southern Oregon from 1875–1883. During this time, he did 28 robberies, never hurt anyone, never robbed the passengers, never fired a shot and supposedly never loaded his shotgun. To gain notoriety, he left poems at 5 sites, and always wore a two hole flour sac over his head. He was eventually captured, did 4 years in prison, and when released in 1888 he disappeared forever."

Wearing casual clothes, we arrived for dinner. Once seated, Sue kept looking around and finally said, "the decor is Western but I don't see why this place is so unique! I did not answer, *I had made a reservation requesting a ringside table next to the the first presentation of the evening, and the lady was to be seated with her back to the show.* We ordered appetizers and wine. As we started eating, it happened–I saw the waiters setting up!

An explosive, loud, and rousing rendition of a show-tune by four waiters and two waitresses–circa 1927, ShowBoat. Sue just about inhaled half of her Mozzarella stick, and spit the other half across the table. She turned around and could not believe her eyes and ears. After several show tunes, the staff went back to work. Sue said, "you certainly engineered this surprise with finesse." I said, "that seat you are in cost me big bucks, but the look on your face was worth it."

At a steakhouse, you order steaks, not seafood. When our meals came the waiter said, "it is customary to not interrupt your meal during a musical presentation, otherwise your steaks would get cold. The entertainers expect this in this location. Besides, you just had a presentation next to your table, the next ones will be at other tables."

Driving to the Grand Canyon, Sue read, "this world natural wonder covers 277 river miles, it's widest point is 18 miles and it's deepest point is 1 mile. Ancestral Puebloan's have lived in and around the canyon for several thousand years, leaving behind dwellings, garden sites, storage areas and artifacts still visible today."

"Early canyon explorers realized that tourism in the canyon would be profitable. In the late 1800's, guides started tours, followed by overnight tents and eventually extended hotels–to today's modern facilities for one of the busiest tourist attractions in the US."

Upon arriving, we walked to the South Rim. Standing next to a low rock wall and looking down, produced a sudden explosive and unbelievable visualization. I said, "WHOA, that is one heck of a big hole." Sue had the same reaction but she stepped back and looked a bit dizzy. Eventually, she came back to the wall, seemed somewhat adjusted, and the camera started snapping away.

There were many tourists at the wall but few were speaking. It was clear, that it took much mental energy, to assimilate the grandeur of this natural and historic site. One tourist spotted some black dots on the canyon floor.

With binoculars, he was able to confirm that the dots were mules hauling gear for backpackers.

We walked the South Rim, then took a bus tour along the Scenic Hermit Road. At one stop, we saw a Condor. I said, "that looks like a big crow." I got that look again, from Sue plus several tourists.

Upon our return, we went to the visitor center to learn about the mules we saw on the canyon floor. The ranger said, "we host backpacking trips to the canyon. It can be an overnight to a week's trip. The trip includes: a guide, camping equipment, tents, food and all necessities packed by porters or mules. Some trips include a base camp with daily excursions, or provide simpler overnight accommodations. The cost is $1,000 per person for three days or some economical trips at $1,500 for a week. The only drawback, reservations begin one year from now and some are even 2 years away–it's a popular attraction!"

The last thing on the canyon agenda was my offer to drive to the West Rim and get on a helicopter to the canyon floor, and or visit the Glass Skywatch. Sue gave me that look again, the one I don't fare well with. She also added, "I can barely walk as it is, and you want me to get in a helicopter, and or stand on a glass bridge–I am still trying to get over that hot air balloon ride. For the next weeks, the only air space I want under my feet is the height, from the ground, of the truck and camper floors." I chuckled!

After finishing our visit, it was too late to leave for NM. We went back to the Flagstaff campsite and headed out the next morning for NM.

Our final tourist site in NM was Founders Ranch in Edgewood. Home of SASS headquarters and location for End of Trail, the yearly SASS Championship. By the time we decided to go on this circuitous Western tour, registration to shoot the main match was already closed. We had planned two days to visit vendors, watch posses shoot the competition stages and many other activities offered on the premises.

This entire event lasts 10 days. The main shooting event has 650 registered shooters that will shoot 12–18 stages. There are side events that include, Cowboy clays, the Wild Bunch, the Plainsmen, Mounted Shooting and a few others. This is a world championship and contestants come from Canada, Australia, Germany, Netherlands, New Zealand and other countries.

After a day of rest at the campsite, a short drive of 30 miles brought us to Founders Ranch. Dressed in CAS accoutrements, we walked through Main Street and headed to Vendor's Hall–now air conditioned. Classic vendors who had advertized in the Cowboy Chronicle for years, were now real and eager to serve us.

The main drag hosted these vendors" Texas Jacks, Cimarron Firearms, Long Hunter, Taylors, Ruger, SASS Mercantile, Copper Queen Hotel, River Crossing leather and so many more. There were vendors selling clothing, hats, boots, shirts, dresses, cowboy carts, guns and accessories beyond belief. There were also gunsmiths present to repair firearms that broke during the shoots. Some gunsmiths were selling and installing speed kits and other firearm modifications.

We were well equipped with guns and supplies, so we were not looking for major purchases. However, as a special for the championship, there was a vendor that was selling repair kits for most guns used in CAS. These kits were based on the most replaced parts, from wear or breakage. We bought a kit for Ruger New Vaquero, Marlin Cowboy rifle, and a Stoeger double barrel shotgun.

With half of the vendors visited we headed to the shooting range. Another spectator confirmed that they had 650 shooters for the main match and a few hundred more for other shooting events. A lady spectator told us she was following her husband's posse which is one of twelve posses to shoot this group of 4 stages today. With 12–18 main match stages, every posse had several days of shooting. The main match, with side shoots, required some massive organization to get every participant processed in 10 days.

We started observing the posses shooting Stage 1-4. The targets were large and up close. It was quickly obvious that there were 4 classes of shooters: the speed demons, the experienced shooters, the JFF, and the clean shooters.

The speed demons were fast beyond belief. They followed the rules of the stage, but would fire with such speed that you had to see it to believe it could be done. I said to Sue, "that Cowboy can draw and fire 5 shots before I can get on the first target." His five pistol shots sounded like an automatic. "Now watch him shoot the rifle, he has 3 spent cartridges still in the air before the first one hits the ground." Later, we saw a shooter load a double barrel so fast that we thought he had failed to load it, when it went bang, we still could not see the next reload.

I asked Sue if there was a difference between speed demons and gamers. She responded, "oh yes, the speed demons shoot fast–a natural talent with practice acquired techniques. The gamers are a group that take every legal trick to have an edge over shooters–an acquired trait."

As examples, "the speed demon walks quickly to the next staged gun, the gamers run. The speed demons place an empty gun carefully on a table, the gamers throw their empty rifle or shotgun on the table. The speed demons never question the RO or spotters on a miss, the gamers act insulted or disgusted at a miss call. Keep watching, you will pick out the different traits and attitudes."

The experienced shooters were the largest class. They were a joy to watch. They moved in an organized fashion, were quick but accurate shooters, and their entire demeanor expressed a sophisticated and well practiced group of Cowboy Shooters. I said to Sue, "your shooting abilities place you in this category."

The smallest class was the JFF group. Sue said, "although this is a common group in our small clubs, that is not the case here. Guess, if you spend the money, you want to compete in some fashion."

The clean shoot group was larger than we anticipated. I said, "I guess I can understand why some shooters are going for the clean shoot. I see the elderly, those with disabilities, the visually impaired, new shooters of all ages, young shooters, serious shooters of all ages and accuracy buffs. I am certain that an award from the National Championship, that attests to no misses in +-400 rounds and no procedurals in all stages, is held in high regards." I remembered Sue's Texas saying, "any job well done deserves respect!"

That being a full day, we returned to the camper and prepared a list of things we wanted to do tomorrow.

The next day at Founders Ranch was even more enlightening. On our walk from the parking area to Main Street, we stopped at the new Cowboy Chapel. This was one of the newest addition to the ranch, and had been paid for by private donations.

Arriving on Main Street, we saw the stagecoach go by. A brand new reproduction of the 1800's style stagecoach, under the control of a 4–Up team of full size horses. We obviously took a ride throughout the ranch and experienced the suspension–giving us a glimpse of the comfort being on an Old Western trail.

We then visited the main tent, site for dinners, entertainment, dancing, and awards. Thereafter, we finished visiting the vendors. We then went to see a side match–the Wild Bunch. Sue explained, "this is a more modern version of Cowboy Shooting, representing the early 1900's, during the era of "Butch Cassidy and the Sundance Kid." These shooters shoot a 1911 semiautomatic pistol in a 45 ACP caliber, a pump shotgun with an external hammer, and a lever rifle in a big bore caliber such as 45 Long Colt."

I added, "I am not sure I am that interested in this type of shooting." Sue added, "this type of shooting is just like the Cowboy Fast Draw we saw at the Bar W Ranch. We do not have these shooting disciplines back home in our local clubs. It becomes totally impractical to gear up with no place to compete."

The last side match we visited was Cowboy Mounted Shooting. Sue said, "this is a shooting and equestrian sport. A competitor on his horse, goes racing between barrels, and poles that have attached balloons. He shoots at balloons with 45 Long Colt blanks, and the hot gases break the balloons."

We watched several contestants. The first ones were a new visual realization. We got use to them, but we were still amazed at the Cowboy's ability to maneuver on a horse at full gallop and still manage to hit the balloons. I said, "this is another of those events, that has to be seen, to appreciate."

For lunch we had a Cowboy BBQ burger. We got to talking to a shooter at our table. His alias was Bo Duffer. We told him that this was our last day visiting NM and we were heading to Durango. He then told us that he lives in a small community outside of Durango.

He invited us to their local range for the next weekend shoot. He said, "we are not a SASS Affiliated club, but we follow SASS rules. We have a great bunch of guys and gals, and we usually get 70 participants at our shoots."

"If you come to the range, to practice shooting at our targets, the clubhouse is locked during the week. We have porta-potties, so bring your shooting gear, and some food and drink. Drop your $5/shooter in the drop box and shoot as long as you wish. I hope to see you Saturday morning."

For the remainder of the day, we went to see how the shooters were doing. We quickly concentrated on the experienced shooter's techniques. I said, "it seems that these experienced shooters all shoot at the same speed and with similar accuracy. What separates the winners from the losers?" Sue quickly answered, "time saving efficiency, since movements on the firing line take energy and time."

"The first example is doing two movements at the same time. As you are holstering a pistol with your right hand, pick up your rifle with your left hand. Now you have saved time in handling one gun, instead of two. As a second example, when you are holstering a pistol with the strong hand, bring the weak hand pistol up to the spot where you will transfer the weak hand pistol to the strong hand. What you saved is the time waiting to bring the weak hand pistol to the transition spot."

"A third example is to choose a movement that takes less time but accomplishes the same result. When you pick up a gun to shoot at an array of five targets, what do you do when you can only see four? Most shooters will move back and forth before they cock their gun. This can take a lot of precious time. The alternative method is to go ahead and cock the gun but only move one foot as you clearly keep the other foot well planted in its original position. Sometimes, just leaning your body, will clear all obstacles. In either case, it is better than stepping around like a cat playing with a strange toy."

"The fourth example is hustling. When you have to travel 10 feet to the next firearm, you can walk and take 5 steps, or you can hustle and take 3 giant steps."

"Now, I just gave you four examples of time saving maneuvers. Let's assume that each one saved 2 seconds.

In this case, you would have saved 8 seconds–enough to win the stage. If you gain similar times at every stage, your final standing will be considerably higher."

"Classes in efficiency movements have been proposed at our annual club meeting. Now that our facades will be built by carpenters, we can schedule these classes, as well as RO1 classes, and others."

Going home I said, "this brings our second base to an end. Next, we are heading to our third base, Durango, Colorado.

CHAPTER 13

On the Road–Durango, CO

The evening before we left for Durango, we started reading Gary McCarthy's book, Mesa Verde Thunder–in anticipation of our visit to this National Park.

The ride to Durango was 225 miles. Sue read the net, "this is a small city with a population of 20,000 and an elevation of 6,500 feet. It lies in the Animas River Valley surrounded by the San Juan Mountains. It was organized in 1880 to serve the mining district. In the past years it became a movie town, where movies were made not only in the city, but also in the surrounding countryside and nearby towns."

"Today, it is a tourist town. Main Street has a plethora of shops, antiques, native jewelry, leather shops, restaurants, hotels, theaters, western bars and products of the area. The buildings all have several levels which serve as apartments for city dwellers. Since Colorado is an 'open carry' state(except Denver), it is common for people to walk around with a holstered cowboy pistol. For those who have a concealed weapon, a permit is needed."

We chose a campsite North of Durango, since our tourist attractions were all located North, East and West of town. Our first day trip was to visit the city of Durango and the Strater Hotel.

Shopping is not my forte, but Sue lives for it. So we walked Main Street from one end to the other and back. Going by the Strater Hotel, we made dinner reservation in the main dining room for this evening. At first we were doing window shopping and moving right along. Then Sue started entering some shops and our traveling speed came to a crawl.

Sue spent much time in jewelry shops, and purchased beautiful western jewelry for upscale events. I bought a few bolo ties for special western events. We found a western wear shop and made several purchases, for casual to upscale western events. To top the western wear, we found an expensive boot shop that sold soft leather boots in half sizes and widths. We both got a perfectly fitted boot with leather soles for dancing–not cheap but a welcome for our aging feet.

We went in two native specialty shops: weaving and pottery. The pottery shop had actual manufacturing and current sales of recent productions. We watched the "turning" of a mud pack to a final product, ready for the oven. Sue chose several items and had them shipped, by special UPS handling, to Jack's house–pottery is not made for a camper.

The weaving shop also had a live demonstration of a weaving machine. Their retail section included all native products to include, rugs, blankets, quilts, table cloths and place-mats. Sue chose, for the camper, some place-mats and a hand made quilt which clearly showed the pattern of hand sewing, on the front and back.

Fortunately, we had paid for secure private parking next to the Strater Hotel, so our purchases were dropped off in the truck. We went back to finish our walk, heard some western music, and entered a western bar. There were locals and tourists dancing a two-step. We took a table, ordered some drinks, and spent a couple of hours dancing the resident dance–the two-step. Eventually, we headed for the Strater.

While at the western bar, Sue read the net on the Strater Hotel. "This is a unique historic hotel with Victorian features of the Old West. Built in 1887 for $70,000, it has endured multiple owners and renovations, but kept the ambience of the late 1800's. We had a 6 PM reservation for dinner in the Diamond Belle dining room.

The place was already packed and so we were herded to the happy hour bar, The Office Spiritorium. A Victorian decor, the bar was a social gathering site for locals and tourists. Daily musical entertainment was provided by local musicians–usually western and country music. It specialized in high class drinks, wine, beer, and a variety of absinthe.

Absinthe was the magic word. I said, "when in Rome etc etc. Let's order some absinthe and get informed." The waitress arrived with a green liquid and explained, "absinthe is an Anise flavored spirit, derived from wormwood flowers and leaves, and mixed with Anise, sweet fennel and other herbs. This drink was outlawed since 1912 because of its hallucinogenic property. Now legal since 2007 because the level of the hallucinogen 'trujone,' is less than 10 ppm. This drink is 130 proof or higher, and can be sweetened by pouring water over a sugar cube in a slotted spoon. The green liquid will now turn cloudy and milky, but sweet."

We had two of these drinks, and we certainly could not handle a third one. Fortunately, we were called to the dining room in a very happy mood.

The Diamond Belle dining room was a world class Victorian masterpiece. There was handcrafted woodwork, period wallpaper, a rustic stamped ceiling, burgundy velour upholstered chairs with matching rug, walnut furniture and antiques. The one thing that will never leave us is the continuous world class ragtime piano players, creating an ambience of the 1800's era.

The waiters and waitresses were costumed as period bartenders and dance hall gals. We noticed several Cowboys wearing their holstered Cowboy guns. Sue commented, "if you put this all together, I feel like I am sitting in a dining room 100 years ago." I added again, "another reason for traveling out West and see the sites in person!"

We both had a premium prime rib dinner. We lingered with coffee, dessert and an after dinner cordial drink. The music was not overbearing but lively, the general conversations were not loud. We were close enough to watch the piano players, and marveled at their talents. The remainder of the customers lingered as we did, and we left only when 50 % of the customers had departed. I commented, "This is going to be a place difficult to forget, and thankfully, this is one place you were allowed to take photographs."

The next day we spent at the camper. We took care of communications and bills that Jack had sent Fed-EX overnight. With ample time, we both read Gary McCarthy's historical fiction, Mesa Verde Thunder, as a primer before our visit to the park.

This book was an unforgettable saga of a nearly forgotten people, the Anasazi. A leader brought his people North to a new home on a mesa. It chronicles the native's lives through hundreds of years, shows their evolution with modern hunting tools, the bow and arrow. It shows their development of planted crops of corn, beans and squash, and the irrigation systems to support these crops. Eventually, they moved to the security of cliff dwellings, and kept the mesas for crops.

The story is intertwined with a modern twist of how one person, in the 1890's, rushed to save the treasures of the Cliff Palace before they were plundered and lost forever.

Arriving at the Mesa Verde National Park, we went to register for the guided tour to the Cliff Palace. We met the ranger at a scenic overlook, which was our first exposure to this wonder of the past. We went down steps to the floor level of the Cliff Palace and entered this massive dwelling–another once in a lifetime event.

The ranger began, "The Anasazi lived on top of the mesa for 600 years, but in the late 1100 AD, they started moving down to structures under overhanging cliffs. This move was for protection from marauding tribes, and harsh winters. It also allowed community formation and ease of living."

As we entered the palace, the ranger continued, "This Cliff Palace was the largest of all cliff dwellings in North America. It faced South to South West for more sun exposure in the winter, was home to 125–150 natives, had 23 Kivas(ceremonial structures), and 100–150 homes."

"The homes were made of sandstone and mortar. The mortar was made of soil, water and ash. The homes were multi stories, with sideways connections for socialization with neighbors. Top stories were accessible through a hole in the ceiling. The entrance doors were small because the Anasazi were a short stature race of +- 5 feet. This square tower, a four level dwelling, was restored to its height of 26 feet."

As we walked about the palace, questions were asked of the ranger. We walked around and could feel the lives of these natives 700 years ago. It was somewhat eerie when you pictured people living in this space so long ago. I said to Sue, "years from now, I will still see us walking about."

At the end of the tour, the ranger added, "in 1300 AD, after years of droughts and social unrest, the Anasazi nation abandoned their cliff homes and moved to Arizona and New Mexico. In 1888 the Cliff Palace was discovered by ranchers and in 1906 Mesa Verde was established as a National Park by President Theodore Roosevelt."

For the last event, we all had to climb a ladder out of the Cliff Palace to reach the top of the mesa, just like the natives did for a hundred years. We then walked about the park another hour visiting landmarks and other dwellings. You could not see it all, since we were told, by another tourist, that some 600 separate dwellings had been documented by the Park Service.

On our way home, we both agreed that reading the book had brought a degree of reality, to generations of native's lives and their surrounding habitat.

After resting at the camper for a few hours, we then went to dinner at the Bar D Ranch. This was a modern version of the classical chuckwagon dinner of the Old West. We had made reservations several days ago and were able to get a ringside table. We arrived early and got in line to buy our tickets for a steak dinner. The arena easily seated 400 plus patrons. Our table was called and we got in line. An attendant handed rolls, another a potato, another a steak, another a vegetable and finally a dessert. We were not an early table, yet our food was hot, especially the steaks.

After the meal, with tables cleaned, the entertainment began. On stage were the Bar D Wranglers. A stage performing quartet with two guitars, a string bass and a fiddle. They sang songs of the Old West, provided western humor, and played western instrumentals. Their specialty were songs from The Sons of the Pioneers. They performed their classic ballad, Tumbling Tumbleweeds, and many jokes were mixed between songs and instrumentals. Sue looked at me and said, "this is a similar presentation to the one we had at the Bar W Ranch. I suspect that this is the way it is at all chuckwagon meals" With great food and entertainment, we headed back to camp.

The next day started as a road trip heading east to Wolf Creek Pass. Sue read on the net, "this is a high mountain pass on the continental divide, elevation 11,000 feet. It is significantly steep on either side, with a 6.8% maximum grade, and a runaway truck ramp on the westbound side."

As we drove upwards, we came onto a well known 900 foot tunnel in the rock. There were several blasting sites to widen the road. We drove right through and turned around in South Fork. The route west was much more impressive since the truck was now in the right lane heading west, with Sue overlooking the cliffs. The real dramatic moment was when we were driving within few feet of a massive cliff's edge. Sue looked out the open window and saw the cliff floor and said, "Wil, this is not time to talk, pay attention to your driving because our lives are in danger." I had to agree there were some breathtaking moments, and I must have been riding my brakes because we could smell the result. Finally, we got through and headed to Pagosa Springs. I said to Sue, "that was the first tourist site that I was glad to leave."

Pagosa Springs, Sue read on the net, "a small town which is the site of the "Mother Spring" that feeds three commercial hot spring soaking locations." We decided to proceed and soak in our first hot spring. The smell of sulphur was foreign to us, but soaking in the rich minerals did seem relaxing. Before we left, we hit the public showers and thoroughly rinsed our designated swimsuits–to be save for our next soaking in the Yellowstone area.

The final stop on our way home was the Chimney Rock National Monument. I read on the net, "in 2012, President Obama proclaimed this 5,000 acre site the nation's 103rd National Monument and the 7th National Monument managed by the US Forest Service. This monument is managed for archeological protection, of 200 ancestral homes and ceremonial structures, of Ancestral Puebloans from the Chaco Clan(mentioned by the tour guide at Mesa Verde and McCarthy's book, Mesa Verde Thunder)."

As we walked in the popular areas of the monument, we saw cliff dwellings similar to the Mesa Verde site. However, we did see a restored Pit House, a classic home for land and mesa dwellers. The real attraction was the double rock spires, Chimney Rock and Companion Rock. These rocks formed a recognizable landmark for pioneer travelers on the westward trails–the Oregon, Mormon, and California Trails.

We then headed home and prepared for dinner and show at the Henry Strater Theater–reservations made the day we visited the Strater Hotel

Our internet review read as follows, "this theater is one of the oldest and prestigious continually running theater in the US, with 50 years of performances. It was last renovated in 2008. It offers: comedy, melodrama, vaudeville, concerts, music revues, dancing, plays and special holiday events. It also is a great venue for weddings, meetings and private parties."

For our evening, we dressed with elegant western outfits purchased two days ago in Durango. We started with a fine dinner at the Mahogany Grille which was adjacent to the theater. After dinner we were seated according to our reservations. The presentation tonight included two separate short comical plays. The mood and story sequence was supported by the expert ragtime piano player. The music produced a varying volume intensity and musical renditions that fit the different scenes of the play. Best of all, the comedy was natural with many hilarious moments. At the end of the presentation, I said, "considering I'm not a lover of the theater, this play was a pleasure to watch and well worth the admission price." Sue added, "well maybe we should consider becoming theater goers when we return to Missouri!" I quickly came back, "let's not go overboard just because of one play!"

The next day, we decided we needed a rest from tourism. I asked Sue what she wanted to do, and she said, "Let's take advantage of BO Duffer's offer, to go to his range and have a day shooting, as a primer for the weekend shoot coming up." "Yes Mam, lets load up our gear with plenty of ammo, drinks, and lunch."

Since we knew we would be shooting at CAS steel plates, we dressed with proper CAS apparel. When shooting lead bullets at steel plates, 99% of fragments land withing two feet of the target. Rarely a piece of hot lead comes back toward the shooter. The shooter is protected by long pants, long sleeve shirt, a Cowboy hat and safety glasses with side shields.

Arriving at the range, we noticed 6 stages set up with standard CAS targets. The stages had modified facades with firing line tables as well as loading and unloading tables. I shot at one stage and Sue shot at the next stage. That way we did not have to wait for each other to shoot, but we did spend twice the ammo. At lunch we decided to change our shooting strategy. I was going to practice drawing, pistol transfer, shotgun loading and speed rifle shooting. These were the four areas that seemed to prolong my shooting times. Sue also did some training.

By the end of the afternoon, we were shot out. I looked at the leftover ammo and said, "I had brought all the ammo we had loaded, some 2,000 rounds. This can has about 200 rounds left in it." Sue smiled and said, "that's why we had so much fun. Guess one of us will reload 38 ammo tonight, while the other cleans 8 guns and reloads some shotgun shells." I suggested, "let's grab some Chinese takeout on the way home and get to the gun room sooner!"

With country music on the radio, we spent the evening working and talking. It was a happy time for us, we were together and doing a hobby we enjoyed. Sue volunteered, "I am so glad you had the forethought of seeing the need for a bunk room camper. Now we have a gun room with an 8 foot long workbench, just enough room for both of us to work at."

The next day we took a road trip through Telluride and Ouray, with our goal being the Old 100 Gold Mine next to Silverton. We drove on the scenic road, the San Juan Skyway, to Telluride. I read the net, "this town has a population of 2,500 and sits in a box canyon with an elevation of 8,700 feet. It was founded in 1878 around a silver mine that also produced zinc, lead, copper and gold."

"Historically, this town was the site of Butch Cassidy's first bank robbery, where he left with $25,000. Today it is a major skiing area as well as a popular foliage viewing venue."

As we rode through town, we saw many tunnels opening out of the mountainside with tall piles of tailings. The town obviously had a preservation society since many buildings had been renovated. Two famous preserved buildings were the Sheridan Hotel and Opera House.

According to the net, I read, "Ouray, population 1000, is surrounded on three sides by high mountain peaks of 13,000 feet, and is known as the Switzerland of America. This is another town, incorporated in 1876, and developed around a mining industry of 30 mines. Today it is known for some interesting events and locations."

"First, it has preserved 23 major Victorian buildings that are still occupied today. Secondly, it has many sulfur free hot springs. Third, it is known as the ice climbing capital of the world with a free ice park that uses natural frozen waterfalls, some of which are 200 feet tall, and some of which are enhanced by a sprinkler system. Fourth, it has an extensive route system for off-roading 4WD in the mountains."

"Lastly, Ouray lies at the beginning of the Million Dollar Highway, a popular road for motorcyclists because of the road's hairpin curves. It is 25 miles long from Ouray to Silverton. It's called such, because of the ore tailings used in its construction, that contained gold. When constructed in 1880 for horse drawn stagecoaches, the road was valued at 1 million per mile."

"This 25 mile route is considered one of the nation's most scenic and spectacular drive. It crosses three mountain passes, and has many scenic sites such as: Animas Forks Ghost Town, Trimble Spa Hot Springs, Molas Lake, Idarado Mine, Uncompahgre Gorge, and Box Canyon Waterfall."

We bypassed visiting Silverton since this was our next trip via the narrow gauge RR. So we drove directly to the Old 100 Gold Mine.

On route, Sue read, "this is a gold mine operated between 1930–1960. Today, a guided tour provides a look into the miner's lives of yesteryear, their equipment, the miles of tunnels blasted by hand, and their living quarters at the mine." Sue stopped reading and said, "I think we should stop researching this site. It says that there is a guide who will take us in the mine and explain everything we see. I think we may ruin our tour with further investigations."

As we arrived, a small group was gathering by the visitor center. We were greeted by an elderly, talkative and pleasant gentleman. He first requested that everyone wear shoes or sneakers–no sandals or open toe footwear because the ground may have water, mud or loose rocks.

He encouraged everyone to wear long pants and consider an extra shirt or sweater, because the temperature in the mine was 47 degrees. After we were all properly dressed, he handed everyone a hard hat and raincoat. He said, "rocks can fall and there is always water dripping from the tunnel ceilings."

We all got into an electric train of ore cars, and traveled over 5 minutes, some ½ mile in the Galena Mountain. The guide talked the entire trip. He said, "those big pipes on the ground carry electricity into the mine, a benefit since the late 40's. The tunnel is well lit today, but was not the case in the 30's. The track we are on, was the worker's way in and out of the mine, and was used for moving ore out of the mine. Notice, the mineral lining this tunnel is called quartz, and where there is quartz, there is gold."

We finally got to a work site full of mining equipment. The first tool presented was the air drill. "This is the tool that started the process of collecting ore. Several holes were drilled in the wall, in a specific pattern, for the type of rock and the depth of harvest. Then dynamite, with differing fuse lengths, was added to the holes for blasting in the sequence desired–this was knowledge passed down through the years, but also required a basic talent."

"Once the blasting was done, the ore had to be picked up–not by hand shovels. A mucker and slusher were used. The slusher was a rake or a drag shovel, hauled on the floor by a hoist rope, and used to bring the ore closer to the loading site. The mucker was a powered tool that gathered the ore, moved on the track and dumped it's load into an ore wagon, which was also sitting on the same track as the mucker."

Our guide activated the hydraulics and demonstrated the mucker. We saw the mucker plow into a pile of ore sitting on the track, it lifted a bucket-full, traveled back on the track and dumped its bucket-full into the ore wagon. I said, "A very impressive powered maneuver deep in the mountain,"

Someone asked about air quality from drilling and blasting. The guide moved on and answered, "air quality has been a major problem since the 30's. In early years, the miners relied on air shafts to the outside, and closed down levels after dynamite blasts to let the dust settle. In the 50's and 60's, ventilation equipment was used. All these efforts were to prevent pulmonary silicosis."

"These air shafts were also used as hoisting elevators. Each elevator had two levels, the top was a cage for workers to travel the different mine levels, to travel to the bunkhouse/dinner building, or to the main ground level. The elevator's bottom portion was the skip. This box contained ore to be transported between floor levels, especially to the tram level. The tram transported ore to the ground level, where it would be processed in the stamp mill. More on the tram as we exit the mine."

Explaining the last piece of equipment, the guide asked, "does anyone know what this tank on the track is?" Someone answered, "The Honey Wagon." The guide added, "yes, this is the holding tank for human waste, that was taken out by the main tunnel tracks every day."

The tour in the mine lasted one hour. After exiting the mine, the guide made a presentation. "Several trams were constructed over the years to access the different levels of the mine. The third and last tram accessed level 7 of the mine. In early 1900's, workers leveled a rock platform off the cliff and built two buildings, the boarding house and an ore transfer building. The ore was loaded onto the tram buckets, and the weight of the loaded tram buckets travel to the ground by simple gravity. This in turn brought empty buckets back up(or buckets loaded with workers)."

"The Boarding House had two levels. The first level was the kitchen and dining area. The second level held 25 bunk beds for short and long term housing of mine workers. Unfortunately, the tram is not operational, pending repairs." Sue said, "isn't that a shame, I could have traveled over a thousand feet on a cable, to be able to stand on a rock perch several hundred feet above ground!" *I thought, I missed my chance, when the guide asked if anyone wanted to take a ride in the cage and get hoisted upwards. There were no takers–I should have volunteered Sue and gotten that look, the one I don't fare well with.*

Arriving at the visitor center, the guide offered a Q and A session to our group since the next scheduled reservation was still one hour away. The first question was regarding the photographs on the wall depicting a small town at the base of the mountain. The guide said, "at its peak production, there were several building and actually it was a small town providing services to support the mine– which included our own stamping mill. Supplies were brought in from Silverton and then were dispersed through the mining town."

"After the mine closed down, the buildings were demolished and the mining equipment sold. The only buildings left over were the bunkhouse and the tram house. These buildings stand today because of a major renovation project in 1998–done by gutsy carpenters, and bold helicopter pilots."

"Does anyone know how many miles of tunnels are in the mine?" With no answer, the guide said, "five miles." The last question brought tears to our guide's eyes. "You appear in your 70's, did you ever work in this mine or any other mine?" "I was a young teenager when I worked in this mine until its closing. For 30 plus years, I worked in surrounding mines, until each one closed. Every mine closing was a major funeral, an end for communities, and eventually an end to the industry. That's why the area has so many ghost towns."

"By the time I was approaching retirement, the industry was sadly near extinction. I was fortunate to get a retirement job as a guide in this mine. I qualified because of my 10 year employment in The 100, as did the other guides in this mine–we all lived part of our life in this mine."

Someone pushed the issue, "why didn't you just walk away, as most of us do upon retirement?" With tears, he said, "for me, mining was not just a job, it was a profession and a labor of love. I work here one day a week and plan to continue doing so as long as they allow me!"

On our way home, Sue commented, "WOW, that was an enlightening and educational experience, for our first visit in a mine. I was totally mesmerized by this guide, I empathized his feelings and I could not hold back my own tears as I felt his sadness."

After a complete day in traveling through, Telluride and Ouray, to our destination the Old 100 Gold Mime, we decided to take a rest day. We had a late replenishing breakfast and then went grocery shopping. By the afternoon we went looking for horse riding locations. We found, on the net, the one that appealed to us. We were assigned a horse and took off for great trails throughout the San Juan Mountains.

I was assigned a grey spotted gelding, called Spot who was a bit overweight. The guide had said that my horse likes to eat and would stop unexpectedly to chomp-on, even a solitary weed. I was to keep a tight hold on the reins to keep his head up. If I let his head down, he was going to stop to eat, and it would take some severe prodding to rejoin the other horses. As we rode along, Spot kept looking around. I didn't think he was looking at the scenery. I eventually became complacent at the smooth ride and eased up on the reins. Spot's head dived for the ground. It took some pulling on the reins and some flank jabbing to get him going, again. I managed to get into the same wave length as the horse and could predict when he would attempt to balk.

There was one event that I will remember forever. We were climbing some 45 degrees out of a deep gully. I was struggling to hold on to the saddle horn, to avoid sliding off the saddle and horse. Suddenly, Spot's head bent down and he started eating. I was stuck, I could not pull on the reins, and could not kick him. Fortunately the rear guide yelled out, "Spot, get going." The guide's voice was menacing, but Spot just picked up the pace, as if nothing happened.

After a short break with a photo op, the guide said, "there is a flat prairie ahead. If anyone feels comfortable, you can push your horse to a trot or slow gallop until we reach the tree-line. For those of you who don't want to speed up, stay with the rear guide and wait for the mount signal. Horses follow each other, if you try to slowly follow the galloping horses, your horse will automatically start galloping to catch up with the lead horse."

Sue and I galloped to the tree-line and enjoyed the thrill. The remainder of the ride was uneventful with beautiful trails and scenery. Getting back to the camper, we had a peaceful evening with an outside dinner, TV news, reading, and e-mails with photos to friends and family.

Our last trip out of the Durango base, was the railroad excursion to Silverton. We were early to board, so we visited the Roundhouse Museum. Our research revealed that this routing building was built in 1989 with 15 stalls. It burned down and was rebuilt in 1998 using 8 stalls of the original 15.

Sue read from the internet, "The museum covers 12,000 square feet, and includes these displays: antique trucks and tractors, a covered wagon, a full size locomotive steam engine, vintage coaches, locomotive tools, and railroad cars of the 1880's."

As we walked around, two items got most of our attention. A locomotive cab was explored. We sat in the engineer's and fireman's seat, handled the different levers, examined the gauges and other workable tools. The other item was a family car from the 1880's which had been renovated in 2001.

Eventually, we boarded the train for our 3+ hour trip to Silverton. I read on the net, "this railroad was opened in 1882, and was originally built to haul gold and silver ore out of the San Juan Mountain mines. The trip back to Silverton was loaded with workers returning to the mines and tourists who wanted to see the magnificent scenery."

Sue asked, "why was it built as a narrow gauge railroad?" "Because it could be built quicker with less blasting of the mountainside. Also, a narrow gauge could handle much tighter curves, which occurred frequently in this track of mountains."

"The construction required creating a rock bed out of the rock walls, building trestles over gullies and chasms, and hanging trestles off the rock walls."

Traveling the route, we would alternate between the right and left seats to view the scenery, which was not accessible by highways. The wonder was seeing the trestles built in impossible locations. We were in awe, "how could this be built in the 1880's? The wildlife was abundant, we saw deer, elk, and even saw a grizzly with her cub.

After a long ride, we arrived in Silverton. The first thing we did was to make a shuttle reservation to the Mayflower Mill and a late bus reservation back to Durango.

We had two hours before our trip to the ore mill. We walked the streets and saw a classic western town, preserved and restored from the 1880's. The tourist attractions were plentiful with every shop imaginable. Sue commented, "these shops look similar to the shops in Durango." I said, "yes, but here is one we missed in Durango–Old Tyme Portraits. Let's go in, change in the appropriate clothing, get the photographs mounted in old frames, and we will display them in Missouri." We went in, took the photos and had them shipped to Jack.

We went into the Grand Imperial Hotel and Saloon. The saloon was a revelation of years passed. We could picture this exact room in western movies. The bar was covered with brass, was over 25 feet long, was made of walnut, had a brass foot bar, had brass spittoons, and a liquor covered backdrop with a full length mirror. The tables and chairs were antique items of the 1800's, and the ambience was simply, Old West.

After a beer, we ordered lunch. While drinking our beer, a lady Cowboy showed up on her horse, tied it to the railing and entered the saloon–moving directly to the bar and ordered a beer. As a ranch worker, she carried a Cowboy pistol and was covered with dust. Sue said, "look at her hat band." "What is that?" "It's a rattlesnake skin!"

Shortly thereafter, several Cowboys arrived, wearing their trail dust and Cowboy guns on their hips. By the time lunch arrived, we were having beans and salt pork amidst Cowboy ranch hands.

After lunch, Sue read from the net. "Silverton, population 700 from a peak population of 5,000 in 1880's. Elevation 9,000 feet. A former mining town, today it is a tourist center providing shops, rafting, hiking, hunting, fishing, 4WD off road trails, and snow sports."

Skiing is a major industry. Despite its 400 inches of snow, the ski trails are not groomed and there are no clear-cut runs. This is expert or advanced skiing only. Helicopters will provide 6 drops per day to incredible locations–with or without guides.

Using the shuttle, we arrived at the Mayflower Mill. Since this was a self guided tour, we started with the introductory movie which showed how the process was done. Before we started the tour, we checked the internet for more information. Sue read, "built in 1929 to recover gold and other metals from the Mayflower Mine. The ore was brought to the mine by aerial tramway. After crushing the ore, the metals were separated by gravity and the new flotation technique. As an average, the ore comprised 5% metals and 95% waste rock(tailings)."

The tour included: heavy steel ball mills, machine shop, tram station, ore bins, floatation cells, recovery systems, and an assay office. Because the mill was intact and functional, you were allowed to turn some of the machines to see how they worked. Self guided tours require reading many display directions. We read most of the important ones, but had to leave as the shuttle arrived.

The 50 mile trip back to Durango was a short scenic one.

The next day was initially planned as a rest day. When we realized that we were heading to Wyoming in two days, we changed the rest day to a household workday. I washed the truck and camper. Sue did the laundry, vacuumed the camper and other cleaning duties. When we were both done, we did groceries to restock the camper. That evening, we visited with our neighbors who had just arrived from South Dakota and were planning their week long visit in Durango. We told them where we visited all week. When they asked us what place was most memorable, Sue said Mesa Verde–Cliff Palace, and I said the Old 100 Gold Mine. To my surprise, they weren't even planning to go to the 100 Gold Mime. It did not take long for me to convince them otherwise. In return, they mentioned places to visit in Wyoming and South Dakota.

The next day we were on the road early to our CAS event. On arrival we went to the clubhouse to register. BO Duffer was the registrar. He spotted us as we entered the clubhouse and welcomed us to their shoot. We were placed on BO's posse. BO encouraged us to check out the local vendors, get some breakfast from the cook-wagon, and review the stages. He said, "I will send all my posse members out to introduce themselves to you as they arrive. I said, "how will they recognize us?" He smiled and said, "I'll tell them to look for the young tall blonde." Sue came back with, "but BO I am 60 years old!" "Well Mam, around here, as you will notice, that is real young!"

At the breakfast wagon, we had an egg/bacon sandwich with coffee. Several of BO's posse came to introduce themselves. We both felt good about this method of making visitors welcomed. We then walked the 7 stages scheduled today. The first six were standard SASS orientation with a few oddities. The last stage was that darn Texas Star.

While waiting for the obligatory meeting, we managed to meet the remainder of our posse. It was certainly an older crowd. There were no ladies on our posse except for Sue, although there were several on the other posses. Anticipating some comment from Sue, I headed it off by saying, "there is a good and a bad side to this arrangement. The bad side is that you are not going to meet any other lady. The good side is that you are not going to tick any off by your high end shooting ability!" And of course, I got that look, the one I don't fare well with.

The meeting started off with the Pledge of Allegiance. Rules were standard, there were few announcements, except for the Texas Star. The master RO2 said, "We finally purchased the darn thing. Your RO1 will demonstrate how to shoot it and how not to shoot it. At the end of the competition, I will stay and reload the thing for anyone who wants to practice, as long as it takes or till dark."

The random shooting order was called. I was shooter #9 and Sue was shooter #12 out of 15 shooters. The shooting began, it was quickly determined that there were good shooters like Sue and average shooters like me. There were no gamers, speed demons or JFF in our posse. People were shooting for pleasure and competition.

It was a smooth shooting event for the first three stages, then we came on the Texas Star. The RO1 did a good job of explaining the dynamics of gravity. Then the RO1 loaded his rifle and shot the 10 and 2 o'clock plate with little rotation, then the 8 and 4 o'clock plate with the same result, and last the still 6 o'clock plate. Many comments ridiculed the potential nightmare. Everyone was saying it was an easy shoot.

Then the RO1 demonstrated the bad moves. He shot the 10 o'clock plate but missed, intentionally, the 2 o'clock plate. Everyone saw some serious rocking and extra time for the wheel to settle. After loading the Star, he shot the 10 o'clock plate followed by the 8 o'clock plate. The wheel made two full turns before rocking into a still position. The RO summarized by saying, 10–2,8–4, 6, or good luck chasing the plates."

The shooters were having beginner problems. They hesitated in shooting the second balancing plate and found it a moving target. Their best times were 20 to 50 seconds. I shot it in 12 seconds with a loud applause and whistling. Sue shot it in 7 seconds, with a long period of silence, followed by many expletives. Lunch was ready and everyone laughed all the way to the lunch wagon.

Lunch consisted of a half, plain or BBQ chicken, over a wood fire, with macaroni or potato salad and a drink– for $8. After lunch we had three more stages, but these were not standard SASS stages. The fun was starting.

The first stage had all knockdowns. 10 pistol, 10 rifle and 4 shotgun. The catch, only one shot per target. It either fell down or it was a miss. Sue and I knew we had to hit them high with the pistol and rifle. We had those hot field loads for the shotgun. We also used the hot rifle ammo in our pistols, for a legal advantage. When the shooting started, the local shooters had an advantage, they had shot this stage before and they were using very, very, very hot loads. Yet we did well, Sue got 23 down and I got 20 down, with our relatively soft loads. In the future, we would consider carrying some very hot loads, when faced with a single shot requirement at pistol or rifle knockdowns.

The second stage was a nightmarish sequence to commit to memory. The only thing that saved us was our shooter's position of #9 and #12. The third and last stage was an exercise in reloading on the firing line. The pistol was 5 rounds with a reload of one round for each pistol, using the shoot one–reload one, technique. The rifle was 2 rounds reloaded after the first 10 rounds. The rifle and pistol reloads could be accessed from the pant's back pocket. The shotgun shells, all four, had to come from one of the pants front pockets. This meant that the gun-belt had to be lifted off the pocket entrance before stepping to the firing line, and hope the belt did not sneak down. Ladies were given a purse if they did not have pockets on their pants or dresses. This last stage was to point out that in a gunfight, reloads can be necessary, and the reloads are not always easily accessible. Our score times were high, but the same for everyone.

This last stage revealed a new accessory. Some shooters added a second set of suspenders, attached to the gun-belt. This prevented the belt from sliding over the pocket entrance. Sue pointed out, "portly shooters wear this extra set of suspenders at all times, to keep their rig up when they lift their arms up to shoot their rifle."

At the awards ceremony, out of 75 shooters, Sue took 4th place in Ladies Senior and I took 6th place in Mens Senior. After saying thank you and goodbyes, we loaded our gear and headed home. I reminded Sue that we were heading to Wyoming tomorrow for our 4th base of operations–some 688 miles to Cody.

CHAPTER 14

On the Road–Cody, WY

That evening we started talking about Wyoming and Cody. Sue asked, "why are we heading to Cody?" "Because it is a nice small city with access to Yellowstone National Park. It also is the site of the Buffalo Bill Museum and other points of interest."

"So tell me about Wyoming." According to my reading, "Wyoming is a large state with a low population. It is the size of England but has the population of Louisville Kentucky. The census bureau calls it the most uninhabited state in the union. The bulk of the population is in its few cities, Cheyenne, Casper, Laramie, Cody, Jackson and Sheridan to name a few. The state has large areas of high plains and high mountain deserts in the range of 3–6,000 feet, which are thinly populated."

"Good info, now what about Cody?" "Cody is a city with a population of 10,000 at an elevation of 5,000 feet. It was established in 1890 by Buffalo Bill Cody as the town developed around his museum, and as an access to

Yellowstone's East Entrance. Today it is a major tourist center and easy access to the East Entrance."

"It's also known for its rodeos. They hold a nightly amateur rodeo during the summer months. Cody also hosts the rodeo championship, the Cody Stampede Rodeo, held every 4th of July. Cody has become: a major outdoor recreation venue, a manufacturing center of western furniture, a small gypsum mining operation, and major housing for visitors to the 5th most visited National Park, Yellowstone."

That night, we started reading Gary McCarthy's historical fiction, Yellowstone Thunder. "It's the story of a California woman, a fortune seeker and a mountain man, who get to know the gentle Sheep-eater and Nez Perce Indians. It's history interwoven with fascinating characters."

Looking at the map, we noted that it was 688 miles to Cody. We decided to break up the trip. Our first day we would travel 428 miles to Rawlins, and the second day we would have 260 miles to Cody.

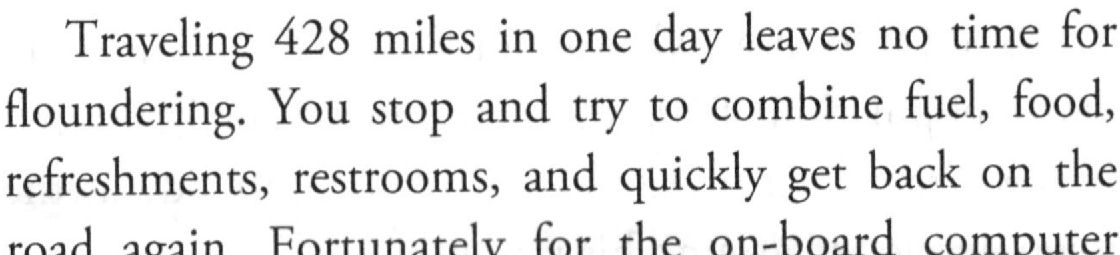

Traveling 428 miles in one day leaves no time for floundering. You stop and try to combine fuel, food, refreshments, restrooms, and quickly get back on the road again. Fortunately for the on-board computer and iPhones, we were able to maintain some internet connection. We prepared ourselves for our visit to Yellowstone.

I started, "Yellowstone was established in 1870 as the first National Park. It covers 3,500 square miles or 2.2 million acres. It lies over a volcanic hot spot, but the last eruption was 600,000 years ago. In linear miles, it measures 63 miles North to South and 54 miles East to West. As previously mentioned, it is the 5th most visited of our National Parks."

"It includes canyons, geysers, hot springs, mud pots and it's the number one photographing location for animals, to include: bison, elk, deer, coyotes, bears, wolves, sheep, antelope and bald eagles. The trees are douglas fir, spruce and lodgepole pines."

"The most popular tourist attractions are: the Old Faithful Geyser for its predictable eruptions, and the Hayden Valley for viewing animals. All viewing areas have an easily accessible boardwalk. It is of note that the safe distance to bison is 25 yards, and 100 yards for bears."

"My research reveals that we will concentrate our visit by traveling the Grand Loop Road. This road is centrally located, and is in the shape of a figure 8. The southern loop is called the Lower Loop and the northern loop is called the Upper Loop. This Grand Loop covers 140 total miles and each loop takes 4 hours, depending on traffic and how many sites you stop to visit." We will spend a full day on each loop, since we will stop and visit at selected sites.

We finally arrived in Rawlins for the night. We fueled up and found a campground. After dinner we finished the Yellowstone Thunder historical fiction and retired early. We were on the road by early AM. The short drive to Cody brought us early enough to set up the camper and head for downtown. We walked the main street and found a family restaurant that was our spot for dinner. This was an obvious local gathering place, with a diner type bar, open tables and private booths. A fair priced home cooked meal was our attraction for further visits

After dinner, we walked right into a gunfight re-enactment in front of the Irma Hotel. We had seen re-enactments before with a large crowd in attendance. This was different, two Cowboys came out of the Silver Saddle Saloon, yelling at each other, stepping in the middle of the main street, drawing and shooting. Each shooter shot once, but one shot a second time, to put the opponent down. The street was full of that acrid smoke from black powder, and of course the sheriff showed up in a timely fashion. The sudden shock of the event, without any warning, was realistic of the Old West ways.

On our walk home, Sue admitted, "when those two Cowboys came out shouting at each other, I honestly thought nothing would come of it. Suddenly the shooting started and I just about jumped out of my britches. I was about to get you to go help the downed Cowboy when I saw you smile, and realized that I had just witnessed a perfectly well staged gunfight." "I agree, it's good that you didn't jump out of your britches, but both your feet came off the ground. That's why I was smiling–boy they got you good, heh!"

The next morning we woke up to pouring rain with the forecast of rain most of the day. Thanks for an indoor tourist site, we headed to the Buffalo Bill Museum. We researched the museum on the net before visiting. "The museum opened in 1927 and then moved to its current site in 1969."

"The museum focuses on the life and times of Buffalo Bill from 1846–1917. Known as a military scout during Indian wars, Pony Express rider, Civil War veteran, medal of honor recipient, hunting guide, buffalo hunter, actor and showman. He became known as the era communicator of the enduring spirit of the Old West."

"The museum is actually made up of 5 separate museums:

1. "Buffalo Bill Museum, life and times with special attention to the Wild West Show.
2. Cody Firearms Museum. Large collection of firearms from around the world.

3. Draper Museum. Wildlife and geology of the state.
4. Plains Indians Museum. Culture of the prairie's first inhabitants.
5. Whitney Galley of Western Art. Famous artists provide a continuum of the Wild West theme."

Shortly after entering the museum and seeing its vastness, Sue said, "how is this museum financially sustained?" I answered, "admission fees and several charity events–invitational shooting events of trap, skeet, and sporting clays. They also have a large charity ball, and support from several philanthropists and private donations."

Our interests centered on the Plains Indians and Buffalo Bill Museum. We spend several hours walking about just to see the exhibits, as small as a bullet to a Conestoga wagon. Eventually we decided to go to lunch at that family restaurant, during which time we would research the Buffalo Bill Wild West Show–our next planned inspection of the memorabilia at the Buffalo Bill Museum.

Waiting for lunch, I read, "the show opened in 1883 in Omaha, Nebraska. It was the opening of the golden age of outdoor shows. Buffalo Bill was a master in the use of the press, poster advertising and parades, as well as giving his shows a dramatic narrative structure."

"His shows covered historical reenactments to include: the Pony Express riders, wagon trains, stagecoach attacks, gunfights, battle scenes with Indians and others. It also included skilled exhibitions in pistol/rifle shooting, wing shooting, roping, riding and survival skills. The most famous of the reenactments was Custer's Last Stand."

"The show's procedures included an orator booming the script from an elevated platform. The Cowboy Band played mood setting music. The actors were Cowboys, Indians and civilians. Famous participants were, Annie Oakley exhibition shooter, Calamity Jane, Sitting Bull, Geronimo, and Chief Joseph. Unfortunately, the Indian's lifestyles were exposed to the world and stereotyped as mounted warriors–the last impediment to civilization."

"The show prospered and its popularity peaked with a performance at the Chicago World's Fair with a crowd of 18,000. The show went to Europe eight times between 1887–1906. It opened in London, giving Queen Victoria and her subjects, their first look at the American Cowboys and Indians. Queen Victoria was known to return for a second performance, before the show moved on to amaze audiences all over Europe."

As lunch arrived, Sue asked, "how did Buffalo Bill get his name?" I read, "Buffalo Bill was a professional buffalo hunter who supplied, by contract, meat for the Kansas Pacific Railroad while building the Transcontinental Railroad. His record harvest was 4,000 plus buffalo shot in 18 months. There was another buffalo hunter by the name of William Comstock, who vied for the name

'Buffalo.' The railroad set up an 8 hour competition to determine the winner of $500 and the coveted name of 'Buffalo.' Bill Cody shot 69 buffalo and Bill Comstock shot 46–and that's how it all happened."

After lunch, Sue read an interesting side story about the show. "The logistics of providing such a massive outdoor attraction included"

1. "Payroll for 500 cast and actors.
2. Three meals a day for 500 people.
3. Generating its own electricity.
4. Maintain its own fire department.
5. Tents or railroad cars as living quarters for 500 participants.
6. Moving the show required two trains of 50 cars each.
7. Feeding and moving 100 horses and 30 buffalo.
8. Setting up a grandstand and canvas cover for 20,000 ticket holders."

Sue added, "thanks to the railroad, the show established a record in 1899. It covered 11,000 miles in 200 days, and gave 341 performances in 132 cities/towns."

And last, Sue read, "the show started fading by WWI, because of motion pictures, baseball, football, rodeos and the Old West was losing its exotic nature. The show finally ended in 1917 along with Buffalo Bill's death. Of note, 18,000 people attended his funeral!"

Upon our return to the museum, we spent several hours reading the captions, plaques and viewing the many photographs and posters. We saw photos of Sitting Bull, Geronimo, Chief Joseph, Annie Oakley and too many to mention. We saw photographs of the many historical reenactments, and a few videos made by the old and modern movie world. It was clear, reviewing the internet before visiting the exhibits, made all the difference in the world in appreciating this museum."

The next morning, with good weather, we left early for Yellowstone. We traveled 50 miles west to the park's East Entrance, and then traveled another 25 miles to reach the Lower Loop at Fishing Bridge.

Sue had prepared a presentation at our last internet connection and said, "this location offers fishing off the bridge, a visitor center, a café and a gas station." We picked up a map of the Grand Loop road, and we drove through heading southwest to Lake Village, "this is a Yellowstone Lake shoreline hub with lodging and cafes. The next location is Bridge Bay, where you could put a boat in Yellowstone Lake or join a fishing guide. Yellowstone Lake is the largest high-altitude lake in the continent at 7,700 feet and it's an anglers paradise. The last site located on the lake is West Thumb with its own geyser basin."

We drove through those four locations and heading west, we finally arrived at the Old Faithful geyser and Inn. This was the first site we stopped to visit. Sue read, "This area is the best thermal zone in the park. It has 150 geysers in one square mile, including Old Faithful."

Old Faithful is the most popular attraction in the park. Sue read, "This geyser erupts regularly and even predictably. It erupts every 60 to 110 minutes with an average of 74 minutes. Their predictions are fairly accurate, and are based on knowing the length of the last eruption and other factors. Eruptions last between 1.5–5.0 minutes and can be as high as 100–180 feet. A 1.5 minute eruption yields 3,700 gallons, and a 5 minute eruption yields 8,400 gallons of water. The water temperature of an eruption is 204° F(water boils at 212° F)."

We walked to the visitor center and we were told that the next eruption was predicted in 30 minutes. People were walking around along the boardwalk. We saw mud pots popping and fumaroles ejecting steam. The earth felt warm and it was clear that we were standing on an active thermal area.

Eventually, we sat on the circular bench around the Old Faithful geyser. The eruption was within 3 minutes of the predicted time. The eruption was +-75 feet and lasted 2.5 minutes. Sue's camera followed the entire eruption as a full video, and I took photos with my phone.

After viewing the eruption, we stayed in the area and moved to the Old Faithful Inn. Sue read, "this is a massive log hotel built in 1903. It measures 700 ft. long, has 300 rooms, and is 7 stories high. A historic landmark, it's actually the largest log structure in the world, and the most requested lodging in the park."

We stopped at the Inn. As we walked in the hotel lobby, we were faced with a massive and towering gathering area. There were etched glass panels, large timber columns, western hickory furniture, a massive multi-face stone fireplace, and a unique copper/steel clock. Surrounding the lobby were restaurants, lounging areas, a snack bar and a gift shop. We had a light lunch in the snack bar and then moved on.

Moving north along the Lower Loop, the first site we came upon was the Midway Geyser Basin. Sue suggested, "let's do a quick stop to view the Excelsior Geyser, with its 200–300 foot crater, and the Grand Prismatic Spring. This hot spring spans 370 feet wide and is a good photo opportunity because of the water's hues of blue, green, orange and gold colors."

Still heading north, we drove through the next three sites without stopping–the Lower Geyser Basin, the Madison Area, and the Artist Paint Pots. We then arrived at the two hubs that connect the Lower and Upper Loops. We saved them for tomorrow and headed to Hayden Valley–our second most preferred tourist site.

The valley was a massive flat, open, and green area with a river. Buffalo were everywhere, possibly 800 animals. The buffalo were so close to the road that they slowed down traffic, as several animals were walking on the paved road. You could stand in one spot and get photos of every size buffalo. The best shots were of the calves, now a few months old, they were a lively and playful bunch.

As we were watching, suddenly there was a ruckus, and buffaloes were gathering in a tight small circle with bulls on the outside and cows/calves inside. The bulls were grunting, pounding the earth and all looking in one direction. That is when we saw a pack of coyotes running along the tree-line. Using binoculars, one person suggested that they were grey wolves. In any event, the pack disappeared in the trees. Sue immediately asked, "what is this about wolves in the park?" I answered, "41 wolves were introduced in the mid 90's as an effort to provide a balance of nature. The experiment had been met with mixed feelings. Today, the wolves have prospered and have grown to numbers, that seem to control the balance the biologists were looking for!"

That afternoon, we did not see any other animals other than buffalo. I added, "tomorrow we will pass through this valley in the early morning and may see other types of animals. Because we are in mid summer, we have missed the early spring calving season, when predators would roam this valley looking for an easy meal–predators such as bears, coyotes and wolves."

We then headed home for an evening's rest. In early morning, we were back on the road to Yellowstone. We again landed at Fishing Bridge but this time we headed north to the Upper Loop. The first place we came upon was Hayden Valley again. This time there was a mix of animals. We saw groups of Big Horn Sheep and Pronghorn Antelope. Sue had to use her telephoto lens on a tripod to capture these animals, since they were at least 100 yards from the road.

Moving on, the next site was the Grand Canyon of the Yellowstone. We stopped to visit the famous waterfalls. Sue read, "The Yellowstone River emerges from the Yellowstone Lake and flows in the Hayden Valley. It then forms two waterfalls as it plunges into the Grand Canyon of the Yellowstone, a steep 20 mile long gorge."

Sue added, "the boardwalk brings us to the Upper Falls which is 109 feet high. A short walk brings us to the Lower Falls where the river, with a deafening roar, plunges 308 feet–twice as high as Niagara Falls."

It was a short walk to both falls. The photo-op was amazing. The walls of the rock revealed shimmering red and yellow tones. A site worth seeing.

Heading north, we came upon Canyon Village, a hub town that is the eastern hub between the Upper and Lower Loops. We drove through to Dunraven Pass, which was listed as an elevation of 8,900, and was the trail head access to Mt. Washburn.

Our next stop was when we started heading west at the upper part of the Upper Loop–Roosevelt Tower. Sue interjected, "the figure of eight map showing the sites along both loops has been very useful. Roosevelt Tower is home to the rustic lodge built in 1920, the area has a waterfall, petrified tree and a fossil forest."

We stopped, saw the lodge, waterfall, petrified tree and took extra time to visit Specimen Ridge, a fossil site.

Our last stop on the Upper Loop road was the most western site at Mammoth Hot Springs. Sue read, "a hot spring that deposits "travertine" a calcareous rock. The hot water dissolves calcium carbonate in the limestone, forming the constantly evolving white rock, travertine, in terraces. A popular site is Minerva Terrace."

We stopped, walked to the sites and viewed another marvel of nature. Photos were taken. We then headed south to Norris, the western hub between the two loops. Sue added, "Norris has its own geyser basin. It is one of the oldest, hottest, and tallest geyser in the park." We drove east to Canyon Village, the eastern hub of the loops, and had lunch.

After lunch, we stopped at Hayden Valley for the third time. Again plenty of buffalo, but isolated and near a tree-line was a nice herd of elk. Sue said, "what is this, they are all bulls with full antler racks?" *I thought of saying something off the cuff, about sexual preferences, but I held back because I knew I would get that look–the one I don't fare well with.* So I said, "my reading reveals that elk possess a strange biological process called 'mimicry." This means that female calves exposed to males with antlers, have the ability to produce antlers as well. So a high percentage of elk have antlers. Since antler production is based of blood levels of testosterone, it is not clear why this happens. Even more strange is the fact that all buffalo have horns. This is one subject we can research, during our evenings at the camper–with WI-Fi."

This finished our visit to Yellowstone. I added, "Grand Canyon was a wonder of the world, Mesa Verde was a historical relic, and now Yellowstone was another natural phenomenon, geysers. The park's special feature is the animals–separating it from other National Parks!"

We had two more days of tourist sites to see. Because the weather forecast was excellent for tomorrow, we headed to Thermopolis. I read, "this is a hot springs State Park, it is known to have hot water cascading down colorful terraces along the Big Horn River. The public pool with its 104 degree water was given to Wyoming in 1896 by the Shoshone and Arapaho Tribes with the provision that it remains free to the public."

We had brought our sulfur smelling swimsuits and changed in the visitor center. We soaked and smelled sulfur for hours, followed by a cleansing shower and permanent disposal of those stinking swimsuits.

When preparing to leave, Sue mentions, "dinosaur fossils were found in 1993 at the Warm Springs Ranch. Today a Dinosaur Center has been built. It is a natural science museum with several dinosaurs displayed, but it also has ongoing excavations going on, where the public can schedule a volunteer work day?" Sue looked at me and I just gave her that look, the one she knew she would not fare well with.

We arrived in Cody by lunch time and had lunch at the camper. After lunch we headed for an afternoon visit at Old Trail Town. I read, "In 1895, Buffalo Bill Cody laid out the plans for the original Cody on this site. By 1901, the town had started to decline and eventually Cody was moved to its present site, and the town became an eventual ghost town."

"Today, it is a mixture of old untouched and restored buildings. It was built to its present status as an attempt to preserve historical buildings and artifacts. Artifacts and buildings came from within 150 miles of Wyoming and Montana. Buildings were disassembled and reassembled in Cody. In 1967 this present site opened to tourism."

As we walked through town, we saw a saloon frequented by Butch Cassidy and his gang. We saw cabins that served as hideouts for historical outlaws such as Butch Cassidy, Sundance Kid, and Kid Curey.

One cabin was for the known military scout, Curley, who had participated in Custer's Last Stand.

Of more interests, we saw many buildings that made up a small western town in the late 1800's. There was a well restored general mercantile that showed the set up of the times, a large shelved counter plus shelves behind the owner with groceries and expensive items, allowing him to serve the customers. A gathering area with a large barrel of soda crackers and a pot belly stove. Larger items and clothing were placed on tables in the open portion of the store.

There were so many buildings, but the problem was that we could not tell if these buildings were original on site or brought in from afar.

The one thing that was overdone, the main street was overloaded and cluttered with the wagons of the times. Too many to appreciate. It would have been better to have one example of each classic wagon with a caption or plaque explaining its function of the times. The duplicate wagons could have been placed in a separate lot for viewing. This was a quick visit, like any self guided tour, it would have been enhanced by a tour guide.

That evening we went to the Irma Hotel for dinner. Sue read from the net, "built in 1902 by Buffalo Bill and named after his daughter, Irma. Buffalo Bill kept two suites and an office for himself. You can stay in his suite, now 100 years later. Wild West tryouts were held in a lot next door. European royalty stayed at the hotel when on their hunting trips. Hotel additions were constructed in 1929 and 1976."

Arriving early, we went in the Silver Saddle Saloon for drinks. We finally saw the famous cherry bar donated by Queen Victoria in 1900. This gift was the Queen's thank-you to Buffalo Bill for bringing his Wild West Show to Europe. Incidentally, it cost $100,000 to build in 1900, today it is worth over one million. As we were waiting, the famous Wild Bill Hickock character/persona was sitting by himself. He left to go outside and ended up in an unscheduled gunfight with an outlaw. This attracted a crowd, and a full reenactment followed.

Eventually, we were escorted to the dining room. A fine Victorian decor similar to the Slater Hotel in Durango. Their specialty was prime rib like the Slater Hotel, but there were no Cowboys with guns, or ragtime piano players. The meal was prepared to perfection.

The next day, after another replenishing breakfast, we headed to Montana, at Red Lodge. While traveling, I read, "in 1851, the area was ceded to the Crow Nation by the US Government. When coal and gold were discovered, a new treaty in 1882 allowed the Crow land to be settled.

As mines closed in the 30's, the area was known in post depression times, as a major boot legged liquor producing town. The area was redeveloped in 1980 for historic and cultural tourism."

"Today, it is a quaint, historic mountain town with a population of 2,500 and real western hospitality. The area is also known for Winter Carnivals, skiing, music/ songwriter festivals and championship rodeos."

We drove through town, walked along Main Street, and had lunch at a downtown café. After a light lunch, we got in the truck and went to the Beartooth Highway. I said, "this is a highway built in 1937 as a major route from Red Lodge to Yellowstone's North Entrance. On TV, Charles Curalt called this road the most beautiful drive in America."

As we drove along, there were certainly scenic views of grandeur. It had steep zigzags and switchbacks in one of Wyoming's highest paved road. We drove as far as Beartooth Pass, elevation 11,000 feet, and stopped at the peak's plateau to view the most spectacular panoramas.

That ended our Cody visit, now we moved on to South Dakota.

CHAPTER 15

On the Road–Hill City, SD

The evening before our departure, we started watching the HBO series, Deadwood. The three season production required getting use to the Old West dialect and accent. There was violence and expletives that also needed some familiarity. However, it was a great production, that depicted the life of settlers in an early mining town–during the Dakota's pre statehood years. The story revolved around characters such as Wild Bill Hickok, Seth Bullock, Calamity Jane, Charlie Utter, and Al Swearengen. It includes historical truths and fictional elements.

We traveled the 375 miles to Hill City in one day. During our trip we got a phone call from Ranger Rooster, our club president. He wondered if we could send him some more photographs of Cowboy storefront facades. He said that they had seven facades already built but were at a standstill in designing the last three facades. I agreed to visit a local CAS club tomorrow and send him some more photos.

Before getting to our destination, Sue asked, "why did you choose Hill City and what is our major attraction?" I answered, "Hill City is a small community that is centrally located as a base of operation. Our major attractions are: Mount Rushmore National Monument, Crazy Horse Memorial, Custer State Park, Deadwood, the Badlands National Park, Wall, Keystone and others."

"Hill City, population +- 1,000, was started in the 1880's around a tin mining area. Today it is a tourist and timber area. Tourism developed because of Mount Rushmore. The timber industry, with a local mill, is the major employer in the area."

Our campsite had full hookups and several log cabins for tourists traveling by car. We watched more Deadwood DVD's that night and headed out the next morning for a local CAS club, which had 10 full facades. We were allowed to take photographs, which we sent by e-mail to Ranger Rooster.

Our first tourist excursion was to Custer State Park. We came south to the visitor center using the eastern portion of the Wildlife Loop Road. At the visitor center we watched a movie and were informed that there was a herd of +- 400 buffalo on the western portion of the Loop Road. The ranger gave a presentation, "the park covers 70,000 acres and has +- 1400 buffalo that roam free–the second largest herd in the US. Every late September we hold the Buffalo Roundup. Since 1965, we roundup 1,000 animals for culling and vaccination. The Cowboys who do the roundup pay for the privilege of participating in this event. The culled animals are sold at auction as building stock, or for commercial meat supplies. The remainder of the buffalo do well with the park's limited forage. This roundup draws 10,000 tourists each year."

"The second issue is the 'Begging Burrows'. Burrows were once used to haul tourists to Black Elk Peak, now an abandoned attraction. The burrows roam free and clutter the roads, especially around scenic overlooks, panhandling for food."

With this information we headed north along the western portion of the Loop Road. Following a bend in the road, we came beside some 300–400 buffalo. I stopped for Sue to take pictures, she opened the door and said, "I can't get out, there is a buffalo laying down under my door!" She eventually took more pictures than we really needed.

Further down the road we saw Bighorn Sheep and Pronghorn Antelope at a distance. Suddenly we arrived at a scenic area full of burrows. They came up to your car windows waiting for a handout. Sue got out and took more photos–again more than we needed!

We then drove to Custer on our way to Sylvian Lake. Sue read, "Custer, population +-2,000, was established in 1874 after the expedition, lead by Lt. Colonel G. A. Custer, found gold and started the Black Hills Gold Rush. The town was nearly abandoned in 1876 when gold was found in Deadwood, the population went down to 14 residents, yet it survived. The town claims to have the widest Main Street in the US–made for a team of oxen, pulling a wagon, to turn completely around. The economy today is tourism, mining of precious metals and industrial minerals, and timber/lumber industry."

As we drove through, the Main Street certainly was the widest we had ever seen. Some 7 miles later, we arrived a Sylvian Lake. Sue read, "this lake was created in 1881 when a dam was built on the Sunday Gulch Creek. Today, with a background of massive rock formations, we have a crystal clear lake known as the Crown Jewel of Custer State Park. These rocks are in the form of pillars, needles, and stacked round and eroded rocks. The rock landscape is reflected in the blue waters creating a photographic mirror image. This is truly a hobbyist's photographic paradise. The lake offers swimming, non powered boats, and a popular destination for weddings."

We walked the path on the lake's shore, with rock formations in the background, and many breathtaking views. We also walked a short path between the rocks and the lake. Sue again took more pictures than we needed. At the end of the walk we stood on the dam overlooking the Sunday Gulch Creek.

After a full and interesting day, we went home for the evening. We watched a few more Deadwood DVD's and prepared for our big day tomorrow, Mount Rushmore Monument and Crazy Horse Memorial.

I read, "Mount Rushmore National Monument was carved in granite and sculpted between 1927 and 1941 by Gutzon Borglund and 400 workers. A government funded project, at a cost of 1 million, some 400,000 tons of rock were removed from the mountain to create four 60 foot sculptured presidential heads–George Washington, Thomas Jefferson, Theodore Roosevelt and Abraham Lincoln."

Sue asked, "who chose the Presidents and why?" "Mr. Borglum chose them because of their role in preserving the republic and expanding its territory."

We paid for parking, but entrance was free. Arriving at the visitor center, the first glimpse of the long archway leading to the distant monument, was an unforgettable grandiose sight. We began with a movie and then started the long walk under the arches. Every state had its flag and a plaque along the archway columns. The more we ascended, the closer we got to the monument.

Arriving at its base, we followed a boardwalk next to the massive tailings. The boardwalk offered magnificent closeup views and photo shots. I said to Sue, "this patriotic monument explains why there are 2 million visitors each year. I am proud to be here today and proud to be an American!"

Walking back to the visitor center, we had lunch in the massive dining room and then headed for the Crazy Horse Memorial. We made plans to return this evening for the evening lighting ceremony.

I read on the net, "the Crazy Horse memorial is on private land and supported by the Lakota Sioux Indians. It is being created to commemorate the life of a Native American leader and warrior who, fought against encroaching American settlers on Indian Territory, and fought to preserve the Lakota's traditional way of life."

Reading further, "This is not a federally funded project. It is solely funded by admission fees and private donations. The project started in 1948 and the sculptor, Korzak Kiolkawski died in 1982. His wife and 7 children took over the project and completed the face in 1998. The face is 87 feet high and the eyes are 17 feet wide. When completed the entire sculpture will be 500 feet high and 600 feet wide. It will depict the Lakota warrior riding a horse and pointing into the distance with an extended hand–which symbolizes the phrase, 'my lands are where my dead lie buried.'"

We took the bus tour to the base of the sculpture and took many closeup photos. They were offering a separate bus tour to the top of the mountain and an opportunity to stand on the arm in front of the face. I asked Sue if she wanted to go, but all she did was give me that look, the one I don't fare well with! Before we left we visited the visitor center and went through many exhibits and artifacts depicting the life and legends of the Sioux Indians. In the evening, there would be a laser light show on the face and mountain, which we would attend at a later date.

After dinner, we went back to Mount Rushmore for the evening lighting ceremony. After an introductory speech and movie, the master of ceremonies started the National Anthem. With everyone standing and singing, the floodlights came on and lit the four President's faces to a white color with the sky as a background. The evening finished with all Veterans in the audience appearing on stage, for a patriotic recognition of their service.

That evening, we finished the Deadwood series and prepared for tomorrow's trip to Deadwood and the Black Hills National Forest.

As we were traveling, I read, "Deadwood is a National Historic Landmark, for its well preserved Gold Rush era architecture. Established in 1876 as a gold mining camp with a peak population of 5,000. The town was named after the dead trees found in its gulch."

"Today the population is +- 1,500. Like all mining towns, that loose their residents when the mines shut down, this area's economy has fluctuated over the years. The community was revived in 1989 when gambling was legalized in Deadwood. Today it is a small city with western charm, much history of the times, and gaming casinos."

Upon arriving, we decided that the best way to see this town was by getting a guide. We booked ourselves with a talkative and charismatic guide, on a bus tour of the city and Mt. Moriah Cemetery.

Our guide was a natural and comedic individual. He did a great job giving us the history of the city, with many anecdotal events. There were many comical stories that related to the city's history and its characters. By the time we left the city limits, we felt quite informed.

Our trip to the historical cemetery, Mt. Moriah, was enlightening. We saw the burial sites of Wild Bill Hickok, Calamity Jane, Preacher Smith, Charlie Utter and Seth Bullock.

Upon returning to the city, we had lunch at the #10 Saloon. Well known in the Deadwood series, as well as real life some 140 years ago. During lunch, they had a reenactment of Will Bill Hickok's death at the poker table, shot by the infamous Jack McCall.

Our next excursion after lunch was a roadtrip through the Black Hills National Forest. Sue read, "This National Forest covers 1.2 million acres from the eastern forests to the western plains. It has an estimated 573 million trees, most of which are Ponderosa Pine, and 17 wood/paper manufacturing facilities that support +- 3,500 jobs. Other main economic benefits include coal mining, and ranching on the plains."

"The history of this region is a contested and an unresolved issue. For hundred's of years, this region was home to many tribes of American Indians. In 1876, during the Black Hills War, the US Government defeated the Lakota Sioux, Cheyenne and Arapaho Tribes, and the US Government took control of the Black Hills."

"The takeover area was contested for 100 years by the Indians. In 1980, the US Supreme Court ruled that the Black Hills was illegally taken over by the US Government, and ordered a remuneration of 106 million. The Indians refused settlement because they want their land back. The amount has grown in interest, and now is worth 1.5 billion."

As we traveled the forested eastern portion of the area, it became clear that the Forest Service had done some serious thinning of the Ponderosa Pines. The forest was manicured, with widely spaced trees in straight rows, and ample grasses growing between the trees. We saw evidence of small and large piles of brush and cut trees. There was evidence of selective cutting with small trees saved for the future. The non harvested areas were wild with dense mixed trees and brush.

Further research revealed an explanation of the forest's appearance. Sue read, "the Mountain Pine Beetle has infected 1/4 of the forested acreage. Beetles thrive in overcrowded Ponderosa Pine trees. Thinning of trees, to increase sunlight and decrease competition of nutrients, yields a healthier forest capable of resisting insect outbreaks. This thinning also promotes grass growth to support wildlife."

"Commercial contractors have been harvesting mature, diseased and poor quality trees for years since the onset of the beetle infestation. They have also followed a method of killing the beetle larvae. It is called 'Cut and Chunked'. Cutting infected trees into chunks 2 feet or less and leaving them to dry, which kills the larvae. Private growers have also sprayed high quality trees with insecticides."

Getting home, after a quick dinner, we went back to the Crazy Horse Memorial for the evening laser light show. This was a panoramic production of the American

Indian's history–from hundred's of years ago, to tumultuous years, and finally to reservations. It presented an attempt to preserve a culture and a way of life.

The next day, we drove east to the Badlands National Park. I read, "the Badlands are an amazing geologic landscape. The northern section is an area of eroded rocks to form butes, pinnacles, and spires which are rich in mammal fossils. The southern section has the largest undisturbed grasslands in the US. The Indians called this northern area, 'land bad' where nothing would grow."

We drove through the northern section. I said to Sue, "this is an other-worldly multi colored massive peaks of rocks. I can see why the outlaws would hide in this unnatural environment and why posses would not enter the Badlands–they were afraid they would not find their way out. This is real desolate area without any evidence of human activity."

On our way out of the park, we stopped and observed a large town of prairie dogs. To our surprise the dogs were white and not fearful of humans. Sue took too many photos, again!

Our next stop was Wall, SD. I read, "population 1,000, it was formed in 1908 as a railroad crossroad. It was named 'Wall' because the town was next to the adjacent steep peaks of the Badlands. We walked the street full of western charm and our destination was Wall Drugs.

I read, "the Wall Drug Store is a shopping mall that operates as a single entity. It started in 1931 as a pharmacy but quickly developed into a large roadside tourist attraction, as tourists would stop on their way to Mount Rushmore. As a town in the 'Middle of Nowhere', their early advertisement was posters all over the state and country and free ice water to parched travelers."

Today, it has a restaurant that seats 500. It serves homemade donuts, buffalo burgers, and homemade ice cream in an old fashion soda fountain. The biggest attraction is their famous 5 cent cup of coffee It also houses: western clothing and boots, a large privately owned western art collection, gifts, souvenirs, drugs, leather goods and more.

Our last stop was Keystone, SD. Sue read, "population +- 1,000. Established in 1883 as a mining town, today it is a major resort town next to Mount Rushmore and Crazy Horse–and boasts of having 800 hotel rooms to house tourists. Other tourist attractions are the railroad to Hill City and the National Presidential Wax Museum." We walked the street full of tourist shops and headed to the Ruby House for dinner, and dancing at the Red Garter Saloon.

I said to Sue, "the Ruby House was first built in 1970 but lost to a flood. The second building in 2003 was lost to fire. The third and present building opened in 2004.

The dining room has a turn of the century decor and also has a room dedicated to the Sioux Nation."

The dining room was elegant with their early 1900's Victorian decor. We had a chat with the waiter. He pointed out that this was an excellent place to experience buffalo meat. We admitted that we had tried Buffalo burgers but could not appreciate the different taste. The waiter strongly suggested their popular buffalo chopped sirloin steak, to experience the unique flavor. The meal was delicious, the buffalo flavor was hard to describe but easy to remember. We both agreed that our next meal would be a buffalo steak.

Before leaving, we walked into the Red Garter Saloon for after dinner coffee and liqueur. The band sounded great and we danced several two-steps. After a great day and evening, we headed to our camper.

Our last excursion was to the Jewel Cave National Monument. I read, "it opened in 1908 and was called Jewel because as you held a lantern, the walls full of calcite crystals sparkled like jewels. It is a fascinating underground world of caves, caverns, chambers and tunnels covered with calcite. It is the 3rd longest cave in the world with +- 190 miles of mapped passageways, formed from ground water eroding the sandstones over thousands of years."

We entered the cave at the visitor center by being lowered to the cave entrance by elevator. The cave was 49 degrees and after entering the first large chamber, you went caving with the guide. You walked a ½ mile loop, went down 40 flights of stairs with a total of 723 steps. You saw formations to include: boxwork, cave popcorn, nailhead spar, dogtooth spar, stalactites, stalagmites and more. The entire caving tour took approximately 1–1.5 hours.

Someone asked the guide why the air was so fresh. He answered, "this cave is a breathing cave. The air enters and exits according to the atmospheric pressure outside the cave."

The last question was regarding how these passageways are discovered and documented. He answered, "we have young, healthy, non claustrophobic volunteers, who can squeeze into tight places, and have previous caving experience. A group of the volunteers will enter a cave with a guide and spend a week in the cave."

"It takes an entire day of walking with backpacks to reach a base camp. From there they walk 3 hours daily to the actual work site. Once at the work site, they search for 'leads', unexplored passageways with strong air flow– the best indicator that large areas are worth discovering. Then the work starts, measuring size and distance of passageways as well as diagrams and sketches of the passageways. They also document the crystal structures of new areas. It is the unproven theory that this cave may also connect to nearby caves and have a distant air access".

We then headed to the camper and took the time to make plans for tonight and the next weeks. Tonight, I said, "we either go to a chuckwagon dinner or go back to the Ruby House for a buffalo steak, and a few dances at the Red Garter Saloon–it is up to you." Sue said, "we have already had two chuckwagon dinners and at the Ruby House we can have alcohol, dinner, dance and set the mood for tonight. It is a no brainer." *I thought, and another replenishing breakfast in the AM.*

Bringing up the final and major issue. I said, "we have to decide our next move, we have two choices. The first is to make our way slowly through 900 miles of Kansas and Nebraska, on our way home. To visit cow towns of Dodge and Elsworth, KS, the fantasy village of Dodge City's Gunsmoke, as well as Fort Kearney, NE and other sites."

"The second choice is to travel the 900 miles directly to Springfield without visiting Kansas and Nebraska. When we get to Springfield, we visit with our families, go to the Country Roadhouse, and then travel 400 miles by car and go to Nashville, TN. Where we can go to: the Grand Ole Opry, the Wild Horse Saloon and stay at the famous hotel, the Gaylord Opryland Resort Gardens and more."

Sue looked at me with a gleam in her eyes and said, "this has been a grand tour of wonderful National Parks and Monuments. I don't think there is much more to see on this route. In my recent life, I always wanted to go to Nashville and dance at the Wild Horse Saloon." I stopped her and said, "say no more, we are heading to Nashville." The embrace and kiss I got finished priming the evening. *I thought, we are going to need a 'high calorie' replenishing breakfast in the AM.*

On route to Springfield MO and then to Nashville TN.

CHAPTER 16

Final Destination–Nashville, TN

Our last evening in South Dakota was spent at the Ruby House in Keystone. The dinner was selected by the same waiter we had yesterday. He chose a wood fired buffalo steak that resembled a delmonico cut, with assorted wood fired vegetables and "smashed" potatoes. Red wine and a fine meal. The buffalo taste was again unique, but a bit stronger than the chopped sirloin steak.

After dinner, we again moved to the Red Garter Saloon for coffee and a liqueur. Several dances later we were satisfied of a wonderful day, evening, and several months on the road. We retired to our camper.

The next day after a super replenishing breakfast, we took off for Springfield, MO. Knowing we had 900 miles to home, we decided to split the trip in either a two day or a three day trip. It came down to 450 miles or 300 miles per day, depending on our road tolerance.

The first day we did +- 450 miles and ended up north of Omaha, NE. Being two drivers made the day travels much easier. That evening we notified our kids and Jack that we would be home tomorrow night. The next morning, after another replenishing breakfast, we took off for the last leg of our circuitous route. We got home at 4 PM and Jack was sitting in our garage with a beer in hand and a cooler by his chair. We had a long visit, described our travels and shooting venues, and informed him of our next trip to Nashville, TN.

That evening we transferred all our refrigerated, frozen and dry goods to the house. Moved all our guns to the garage safe, and we were both on the phone most of the evening calling our families and telling them of our plans.

The next day Sue packed our wardrobe. I made reservations at the Opryland Hotel, the Wild Horse Saloon, the Grand Ole Opry and the General Jackson Showboat. Several family members, who were not working, came to visit. That evening we went to dinner at the Country Roadhouse. It turned out to be a visit with all the people we got to know before leaving. We danced several two-steps, waltzes and line dances.

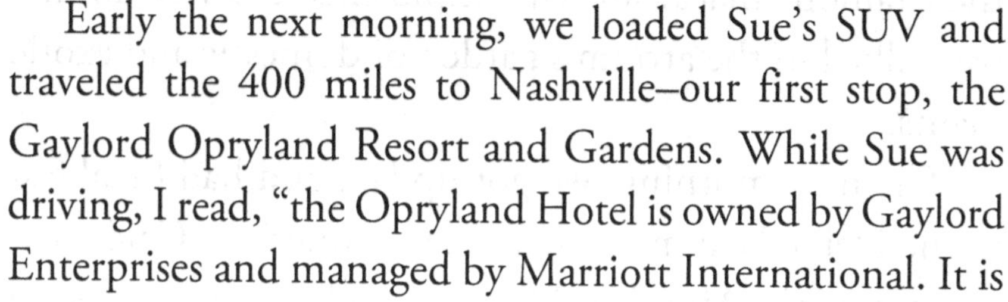

Early the next morning, we loaded Sue's SUV and traveled the 400 miles to Nashville–our first stop, the Gaylord Opryland Resort and Gardens. While Sue was driving, I read, "the Opryland Hotel is owned by Gaylord Enterprises and managed by Marriott International. It is one of the world's largest hotels. It has 2,888 rooms, 18 restaurants/bars, 3 pools(one indoor), a nightclub with entertainment, a fitness center/spa, multiple retail stores, and a convention center with 600,000 square feet of non gaming exhibition space."

"The central attraction is a glass roofed atrium, covering over 4.5 acres, and called the Delta Atrium. In the atrium are found the restaurants, bars, gardens, waterfalls and a winding river." Sue asked, "who is Gaylord?" "Edward Gaylor, 1919–2003, was a billionaire and media mogul, owner of the Oklahoman Newspaper and Publishing Company. In 1982, he made a multi million dollar purchase to include: CMT(Country Music Television), hotels to include the Opryland Resort, and the Grand Ole Opry at Ryman Auditorium."

At registration we took a small two room suite. It was early evening when we settled in, changed to dress code, and went to the atrium for dinner at the Old Hickory Steakhouse–the hotel's signature restaurant. With a cheese and wine sommelier, and a helpful waitress, we had a fine meal. Of course we had cheese appetizers, wine, Chateaubriand, potatoes au-gratin, with a side of their famous macaroni with triple cheese. After dinner, we walked in the atrium's garden of domestic and exotic plants.

The next morning. we got up late and had breakfast in the Delta Atrium at the Cascade American Café, next to a waterfall. After breakfast, we had plenty of time to enjoy the atrium before our next stop. We then decided to take a boat ride down the river. The guide provided information about the river, plants, fish and the atrium. He answered our questions throughout the 15 minute boat ride as we quietly drifted with the river current.

We then walked through the retail shops, Sue was trying on some dresses in the ladies Western Wear shop, so I went shopping at the store next door and made a purchase for a future occasion. Upon my return, Sue had already chosen some pants, shirts and one more sports coat. I tried them, and they all fit–*I like someone choosing my clothes.*

We then changed into western clothing and headed to the Wild Horse Saloon in downtown Nashville. On the way, I read on the net, "the Wild Horse Saloon opened in 1994, encompasses 66,000 sq. ft., has three levels, and has the largest dance floor in Tennessee. It holds 2,500 people, has a large restaurant, snack bar and alcohol bar. It is a known venue for country singing stars and bands. It has held 4,000 TV shows or tapings since 1994, and has had an attendance of 1.5 million people last year."

Sue asked, "why are we going there in the middle of the day and on a week day?" "Over the years, the Wild Horse Saloon has become a line dancing center. Look at the day's and the evening's schedule. The hourly schedule is a one hour line dance lesson followed by dancing to a band for one hour. In the evening, the line dancers commandeer the dance floor and the couples cannot two-step, waltz or do partner dances. The daytime is when there is a lower attendance of line dancers, and this leaves room on the outer perimeter. Dance groups, who do couple's dances, generally come in the afternoons for that reason."

When we arrived we took a table on the first floor bar next to the dance floor. The dance instructor was in the middle of a line dance lesson. We ordered drinks and waited for a local band to start playing on the hour. When the band came on, the leader explained the floor etiquette and said, "since we have a large dance group from Texas that do partner dances, please leave them room on the outside perimeter."

I looked at Sue and said, "boy did we luck out. We will be able to join this group and do couples dances(two-step, waltz, and partner)." The band started and about 20 couples, with the same uniforms, got on the dance floor and performed the Side Kick. Thanks to Sue's private lessons, we joined in as well as several independent couples. The next dance was a great lively two-step. We now had 35 couples dancing and we were beginning to match the number of line dancers.

The band must have had a meeting with the Texas group, because they played and announced dances that the group could perform. The next dance was the Schottische to a Maverick's song. One thing became very clear, no matter what song was played, the dance instructor started a different line dance to match the song played by the band.

The last dance before the next line dance lesson was a waltz by a Brooks & Dunn song. The Texas group got up and performed the West Texas Waltz. We and several couples did a standard waltz. After the band completed their hour, a new instructor was about to begin the new line dance lesson.

A member of the Texas dance group approached us at our table. The gentleman said, "we noticed that you performed a beautiful waltz, and know how to two-step and perform partner dances." He said that they were from Amarillo. I said, "we are from Missouri, but were close to you a few months ago. We were at the Bar W Ranch for a Cowboy Shoot." The gentlemen was visibly surprised, and looked like a light bulb had just come on. He looked at me and said, "I thought you looked familiar, I was there in another posse, and I saw you bring Mr. Whitehouse back to life. I am good friends with the Whitehouses and will mention that I met you in Tennessee." Sue added, "small world isn't it, heh?"

After several hours of Sue taking advantage of the free line dance lessons, and us doing couples dances, we went upstairs for dinner. Their restaurant was known for BBQ, Southern Smokehouse Cuisine, fried pickles and hot chicken. We both had smoked ham, yams, black beans, and fried pickles.

After dinner, we had to keep our table since the first floor was now full of line dancers and singles at the bar. The floor quickly filled with line dancers and even the Texas group could not get any dancing space. As they were leaving, the same group spokesman said that they were here all week till Friday and hoped we would join them again this week. Sue added, "we will be back, but in the afternoon till dinner."

Our next day was well planned, an AM visit to the Belle Meade Plantation, afternoon dancing at the Wild Horse Saloon, and dinner on the General Jackson Showboat.

The Belle Meade Plantation, I read, "was founded in 1807 by John Harding and grew to 5,400 acres. It was known for developing a fine thoroughbred line of horses. A rock quarry supported five generations of owners and their enslaved workers. Today, it sits on 34 acres and it is dedicated to preserving Tennessee's Victorian Architecture and equestrian history."

A guided tour included a tour of the Greek Revival Mansion and other historic sites to include a dairy, horse stable, carriage house and wine tasting at the winery.

On the mansion tour the guide said, "the mansion's facade has a base of limestone blocks and the pillars are made of solid limestone. The mansion has three floors, the first two have 14 foot ceilings, and the third floor has 8 foot ceilings. A circular cherry cantilevered staircase spirals to the third floor, There are Palladian niches for holding lamps in the staircase. There is a separate staircase for servants to reach the kitchen and their living quarters.

We went through several rooms to include living rooms, dining rooms, bedrooms, library, private offices and more. Displayed in all the rooms were pictures of the families throughout the generations, antique Tennessee furniture, and Victorian architecture of the 1800's" After a nice visit, we went back to the Wild Horse Saloon for the afternoon.

We arrived at their noon opening, sat in the first floor snack bar, had a beer and burger for lunch and visited with the Texas dance group. Come to find out that there were four men and one lady that were Cowboy Shooters, and three had been at the Bar W Ranch. They were a pleasant bunch, and we had a long visit before public dancing started.

We danced on and off and Sue took more lessons. It was a pleasant place to spend the afternoon with good dancing music, nice people, nice ambience and basically our kind of place. We left in time to go change to dinner clothes and then went to the General Jackson.

On route, Sue read, "this showboat was launched on the Cumberland River in 1985. It is +- 300 feet long and +- 65 feet wide, and has a capacity of 1000 passengers and 150 crew. The paddlewheel is 36 feet long and has a diameter of 24 feet. The 3 hour round trip to Nashville covers 14 miles of scenic views, a full course meal and entertainment after dinner."

At the beginning of the trip we watched the land scenery, but quickly entered the two story Victorian Theater for dinner. The dining area was a packed house. Dinner was a superb roast pork with all the Southern fixings.

After dinner, a cast of seven entertainers backed up by a 6-piece band, provided us a musical journey, Tennessee style. This included: Bluegrass, to Gospel, to Country Music. They presented songs from the old classic singers to the modern entertainers. Their final performance was dedicated to our first responders and our military.

On our departure, Sue mentioned, "this was a wonderful day, what do you have planned for tomorrow?" I said, "after a replenishing breakfast(hint), we will visit the Ryman Auditorium in the AM. The afternoon will take us back to the Wild Horse Saloon for dancing and an early dinner. In the evening, we are going to the Grand Ole Opry."

Reading from the net, "the Ryman Auditorium was founded in 1892 by a steamboat captain, Thomas G. Ryman. First named as the Union Gospel Tabernacle, with religious music and song. In 1920, it became known as the Carnegie of the South, hosting entertainers of the times, J P Sousa, Roy Rogers, Bob Hope and even President Theodore Roosevelt."

"In 1943, it became known as the Grand Old Opry, with entertainers such as: Elvis, Hank Williams, Johnny Cash, Patsy Cline and others. In 1974, the Grand Ole Opry moved to their new building called, the Grand Old Opry House. The Ryman fell to disrepair until it was purchased by Gaylord Enterprises in the 1980's and renovated in the 1990's. Fortunately, the circular church pews were restored and returned to the circular theater. It was again renovated in 2015. Today it is a vivacious entertainment center and considered one of the best performance centers in the US."

As we entered the auditorium, we were amazed at the design. A semicircular layout, seating 2,362 people, on multiple levels. All the seats were circular church pews, and no matter where you sat, you were looking down at the stage. This elevated and circular design contributes to excellent acoustics. This is a historical and spiritual location, thinking of all the great entertainers that have graced this hall with their presence."

For the afternoon, we returned to the Wild Horse. Sue asked, "do you mind coming back here tor the afternoon?" "Heck no. We came to Nashville because of this place. For years I watched it on TV, saw their weekly dances, their concerts, and the superstars performing. I know we are 25 years late, to me it is still a viable place and represents the ultimate dancing location. I like it here and will gladly be back tomorrow."

Around mid day we had their special menu item for the day, smoked meat sandwiches with fries and coffee. We danced on and off and talked with the Texas dance group. We went to the third floor and the group leader with another couple taught us a nice partner dance for a waltz, Just Another Waltz.

When time came, we drove directly to the Grand Ole Opry.

Sue read, "It started in 1925 as a simple radio broadcast, and grew over the years as a showcase for classic legends and contemporary chart-stoppers performing at the Ryman Auditorium's Grand Ole Opry. In 1974, the Grand Ole Opry moved from the Ryman Auditorium to their new home, the Grand Ole Opry House. The first show was attended by President Nixon who sang and played the piano."

"Today, each show presents 8 or more artists over a 2–2.5 hours. It holds 4 nightly shows per week, with two shows on some days. It seats 4,400 people, and it is considered one of the largest broadcasting radio and TV studio in the world."

"The Opry has +- 60 members that commit to performing 10 shows per year. The longest running member is Jean Shepard. Some artists cannot commit to membership because of their rigorous entertainment schedules, such as George Strait, Brooks & Dunn and many others. These entertainers still perform at the Opry but are labeled as guest artists. Now, membership concessions and exemptions are allowed for health, age, retirement, and other individualized situations."

"The latest news, the Opry House owners, Ryman Hospitality, has announced a 12 million improvement project. They are adding an extra parking lot, retail stores, and an area for backstage tours."

As we walked into the theater, we were faced with a massive structure. There were two stories of pews with a large row of lights separating the two floors. Each floor had straight church pews laid our in a circular fashion, like an amphitheater, and surrounding an elevated stage. The church pews were cushioned, the elevated stage had a hardwood floor, and the backdrop was a red barn with a large TV screen on top for artist viewing. In the middle of the stage was a 6 foot circle of dark oak, a piece of the old Ryman Auditorium stage, where legends of Country Music once stood and performed.

Bill Anderson was the show's master of ceremonies. We had a great lineup of performers. For oldies, we had Ricky Skaggs and Connie Smith. For more current entertainers, we had Trace Adkins and Lorrie Morgan as scheduled performers. This evening we had several unscheduled artists who were added today. One surprise was Alan Jackson, who came to Nashville without notice. He sang his new #1 single. The remainder of the show was excellent with great musicians and singers. Upon leaving, it was clear that this organization had done so much to promote Country Music and bring it to our homes.

The next day was our last day in Nashville. We planned to visit the Jack Daniels distillery in the AM, the Wild Horse in the afternoon, and our closing dinner at the Opryland.

We were up early to travel the 75 miles to Lynchburg. Sue asked why I had chosen this attraction. I said, "I have never been to a distillery before and I thought this would be a different place to visit. Besides, I want to know about this process of charcoal mellowing I have heard so much about."

As Sue was driving, I read, "Jack Daniels developed his recipe and mellowing technique in 1866. He died in 1907 and a family member took over the business. The distillery was closed during Prohibition of 1920–1933 and during WWII. The whiskey was stored in barrels and placed in warehouses during those years."

"The distillery started to make the original Old # 7, but over the years, they introduced several new flavors. Of note is the popular Doubled Mellowed Gentleman Jack and the 2015 Single Barrel Rye."

We signed up for the tour of the day that include a sipping and tasting of their product. The tour guide gave us an introductory history of the distillery which was similar to our internet research. At the end of his presentation, he said, "well folks, if you follow me, I will take you on a 'chour'. Sue immediately asked, "what is a chour?" I said, "that is the Southern accent for tour." I got a new look, one with a smile!

The tour was great. The guide said, "the original recipe is 80% corn, 12% barley, and 8% rye mixed with iron free water, and yeast from a previous batch–a starter. It ferments for +- 6 days then is singly distilled to 140 proof. It is then mellowed in charcoal. The whiskey is filtered through 10 feet of sugar maple charcoal for 5–7 days. This charcoal filtering imparts smoothness and can accomplish in days what barrel aging can take years."

The guide added, "the last step in whiskey production is barrel aging. It stays in the barrels until the whiskey tasters say it is ready, not because of the number of years in the barrels."

There were several questions but the interesting one was, "is there anything special about these barrels?" The guide answered, "we make our own barrels. They are made of white oak, are uniform in size, and the interior is toasted and charred. This process coaxes the woods natural sugars, which gives the whiskey its flavor."

After a wonderful and well organized tour, we stepped in the tasting center, we tasted half a dozen flavors. We like the smooth nature of all their flavors. We said, "we will take a bottle of your Double Mellowed Gentleman Jack." To our surprise, the guide said, "it is against the law to sell alcohol in this 'dry county'. I can sell you the commemorative bottle and the whiskey is free–with a smirk and smile."

So we laughed all the way back to the Wild Horse, from a wonderful 'chour', free whiskey and an expensive glass bottle. By the time we arrived, it was lunch time and we had their special of the day, BBQ chicken and coleslaw.

Our last day was a repetition of the previous day with line dance lessons, and dancing for all. By 2 PM the lessons and dancing stopped. Trace Adkins and his band were setting up for a special TV show tomorrow night. It was obvious, that since we had seen him last night at the Grand Old Opry, he would take the opportunity of a double venue.

We watched and it was clear they were practicing. Sue added, "they have sung this song 4 times already. "Until their producer approves the quality of their presentation, they will continue playing and singing it. Some presentations need instrumental modifications, or different audio settings to match the acoustics of this multilevel theater." The waiter told us we would be able to watch this show on CMT in two weeks.

Since the dancing was done till evening, the Texas dance group prepared to leave. We said our goodbyes, and hoped we would see some of them again at next year's Bar W Ranch shoot.

We got to the Opryland Hotel, changed for the dress code of the upscale Ravello Italian restaurant. We arrived and my reservation brought us to a semi secluded table for two. Sue looked magnificent in her little black dress, high heels, and with her bright white earrings. *I thought, perfect for the occasion!*

The ambience was elegant Italian and a romantic atmosphere, with a 4 piece string ensemble. The master violinist would parade amongst the customers, on some occasions, depending on the mood of the song.

We had a Chianti red wine and Calamari as an appetizer. For our main meal, we started with hot potato soup, and we ordered the specialty of the house, a mixed serving of veal parmigiana, cheese ravioli, and lasagna. For desert it was coffee and Tiramisu.

We lingered after dinner and enjoyed each other's company. I finally said, "this is the end of our wonderful western tour. I have enjoyed the Cowboy Shooting training, the CAS events, the Bar W Ranch, our five tourist bases, our three major National Parks, many National Monuments, and now our sixth tourist base, Nashville, TN."

"More important than these places we have been, my real pleasure has been spending the past four months with you. Living with you is a new experience each day, and you have become the joy in my life. Sue, I love you so much, *as I open the black box with a diamond ring,* would you consider marrying me and spend the rest of our lives together?"

Sue touched my hand, started crying with tears all over her face and finally saying, "how many ways can I say yes. Yes I will marry you, you have made me the happiest woman in the world." We kissed, and the master violinist started to play, 'Here comes the bride'. Of course the place erupted in applause and we were both smiling with happiness in our hearts.

Back at the hotel, Sue went to the main desk and retrieved an envelope. In out room, Sue asked when and where I had the time to buy a diamond engagement ring. I said, "when you were trying on dresses at the Western Wear shop in our hotel, I went next door to Jareds. I said to the saleswoman, I want a single bright white, flawless one carat diamond with a yellow gold ring. She handed me exactly what I wanted, paid for it with our credit card and hid it for days in my underwear drawer." Sue added, "what if I had said no? According to my court ordered alimony settlement, It cancels my alimony if I marry." I said, "the lost income never had any bearing when it came to having you as my wife."

Sue then opened the overnight envelope and handed me a check for $100,000 and a signed court order termination of alimony. I said, "when did this happen and how come." Sue said, "my X called me upon our arrival at home, the night I spent on the phone. Basically, he wanted to know how our trip was, if I was happy, if I was in love, and if I planned to marry you. He reminded me of our court agreement and the loss of a fortune, but then he said he was sending me this check, as a presumptive wedding present, and wished me sincere happiness. So now I give this to you as my dowry to be placed in our joint account."

The next morning, after a replenishing breakfast, we headed back home. Sue couldn't wait to call her daughters with the good news of the engagement and the early wedding present. Later, I called my kids with the good news, but without mentioning the wedding gift.

Our wedding plans were made. We reserved the Country Roadhouse for a midweek evening event. We invited our friends at the Desperado Club, all of Sue's friends at the Roadhouse, our condo neighbors, some of my old medical partners and most important our children and grandchildren. Thanks to our e-mail combined address book, our e-mail invitation read as follows:

> "You are invited to a free evening of celebration at the Country Roadhouse. Come witness, the nuptials of Sue Austin and Wil Sumner, followed by dinner and dance. Come share our joy. RSVP by e-mail. Wil and Sue.

With 200 guests in attendance, the ceremony began. I was standing on the stage with our minister and Jack as my best man. The music started with "Here comes the Bride" and as I turned, I saw Sue with a beautiful light blue floor length gown escorted by Ranger Rooster.

All I remember was, "Do you take this woman....... I said Yes. And do you take this man......, with a look I knew I would fare well, she said Yes."

Abbreviations

AD	Accidental discharge of a firearm
CAS	Cowboy Action Shooting
CWL	Concealed weapon license
D/Q	Disqualified
EMT	Emergency medical technicians
FYI	For your information
JFF	Just for fun
POA	Point of aim
POI	Point of impact
PPM	Parts per million
RO	Range Officer
RO1	RO with training and capable of running a stage
RO2	RO with training and capable of designing a stage
SASS	Single Action Shooting Society
TMI	Too much information

Printed in the United States
By Bookmasters